T0247952

HEAVY ARE THE STONES

Also by J.D. Barker

Forsaken

She Has A Broken Thing Where Her Heart Should Be

A Caller's Game

Behind A Closed Door

4MK THRILLER SERIES

The Fourth Monkey

The Fifth To Die

The Sixth Wicked Child

WITH DACRE STOKER

Dracul

WITH JAMES PATTERSON

The Coast to Coast Murders

The Noise

Death of the Black Widow

Confessions of the Dead

HEAVY ARE THE STONES

J.D. BARKER

CHRISTINE DAIGLE

"Basically I was a normal person."

— Ted Bundy

"If you believe you've lived your life the right way, then you do not have nothing to fear."

— Ted Wayne Gacy

Pittsburgh Post-Gazette

Monday, April 10

Actor Michael O'Neill, 46, Found Dead

by Matt Burkhart

A body found on Saturday in a field behind the Carrie Blast Furnaces was identified today by the city medical examiner as that of Michael O'Neill, Emmy Award-winning actor and star of the hit show *Werewolves of Paris*. The cause of death was reported as blunt force trauma to the skull. Michael kept a home in Mt. Lebanon. He was 46.

Mr. O'Neill was initially found by a source who wished to remain anonymous. The source shared that, upon discovery, Mr. O'Neill was buried in the field up to the middle of his chest, with his arms below ground. Multiple rocks about the size of a large fist were found at the scene and appeared to have been thrown at the body. The rocks were covered in dried blood. Police declined to comment. However, based on the eyewitness account, there is speculation that the killer may have been engaging in "*stoning*," a method of judicial execution during which stones are thrown at a condemned person until they die. Death by stoning was outlined in the Old Testament Law as a punishment for various sins including murder, idolatry, practicing necromancy or the occult, blaspheming, adultery, and other sexual sins.

The source also shared one additional detail. When Mr. O'Neill's body was excavated, he was found with a diamond clutched in his hand.

Mr. O'Neill's professional acting career began when he played Sly Norris in *Male Burlesque* before landing his breakout role as werewolf Keen Howell in *Werewolves of Paris*. His directorial debut came soon after with the documentary feature *Pittsburgh Steel: The NFL's Toughest Team*, which documented 20 years of the Pittsburgh Steelers football team. Mr. O'Neill had been active with several charities; however, he'd recently been rumored to have involvement in operating a sex trafficking ring and was a person of interest in an investigation dubbed L-Voyager launched earlier this year. This ongoing investigation is a collaboration between the Pittsburgh Bureau of Police and U.S. Customs and Border Protection. According to the PBP, another suspect was advertising internationally for laborers to work in the USA. Upon arrival, police say the victims reported their travel documents were taken from them, and they were forced into sex work. At the current time, it is unclear if these allegations are related to Mr. O'Neill's death. Police investigations are underway.

267 Comments ADD COMMENT **Sort by: NEWEST**

This conversation is moderated according to The Post-Gazette's community rules. Please ***read the rules*** *before joining the discussion. If you're experiencing any technical problems, please* ***contact our customer care team****.*

Anonymous
R.I.P Michael
Monday, Apr 10 2017 @ 8:32 AM

2Cute2Poot
So sad. Loved you in Werewolves!!!! xoxoxoxo
Monday, Apr 10 2017 @ 8:36 AM

X-Factor

The man was a criminal. Good riddance.

Monday, Apr 10 2017 @ 8:37 AM

> CriticalBean
>
> Right on, X-Factor! Spread those rumors about the deceased. Not like he can defend himself!
>
> Monday, Apr 10 2017 @ 8:39 AM

OldTestament

"You shall stone him to death with stones, because he sought to draw you away from the LORD your God...So you shall purge the evil from your midst." ~ Deuteronomy 13

Monday, Apr 10 2017 @ 8:43 AM

> GuyFawkes
>
> I'm all for anarchy, but this is messed up. For real.
>
> Monday, Apr 10 2017 @ 8:45 AM

RockStarGamer

This is like something straight out of a horror game; out of the box thinking and embracing that all important shock factor. As a gamer, I appreciate creativity.

Monday, Apr 10 2017 @ 8:48 AM

<u>LOAD MORE</u>

ALMOST FIVE YEARS LATER

1

JENA

Sunday, 7:00 a.m.

THE SONG HAUNTS my dreams.

It repeats over and over. "Glory Days"—the peppy guitar riff and '80s drumbeat leading up to Bruce Springsteen's rousing "Woo!" It is the ringtone I've set for my boss, Captain Jim Price. *The Boss.* An inside joke. Because it is important to be funny when you're a woman on the force. Competence without humor gets you dubbed an unlikeable bitch. And if you want success in the Pittsburgh Bureau of Police, which is still covertly a boys' club, popularity is a must. The Springsteen ringtone works like a charm. It cracks everyone up, every time.

But hearing that joke ring early on a Sunday morning brings dread instead of humor. My stomach flips, and I open one eye to a slit, squinting into the too bright morning streaming in through the gap between my blinds and the windowsill. Price wouldn't call. Except for an *oh shit* level problem.

I reluctantly slide out of my cocoon of blankets, chilled air hitting my bare legs beneath an oversize shirt. Snatching my phone from the nightstand, I fast tiptoe into the cramped walk-in closet, not wanting to disturb my boyfriend, Mason, who lies sprawled across the mattress, a long, muscular leg dangling off the edge, his big toe grazing the hardwood. Once inside the closet, I shut the door and click on the light before answering the call.

"Detective Campbell," I say. "What is it?"

"Campbell," Price booms, always talking like he is trying to shout over a crowd of people. *"The governor called. His son, Jack, is missing."*

My eyebrows knit. Missing person. Not the earth-shattering disaster I was expecting, but still urgent. And being Governor Ted Taylor's son pushes *urgent* up to *crisis.*

"How long?" I ask, shoving my legs into work pants with the phone wedged between my shoulder and cheek.

"He was supposed to be home eight hours ago."

I stop getting dressed and palm the phone, doing the math as I stare at Price's name on the screen. Bold white against the dark background.

"Campbell. You there?"

I shake off my surprise. "Yeah, I'm here. Isn't Jack seventeen? You got me out of bed at 7:00 a.m. on a Sunday for a kid who stayed out past curfew?"

"I know, I know. And if it were any other seventeen-year-old, I'd agree with you. But the governor says this is completely out of character for Jack. His wife is insistent."

That means I have no choice. I'm on the case, ridiculous or not.

A weary sigh slips out as I say, "On my way," before hanging up and snatching my Glock service pistol from its wire-basket drawer, concealing it beneath a business-casual jacket along with a bare-bones utility belt. Scooping up one of the many hair ties on the floor, I secure my long chestnut hair in a high, messy bun. After a quick dash to the bathroom to brush and gargle away morning breath, I go back to the bedroom for the keys I forgot in the nightstand drawer. Rushing, I stub my toe on the corner of the bed frame, cursing under my breath at the shaking bed.

Mason rolls onto his back, drawing his exposed leg back beneath the covers, but revealing a perfectly sculpted chest, rich sepia skin luminous in the sunlight.

"What time is it?" he mumbles in confusion.

An attorney for the Department of Justice, Mason values his weekend sleep as much as I do and fights being woken up.

"Early," I say. "Sorry. Didn't mean to wake you."

I perch on the edge of the bed and press my lips to his cheek, electricity coursing through my body as his well-trimmed goatee tickles my face. Mason smells like freshly cut grass and lemon tea—a scent uniquely his. I so want to crawl back under the blankets and snuggle up next to him until we both fall into blissful asleep.

Tearing myself away, I look into his eyes, his gaze heavy with sleep. "I need to go. Snooze as long as you want. I'll call when I can."

Mason yawns and stretches before peering up at me with groggy eyes. A wolfish grin spreads across his face. "Move in with me," he says, reaching out to hook me in his arms. "That way, I'd still be here when you get home. You know I'd take care of you."

Laughing, I dodge out of his reach as he tries to lock me down.

"Not the time for this discussion," I tease, hoping to avoid having this talk again.

Mason pouts and shoots back, "It never is."

"Living separately has worked for us so far," I say. Plus, my job is too dangerous for all that marriage and kids stuff. That is the only reason. It has nothing to do with my parents' relationship and my emotional damage. Nope. Nothing at all.

"It's been seven years." Mason props himself up on his elbows, his face more serious. "I haven't forgotten your lease is up next month. And you living alone in this apartment, in this neighborhood, worries the crap out of me."

"I can take care of myself."

Mason's gaze turns to full alert. "But you don't always have to."

When I lean in for another kiss, he wraps me up like a defensive lineman sacking a quarterback. After a few moments, he pulls away and raises an eyebrow. "Is that your gun? Or are you—?"

"—Pervert." My eyes wander south. "It looks like I'm not the only one who's packing." I laugh before pushing him back down onto the bed and bolting for the exit. "I really need to go!" I call behind me as I run down the hallway.

Mason's voice echoes off the walls, chasing me. "Don't think I won't ask you to move in again."

I grin and shout back, "I'd expect nothing less. But you won't win!"

I sprint out of the front door when my next-door neighbor, Dustin Small, steps in front of me.

"Whoa!" Dustin spins to the right, avoiding a crash. In his arms, he cradles a bag of cheese puffs and a large slush drink. Artificial blue, by the smell of it.

"Sorry," I say, surveying his snacks.

"No worries."

I motion toward his munchies. "Please tell me you slept at some point. You do sleep, right?"

His mouth curls up in a mischievous grin and he shrugs, the bag of cheese puffs crinkling. "You know how it is. Hashtag gamer life."

He holds up his snack-filled arms in a gesture that represents a hashtag—an effort that has me laughing despite the situation. In his mid-twenties versus my thirty-three years, his *YouTube famous* way of speaking cracks me up. His comical face only adds to his goofiness—wide-set ice-blue eyes and slightly flat nose complementing each other in an odd way.

"What about you? Rushing out so early. Had a one-night stand and you're sneaking out of your own house? You know that's not how it works, right?"

"Ha ha. Got a case. The boss wants me in pronto."

"On a Sunday? The heathenry."

"The boss thinks it's important, so…" I shrug.

Dustin purses his lips as if he is in deep thought or trying to look cool. I'd bet my money on the latter.

A static-riddled tune plays from inside Dustin's apartment. *Bah dah bah bah-dah baaaahh daahh. "Take me out to the ball… game."*

It is the intercom. I used to think the tune was charming. It brought me back to my college days pitching softball. But now it gets more annoying every time it plays. I'd give anything just to have the standard mechanical buzz.

"Whoa," he says. "Must be my pizza."

"At 7:00 a.m.? Right after a snack run?"

"Don't you have to fly?" He waves me away. "Catch you later."

He fumbles the doorknob to his apartment, the cheese puffs

crunching and slush drink teetering in one arm. Upbeat video game music streams out as he opens the door a crack. I suppress a laugh and end up snorting. How can someone live a virtual life like that?

But as I trudge down the stairs and out into the frigid Pittsburgh morning with no time to grab a coffee for what will no doubt be a thankless task for a privileged kid breaking Daddy's rules, I can't help but wonder if Dustin has chosen the wiser path. After all, there is something to be said for embracing a minimalistic lifestyle. At least you don't have standards to live up to.

2

JENA

Sunday, 8:00 a.m.

MARY SARKIS, MY partner, hops into the car when I arrive at the station. Her shoulder-length dark hair is meticulously brushed, olive skin glowing beneath recently applied lotion. She snaps her gum and hands me my usual black coffee, her bright pink nails wrapping around the cup. I don't get how she is so put together this early on a Sunday. Probably she was already up and getting the family ready for church. Whatever the reason, I could kiss her.

Mary and I are like Thelma and Louise, except without the crime sprees. Or double suicide. Hmm, you know what? Not like Thelma and Louise at all. Let's go with Laverne and Shirley. I'm Laverne. Mary is Shirley. Much better.

I pull out of the lot, speeding through the city, then along Route 1-376 to the Squirrel Hill North neighborhood. The car is fragrant with coffee and bubble gum as we drive. Mary rests her loafers on the dashboard, short legs extended, the hem of her tailored slacks a touch too long. Soon, we arrive at our destination, a haven of wealth.

"Nice neighborhood," Mary remarks.

The mansions in the area come in various architectural styles—Contemporary, Victorian, and Edwardian—with Governor Ted Taylor's being an impressive Art Deco beauty, the windows graceful arches. Two stories of smooth stucco with rounded extensions make up the exterior. Manicured hedges and trellises surround decorative iron double doors wide enough to drive two cars through.

Mary glances over and raises an eyebrow. "Usual method of questioning?" Mary jerks a thumb at herself. "Nice cop." Next, she points to me. "Serious cop."

"Do you even need to ask?" I say. "Don't tell me the governor makes you nervous."

In response, Mary blows a tremendous bubble. I pop it with my pinky, the gum leaving sticky wet residue on my skin. Mary laughs, peeling gum from around her mouth, her vibrant nails shimmering in the sunlight.

As I ease the Ford Explorer into the very long, patterned-concrete driveway, a hulking man in a black suit emerges from the front doors, descending the stone steps. Mitch Daniels. Governor Taylor's bodyguard and a Pennsylvania State trooper. He has been watching, awaiting our arrival.

As I lower my window, Daniels lowers his sunglasses. "Campbell." He nods slightly in greeting. "Governor Taylor is waiting for you."

A small package of gummy bears sticks out of his breast pocket like a pocket square. I don't understand Mary's weakness for bubble gum or his soft spot for gooey sugar.

"Thanks," I say, killing the engine.

Daniels opens my door as Mary emerges from the other side of the car. He escorts us up the front steps, leading us through the ornamental iron doors. We enter a foyer with high ceilings and vintage brass light fixtures. Gleaming Pittsburgh-limestone flooring runs all through the house. Those style of floors are a staple in many homes, courtesy of Ridge Limestone Quarry just outside the city. You can find the white slabs in pretty much every government building, school, and church in Pittsburgh. Daniels goes on ahead, past a grand birch staircase, into a sitting room with a marble fireplace and enormous hexagonal mirror. Governor Ted Taylor, his wife Shannon, and their youngest son, Jude, await our arrival. Daniels vanishes through another doorway, affording us some privacy.

Mrs. Taylor perches on the couch, her hands folded in her lap. The only sign of anything amiss is a stray strand of hair that has broken loose from her coiffed First Lady bob. Her son, Jude, sits next to her, cradling a football. He is an adolescent version of the governor: athletic, with a thick wave of dark brown hair.

Governor Taylor is situated in an armchair. Behind him, an immense wooden cross hangs on the wall. The crucified Christ's head bows heavy, fat drops of blood spilling from the thorny crown. The governor rises to greet us, a politician's smile stretching across his face despite the unsettling situation. Straight, white teeth glimmer radiantly—the unmistakable aftereffect of tireless dental work. His grin is corporate and cool, not a single line crinkling around his eyes. Or maybe his smile is genuine and cut short by Botox.

"Detectives. Thank you so much for coming so quickly." He shakes both of our hands in turn, the tension in the room palpable.

"Governor," I say, carefully choosing my next words. "I'm sorry to hear about Jack's unexplained absence."

Mrs. Taylor covers up a small cough. Jude puts a hand on her shoulder. At a subtle shake of her head, he drops it.

Mrs. Taylor checks her diamond-encrusted watch. "How long will this take? We need to make an appearance at church."

The governor's eyebrows raise, giving her an incredulous look. "Please, make yourselves comfortable." He motions toward the love seat. "I appreciate your discretion. Obviously we need to keep this quiet. The last thing we need is the press running with some nonsense."

"He's a teenager and he hasn't been gone long," Mary says in her gentle way. "Do you have reason to believe something is wrong?"

The governor nods. "He has never *not* come home by curfew. Not once."

"You expected him home by midnight last night, correct?" I say.

Again, the governor nods.

"Where did he go?"

"It's difficult to say. We don't keep tabs on him. Jack's almost an adult. Well-behaved, never been in any trouble." The governor pinches his chin, perhaps a rehearsed gesture when he wants to look thoughtful. "He took off in his car. Said he was going out to meet some friends."

"Jack doesn't have any friends," Jude blurts.

Mrs. Taylor clicks her tongue at him, and he drops his head, picking at the lace on the football.

"No friends at school? Or in the neighborhood?" Mary asks softly.

"Not one," Jude says. "He hangs out in his room, alone, on his computer."

With the voice she reserves for the most difficult conversations, like delivering bad news, Mary asks, "Any chance he ran away?"

At this, Mrs. Taylor's nostrils flare, her chin raising. "He wouldn't just run off. He's very happy here."

Jude reaches for his mother, then thinks better of it. His eyes lock with mine. "He hates it here," he says with regret in his voice. "He feels like he doesn't exist."

Mrs. Taylor glares at her son, but she does nothing to silence him.

"They need the truth," he mumbles at her.

She shakes her head and looks up at Jesus on the wall.

Jude straightens, squeezing the football, eyes darting around the room, unsure where to look or what to do. Looking at anything but his mother.

I press on as if they're not in a silent boxing match and focus on the governor. "Did anything happen that's out of the ordinary?"

He rubs the back of his neck. "We had a slight disagreement a few days ago."

"You had a fight," Jude mutters.

"A disagreement," the governor insists, folding his arms. "Jack is in his senior year of high school. He was on his VR headset. I was telling—"

"—Yelling," Jude cuts in.

"Jude, enough," Mrs. Taylor barks. "Let your father speak."

The governor pauses a moment, lets the quiet build. "I was *telling* him to do his homework. He argued that the 'coding' he was doing in VR was better than homework because it would help him get a job, and that if I *really* wanted to help him, I'd get him a better headset. I told him I'd consider it if he made some real friends. He insisted his online friends were his real friends."

"We don't know who's on the other end of those computers, and Jack's a vulnerable child," Mrs. Taylor admits. The way her nose wrinkles, it is clear giving out any personal information is making her ill. "He realizes he's different, not good at socializing, and it can get him down. He copes by escaping online."

"Does he cope in other ways? Drugs or alcohol?" I ask.

Mrs. Taylor shakes her head, then glances at her watch.

There is never an easy way to ask the next question, so I take it head-on. "Has he ever threatened to hurt himself?"

"No!" Mrs. Taylor says. Then her voice drops low. "He wouldn't do something like that. He couldn't."

The governor shifts in the armchair, like maybe he has more to add, but he stays silent.

"Did he take anything with him?" I ask.

"His laptop and phone," the governor says.

"Have you tried to locate him with any of those Find My apps?"

Mrs. Taylor gives a mirthless laugh. "Jack would never have it. He's a tech genius and we're all Luddites. He disables tracking for everything he does."

I nod. "We'll need his phone number. We can get the call log through his carrier and possibly find his location. Do you have the serial number for the laptop? We may be able to track it down, too."

The governor rises from the armchair, straightening his tie. "Yes. I save all my purchases in my files. I'll get them for you."

"You can do that?" Jude asks. "Like, track it down just from the serial number."

Mary gives a reassuring smile. "We can. Our cyber investigator is the best. We'll find him."

"Quietly," the governor adds with insistence. "You'll find him quietly."

3

JENA

Sunday, 1:00 p.m.

IN A STERILE conference room in the middle of the PBP Headquarters, Mary and I work at the laminate oval table that takes up most of the small room. A festive gold bow hangs upside-down from the drop ceiling. Perhaps a leftover from a holiday party. Or perhaps someone's attempt to add some cheer to the dreary space. An industrial coffee pot, two dirty cups, and a tray filled with hard-boiled eggs and fruit occupy the middle of the table. My attempt to keep our breakfast healthy. The smell is getting a bit ripe, though.

A smart board stretches in front of one faux wood-paneled wall. We've outlined our next steps on the digital writing space. Mary is the designated writer because of her meticulous penmanship. My handwriting hasn't developed beyond that of a third grader. So far, our "to-do" list is very brief. Visit Jack's high school when it opens tomorrow and his classmates are available for questioning. Hope we get a hit on Jack's license plate. Look at the call logs when they come through. Wait for Brian Collins, whom Mary previously dubbed "the best" cyber investigator, to track down Jack's laptop or phone.

"I've got nothing, ma'am," Collins barks as he bursts through the door. No greeting. Just typical IT straight talk. Except Collins is anything besides the standard computer nerd. An inactive Marine with a face like a boxer, he wears too-tight t-shirts sized for an eight-year-old and refers to everyone as *sir* or *ma'am.*

I push the rolling chair away from the table. Mary looks up from where she is doodling a flower with the digital pen that she now covertly "erases" with the edge of her hand.

"What do you mean, nothing?" I say with a tight voice.

Collins grabs the coffee pot, reaching for the soiled cup with a purplish-pink lipstick mark on the rim. He squeezes himself into a chair and pours, his face falling with disappointment when no dark liquid pours out.

"You were going to use my dirty cup?" Mary wrinkles her nose in mock disgust.

Collins abandons the pot, scooping up an egg. "Waste not, want not."

Mary smiles with fuchsia lips. "Is that a Marine motto or something?"

I clear my throat. "What do you mean, nothing?"

Collins sniffs the egg, makes a face, then puts it on the table. He folds thick, corded arms across his Schwarzenegger chest. "The only calls and texts are to his family, ma'am. Last pinged cell tower was Saturday night just after 2300 hours, four blocks from his house. Both devices are either off or totaled. I combed social media and any other possibilities for a net presence I could think of. You're welcome. He has very little social media activity, besides Instagram, which isn't saying much because he just follows twenty people and has only posted three times. Nothing of note in cyberspace. Not in public, using his real name, anyway. If his laptop was on, I'd have a whole lot more to go on. Wouldn't take me two seconds to crack it and get access to all his sites. But like I said, without knowing where to hack, I've got nothing."

"Terrific," I say, at the same time my phone dings. I read the message with wide eyes, then look up at Mary. "They found Jack's car. And he's not in it."

Mary puts down her digital pen and says, "You're driving."

We're out of the precinct in a flash. Five minutes later, I steer the Explorer down I-279 South, the freeway almost vacant. Typical for a Sunday, unless there is a game. PNC Park races by. I've seen the inside of that stadium more times than I care to admit, particularly when Mason and I were first dating. He is a super fan. Go Pirates. I'm not complaining. I love a good ball game, but I'd rather play. The best thing about watching a Pirates' game is the nachos.

The surrounding bars and pubs fade away as we cross the Fort Duquesne bridge. We arrive at Point State Park just after one thirty, the 150-foot-high fountain spouting majestically in the distance.

An underground walkway leads to a triangle of lush green where the Allegheny and Monongahela rivers converge to become the Ohio River. On the grass, quite a few people meander around. Families strolling. Children playing tag. Couples lounging on picnic blankets. Some folks venture closer to the water's edge, descending the steps to dip their feet in. Everyone is enjoying a break in the mid-afternoon sunshine. Including the hopeful gulls gliding overhead in search of an easy meal. Idyllic. That is the only way to describe the scene. A stark contrast to the parking lot, where a few officers have yellow-taped a small section of asphalt.

I park the Explorer a few feet away from an orange parking cone and hop out with Mary following suit. I flash my badge at the nearest officer, and he waves us on. Amanda Anders, the CSI tech, photographs the car. A burgundy Honda Civic, perhaps a few years old. A nice, respectable ride. Anders glances up from her camera. She wears a motorcycle vest over a spandex t-shirt, hair divided down the middle and pulled to each side of her head into what she calls *power puffs.*

"I haven't been here long," Anders says, clicking away. "Looks abandoned. We've got blood inside."

The driver-side window is rolled down nearly all the way. Pulling a pair of nitrile gloves from my pocket, I move closer. The powdered insides dry against my skin.

I find the blood on the driver-side armrest. There is more along the left edge of the seat, the steering wheel, and the floor mat.

"Passive drops," I say.

Mary stands beside me, craning her neck. "Like from a puncture wound," Mary confirms.

"Two wounds, by the pattern." I bite my lip, tugging at one finger of my gloves as I study the spatter. "We've also got blood transfer smears. Like he was dragged from the car." I step back, scanning the pavement. "No blood on the ground. Probably carried. The wound could be from taser barbs that got stuck or lodged too deep."

"Makes more sense than a double fishhook to the face." Mary's peppy demeanor tapers off as she realizes the implication. "A meetup gone wrong, then. Poor kid. He was having a hard time at home and school, and now this."

"Yeah."

This awkward teen could now be dead, or worse. My thumb moves to the scar beneath my chin. It was the fishhook comment that did it. A little too close to home. When anyone asks, I joke the scar is from the stupid placement of an old piercing, never telling the truth about it. That I did it myself with the tip of a scalpel while being haunted by the memory of my father's disappointed face when I told him I didn't get into med school. That I was going to be a cop instead. That is something Jack and I have in common: knowing you're unwanted in your own family.

I pull my hand away from my throat and look up, shading my eyes from the sun, scanning the area. "A kidnapping makes sense with the site selection. No video surveillance in the vicinity. But whoever took him wanted him alive. At least for now." I glance back down, catching a glimpse of Anders off to the side, waiting patiently with fingerprint powder. "I'm sorry, we'll let you finish your job."

Anders quickly swoops in, dusting the interior. Prints everywhere, but I bet they're all Jack's.

"Is that a cell phone?"

Mary's pointing between the seat and center console. Anders fishes it out, holding it up between two pinched fingers. It is completely smashed. The screen is a spiderweb and the plugs have been obliterated. "SIM card is missing."

"Lovely," I mutter, my shoulders dropping. That means no way to find out if he messaged anyone through an app before he went missing.

"I'll send it to Collins," Anders says, bagging the phone. "Just in case."

"Ooh, yes," Mary says. "I'm sure Collins can fix it."

I'm about to reply when my phone beeps with a message. "They've found Jack's laptop. Well, part of it. The hard drive. Without the casing. They found it in the rocks near the fountain. But it's completely soaked through."

Mary's eyes sparkle with possibility despite my bleak news. "Collins can stick it in a bag of rice or something to try to dry it out. Right?" Mary. Always the optimist.

"Sure. Or use a hair dryer."

Mary raises an eyebrow.

"Or the shoe rack in the dryer."

"You're teasing me."

"Maybe Collins can blow on it."

I quickly type a response before looking back at Mary. "I'm having it sent there now. Let's hope Collins can pull off a miracle."

4

JACK

Sunday, 10:30 p.m.

JACK IS FREEZING. Convulsing with whole body shakes. Teeth chattering. Skin tingling with a dull ache throbbing at the base of his skull. His tongue is thick. His mouth cottony and dry. Muscles twitching, a raw soreness radiates from a spot he can't quite pinpoint. A wave of nausea sweeps through him, mixing with a sense of helplessness that makes his stomach churn. Like he is a sitting duck.

He tries to focus, head swimming. He can't open his eyes. But he listens. Footsteps. Shuffling toward him.

He is coming for me.

The message he'd received on his chat app flashes in his mind: "*Wanna meet IRL?*"

The parking lot. Gloved knuckles rapping on Jack's window. His online friend arrived wearing a skeleton gaiter and sunglasses. A secret identity, he said. Couldn't have his streamers knowing who he was. He'd never live a normal life again, always getting mobbed. Revealing his true self was for Jack alone. In private.

Jack was so excited.

When he rolled down his window, the skeleton shot him with a taser. Barbs lodged into his face. One in his cheek, the other just above the eye. Blood dripped down before his brain started shaking like a rock in a jar. Bees swarmed beneath his skin.

And now…

He is going to kill me.

Pain flares in his face. A taste like sour milk curdles at the back of his throat. Why can't he stop shaking? Cold. So cold. Stay still. Don't let him know you're awake.

Pressure. To his right eye. A finger peels his eyelid open.

Standing above him, blurry, out of focus, is the skeleton. No eyes. The tint on the sunglasses so dark.

"Good morning, Princess." The skeleton's voice is distorted. *"Thought you'd never wake up. Gave you a little narcotic cocktail after the zap. Couldn't have you rise-and-shining before we were ready to roll. But shit, I'm no anesthesia doctor. Thought I might've OD'd you. That wouldn't have been a good start. But you've got to take risks if you're going to win the game. Right?"*

The skeleton releases his eye. Jack blinks, staring up at an industrial ceiling, unable to move. Except for the shaking. Skeleton touches the wound on his cheek. Jack gurgles, waiting for him to press harder, for the white-hot stab of pain. But Skeleton only rests a light finger there. Not even enough force to make contact despite the tremors rolling through Jack's body.

"Listen up. I'm only saying this once. You're a hostage, understand?"

Jack tries to nod, but only ends up groaning.

"Good. I like you, Jack. Seriously. We've had some solid conversations, right? I don't want to hurt you. But I will if you don't do

what I say. Got it? Follow the rules of game play, and you'll go home in one piece."

Jack moans in response.

"I'll take that as a yes. But I'm not ready for you yet." Skeleton takes his hand away. *"This is going to sting a bit."*

And then heat burns up into Jack's hand, flooding his left arm as his mind screams. Panic grips him as he fades out.

When he comes to again, he is wracked with the same cold shakes. Anesthesia wearing off. Like when he had his wisdom teeth taken out. Now he understands. He doesn't know how much time has passed. He tries to get his bearings, but the screams of terror inside his head won't stop, heart racing so fast he thinks it will seize.

He swallows, working to calm down his breathing so he can hear. The hum of static presses against his ears. Further away, shuffling footsteps. The greasy scent of pizza turns his stomach. He swallows down the bile.

Not lying on the floor anymore. Now he is upright. It is like he is hanging. Sweat drenches his forehead but doesn't drip into his eyes.

Finally, he opens his eyes. Into darkness. He blinks. Blindfolded? No, something else. He can't see. *Why can't he see?*

There is screaming, echoing inside the space. Then he realizes it is his own.

Cold metal touches his bare bottom. A flash of white blinds him. His body seizes, a loud buzzing in his head. Chest, arms, legs—all cramping. His whole body tingles like needles are being pushed through his blood.

And then it stops.

"No screaming." Skeleton's distorted voice rings in his ears.

"That was a small shock. The next time you break the rules, it'll be longer."

Jack swallows hard, screams turning to sobs. Tears pour down his cheeks, pooling before they hit his chin. He is wearing a mask. And ear coverings. What the hell is going on?

A dark room materializes in front of him. A window. A closed door with a faint glow shining beneath it. Not complete. Not *defined.* Digital? A VR headset? Has to be. There is an outline of goggles around his eyes, over the bridge of his nose.

"This is my room," he says.

A replica of it, anyway. But he never sleeps in the dark. Lights on; always. It is his security blanket. And he keeps the bedroom door wide open.

The room writhes, darkness slithering on top of darkness, crawling from the corners, alive and amassing and peeling away from the wall.

He jumps back, moving in a weird floating motion, gravity too light. Like the room is passing him. And he hasn't moved at all.

A figure congeals inside the room. An enormous silhouette of undulating darkness, growing in stature, and moving toward him.

"I made it for you. Do you like it?" It is Skeleton's distorted voice coming from inside the black mass.

Jack's body is trembling. He doesn't want to be here with this oversize oil slick. Not at all. He breaks out in a cold sweat and shuffles another step back. He needs to get out of here. He paws at his chest, trying to rip off whatever holds him, but his empty hands feel full.

"Deep breaths, Jack," the shadow monster says. *"Deep breaths. Why don't you relax and take a look around?"*

He remembers the electric shock and goes still. He needs to do what the Skeleton-Shadow says if he doesn't want to get hurt.

The room looks like his. Same comforter with the black-and-white graphic owls on his bed. Corner desk with his gaming chair. But there is a full-length mirror on the wall. He doesn't have a mirror in his room.

He glides closer, the motion disconcerting as he slips in front of the glass, turning to see himself. He is confronted with a grotesque reflection. Thin limbs and an elongated body. Emaciated. Skeletal. Warped.

Not him. It can't be.

"Help," he cries. "Someone, help!"

Jack looks down at his wraithlike body. "This isn't me." He whips his head around, but the room is everywhere. No escape. The headset on his face is so heavy. His heart is a slide whistle skating up and down his throat. Worse yet. He has lost track of the shadow.

"Shadow?"

The dark monster materializes from the wall.

Jack floats away from him, landing against a darkened window that overlooks the Pittsburgh landscape. Not the view from his room.

"What do you want from me," Jack sputters. "Is this—"

"—A game," Shadow finishes. *"And like all games, there are rules."*

Jack holds very still, listening to his shallow breathing and the blood rushing past his ears.

"I need to get a message to dear old Daddy, understand?"

Jack nods, his head too heavy, his body too light. "Yes," he rasps, a chill crawling up his spine.

The warped voice continues, *"It's simple. Nine days. Nine games."*

Nine days? But Jack has a history test tomorrow, and he studied all weekend. It is a stupid thing to worry about now, but he can't help it.

"Each time you win, your dad gets a message from me. If your dad answers the message and does what I ask, you go free."

Jack swallows hard. "And if he doesn't do what you ask?"

"We keep playing."

Jack's mouth goes dry, his tongue thick. "And if he doesn't answer after all nine days?"

"Then the game ends."

Jack's heart punches the inside of his rib cage like a speed bag. "TPK? Total Player Kill?" Jack whispers, but Shadow stays silent. "Whatever you want from him, you won't get it."

"You'd better hope I do."

"He doesn't give two shits about me. He'll leave me to die. My mom, too. Jude wouldn't. But what can Jude do? He is only fifteen. Nothing. That is what. I'm going to die here." Jack weeps, full-on.

"I guess we'll find out."

The press of metal to his backside makes him stop bawling.

"No shocks," he whispers, the words strained. "Please. I'll be good."

"Oh, I know you will." Shadow clears his throat, the sound thick with static and reverb. *"Game number one."*

The room around Jack morphs. He now stands on the bow of a majestic sailing ship. A towering mast and billowing sail behind him, a swivel-mounted harpoon gun in front. Old, knotted wood planks run beneath his feet. A clear blue sky stretches above. Ocean surrounds them on all sides until it vanishes in the distance. Everywhere whales surface and dive, sending enormous splashes up into the air. An ambient sea shanty plays softly; an instrumental song with a fiddle and squeezebox.

"Shoot the golden whale," the shadow says.

Jack spots it immediately. The glint of gold in the sunlight. It is close by and moving slowly. If he were in his right mind, this would be simple. He isn't good at much, but he is the Mozart of VR games. He floats forward and grips the harpoon gun's trigger, taking aim. His hands are shaking, his breathing ragged. *Get it together.*

"You have two minutes," the shadow says. *"And if you're enjoying your current lack of debilitating pain, don't miss."*

Jack clenches his teeth, holding back a scream.

"Your time starts…now!"

Jack squints, checking the harpoon gun's alignment, then lets the spear fly. The harpoon sinks into the golden whale, and Jack exhales with relief that his skills didn't let him down.

Direct hit.

Pittsburgh Post-Gazette

Monday, May 15

Leviticus Killer Strikes Again

by Matt Burkhart

The body of amateur-wrestler Dante Inferno was discovered next to the leaf-covered train tracks of the long-abandoned Seldom Seen Village in the Beechwood neighborhood of Pittsburgh. Cause of death, as reported by the medical examiner, was blunt force trauma to the skull. Dante was 32.

Dante's death occurred under similar circumstances to that of actor Michael O'Neill, whose body was discovered last month. Dante was buried in the ground up to his chest, surrounded by a pile of bloodstained, baseball-size rocks. When he was unearthed, he also had a gemstone grasped in his hand. This time, the gem was an emerald. It appears likely the jewels are the birthstones for the month of each kill, although they are neither of the victims' birthstones, with Michael born in July and Dante born in January. Given the method of stoning as the choice for these lethal executions, the name *"The Leviticus Killer"* has been trending on social media. The Pittsburgh Bureau of Police had no comment, but we hope they will find and bring this killer to justice sooner rather than later.

Dante had a colorful career as a wrestler. Known as affectionately as "Loudmouth," Dante was an opulent dresser and known womanizer. His string of affairs and deviant activities were made very public when explicit photographs were sold to *Hush Hush* magazine last spring. His wife of two years, Gloria-Jean, committed suicide three weeks later.

452 Comments **ADD COMMENT** **Sort by: NEWEST**

This conversation is moderated according to The Post-Gazette's community rules. Please ***read the rules*** *before joining the discussion. If you're experiencing any technical problems, please* ***contact our customer care team****.*

T-Bone
Loudmouth!!!
Monday, May 15 2017 @ 11:22 AM

Ken
I have one of his crystal-studded robes. Got it at an auction for cheap. Maybe the price will go up!
Monday, May 15 2017 @ 11:23 AM

T-Bone
Have some respect. He's still warm.
Monday, May 15 2017 @ 11:25 AM

Ken
DM me if you're interested!
Monday, May 15 2017 @ 11:28 AM

T-Bone
Ok. Message sent.
Monday, May 15 2017 @ 11:33 AM

Muffin69
My best friend and me both slept with him. At the same time.
Monday, May 15 2017 @ 11:27 AM

Ken

Feel free to DM me, too.

Monday, May 15 2017 @ 11:29 AM

Dangerfield

It was the ball-gag and granny panties that pushed Gloria over the edge.

Monday, May 15 2017 @ 11:35 AM

CriticalBean

Is everyone on here an a-hole?

Monday, May 15 2017 @ 11:37 AM

LuvTrueCrime

At least Dahmer ate what he killed!

Monday, May 15 2017 @ 11:41 AM

CriticalBean

Yep. Everyone.

Monday, May 15 2017 @ 11:42 AM

RockStarGamer

The Leviticus Killer sure understands how to make a statement. Bringing a whole new level of notoriety to the game. What a buff ace!

Monday, May 15 2017 @ 11:46 AM

LOAD MORE

5

JENA

Monday, 7:45 a.m.

THE LINE AT the coffee shop drive-thru stretches out of the parking lot and onto the street. Mary volunteered to go inside to speed up our coffee acquisition, so I'm in the Explorer on my phone, watching the old news piece again while I wait. I click the screen and the video plays. The camera zooms in on a large room with fluorescent lights stretching across a drop ceiling and hideous floors of oversize linoleum tiles in beige, white, jade, and burgundy. Cinderblock walls are painted in contrasting colors, eggshell on the top half and battleship gray on the bottom. The words *Pittsburgh's Action News 4* hover inside a blue box in the bottom right corner, while *SCI Fayette* is plastered in the top left.

In burgundy chairs, all of them a single piece of molded plastic, sit rows of inmates. They wear matching burgundy jumpsuits with "D.O.C." stamped on their backs in large white letters. Their faces are all tilted up in rapt attention to a man at a faux-wood pulpit. Silas Halvard. Over six feet, but slender, his medium brown hair forms two perfect arches. He holds a wireless mic in cuffed hands, his left one missing the ring finger. From this angle, you can't see the manacles on his legs. They're hidden behind the pulpit. As much as I want to deny it, Silas is devastatingly handsome: a stark contrast to the emptiness of his eyes. Those stormy blues raise goose bumps on my arms every time.

I'm back at the field in Windgap when I discovered the body. Joseph Burton, a name burned into my memory. A fiery redhead, buried in the ground up to his chest. Shattered front teeth. Streams of dried blood running from the corners of his mouth to his chin. Head wrenched back. Mouth stretched wide as if crying out to be spared from this horror. Face a smear of purple, orange, and yellow beneath more blossoms of dried blood. Right cheek viciously caved in. Scalp partially ripped away.

On the phone's screen, Silas's lips are moving. No doubt an impassioned speech. I imagine the hint of New Orleans "*yat*" accent he works so hard to cover up flavoring his words. But all I can hear is the reporter's voice-over.

"The Leviticus Killer's murder spree shook Pittsburgh to its steel core. Eleven male victims. All of them buried up to their chests and stoned to death over the span of eleven months. The brutal murders involved fist-size rocks thrown at the victims until they died from blunt force trauma. The crime scenes were said to be so gruesome, seasoned officers found themselves stepping away.

While only convicted of one murder, with no evidence linking him to the other ten, many are convinced Silas Halvard, a professor of Biblical Studies, is the Leviticus Killer. And that he has gotten away with a string of monstrous deeds, killing "sinners" as part of some biblical opus. Still others think him a copycat. And then there are those who believe the court convicted an innocent man.

Whatever the truth, Silas has found solace in religion, giving motivational speeches to fellow inmates."

The video cuts to show Silas's musical backup. A middle-aged woman playing an old keyboard. A long-haired man strumming an emerald-green electric guitar.

"And his message will go beyond prison walls. The Pennsylvania Prisons and Parole Podcast will feature special episodes of Silas's speeches every Sunday. Silas is also credited with the donations pouring in from regular citizens to build SCI Fayette's first chapel. Silas has come a long way since his arrest by PBP's Detective Jena Campbell—"

The Explorer's passenger-side door swings open, bringing the aroma of coffee. I flick the video away. Mary follows the scent inside, a tray with two paper cups in her hands. Her eyebrows almost reach her hairline. She saw the video.

She puts the coffee in the middle console's cup holders and stuffs the tray down along the side of her seat. "Not the video again. You've got to stop watching that nonsense. It's not healthy."

I hunch protectively over the phone. "In ten days, it will be five years."

Mary puts a comforting hand on my leg. "Yeah. Five years since you locked up a very dangerous man. You should be proud."

Nothing about today deserves an ounce of pride. I chuck the phone onto the dash and sigh.

I didn't put that monster behind bars so he could hoodwink all the fools with his charm. His followers think he was wrongly convicted. That or he only committed *one* murder, and now he is reformed, peaceful. But I don't buy that rehabilitated act for a second. I just want to figure out what game he is playing. What operations he might be running from inside.

My phone lights up, so I grab it. A message from Collins.

"What? It's bad, isn't it?"

"More disappointing. Collins couldn't recover anything from Jack's laptop or phone."

Mary gives my knee a pat. "Let's get to work, huh?"

Even though I can't stomach it, I take a sip of my coffee, scalding my tongue. After another burning sip, I pull out of the parking lot, heading for Jack's high school.

Ten minutes later, the dispatch radio clicks to life.

"20?" the dispatcher barks my badge number.

"Copy." The radio makes an electronic chirp as I release the transmit key.

"A 187 at 158 North Drive. RP found the victim in a hot tub. No suspects on scene. You're the closest unit."

My heart skips a beat. *Don't let it be Jack*, I silently beg. It can't be him.

"Is the victim young? Male?"

Only static from the radio, but after a moment, the dispatcher replies, *"Female."*

I expel a held breath with a mix of guilt and rage. Relief it is not Jack. Pissed there is another homicide in my city. "Check. On our way."

"North Drive. That's close," Mary says as I do a U-turn.

Case notes – Monday, October 16, 2017

Detective J. Campbell

INITIAL SCENE INFORMATION

At approx. 06:30 AM, Monday October 16, 2017, Garth Raycroft, a custodian, arrived at 590 Crane Ave, Brashear High School, to open the building and begin his shift. The building had been closed for the weekend with no custodial staff due to fumigation on the evening of Friday, October 13. Upon parking his vehicle, Raycroft spotted a body in the back field, buried up to mid-chest, in the sand pit used for track and field events. He dialed 911 to alert authorities.

Decedent was found by first responder Officer Tom Dale, to be male, fully clothed, medium build, dark hair. Appearance of heavy bruising and bleeding wounds. Major cranial injuries to the skull. Fracture of left occipital bone. Dislocation of right jaw. Blood-soaked sand under head and neck area indicates profuse bleeding. Decedent was surrounded by a pile of bloodstained stones. Appears to have been deceased 8 to 20 hours prior to discovery. Complete rigor mortis. Upon excavation, hands found closed, right one clutching a beryl gemstone.

Decedent is wearing a blue-collared shirt. No jewelry. No weapons found. The decedent was removed from the sandpit and transported to the Allegheny Medical Examiner for autopsy.

MEDICAL EXAMINER INFORMATION

ME, Rowan O'Reilly, identified the decedent as Leslie George, age 44. Cause of death was reported as blunt force trauma to the skull.

INVESTIGATION NOTES

- Leslie George is the seventh stoning victim in Allegheny County in the last seven months. He had a prior conviction of statutory sexual assault and was a registered sex offender.
- All victims have likely involvement in sex crimes and/or serial adultery.
- Gemstones found in order: diamond, emerald, agate, turquoise, carnelian, chrysolite, beryl.
- While the stoning is likely tied to religious ideology, the significance of the gemstones remains unclear.

NEXT STEPS

- Collins to continue search for any mention of or acquisition of the seven gemstones.
- Expert consultation regarding possible biblical significance of the crimes.
    - ~~Fr. Ian Dorman, Priest, St. Marcy of Mercy Church (interviewed)~~
    - ~~Abdullah Abbas, Imam, al-Masjid al-Alwwal Mosque (interviewed)~~
    - ~~Silas Halvard, Professor of Biblical Studies, Geneva University (no return call so far)~~

6

JENA

Monday, 8:06 a.m.

WE ARE AT the house in no time. It is in the East End of Pittsburgh, where cookie cutter colonial homes with child-friendly backyards make up nearly all of Stanton Heights. This home is a bi-level. Nicely kept landscaping dotted with hostas and a Japanese maple.

An ambulance and the cherry red Mustang belonging to Anders are already there. The paramedics shuffle down the driveway as I kill the engine.

"In back," one paramedic mumbles.

I fly around the side of the house, squeezing between the white brick exterior and the neighbor's cedar fence. Unlatching the gate, I pass through to the backyard. Once there, I try to make sense of what I see.

I stare at what is technically a hot tub, but the setup is so lavish calling it that is blasphemous. It is more like an outdoor spa. A teak pergola covers the oasis, lined with tropical foliage: bromeliads, birds of paradise, philodendrons. A concrete slab of a bar stretches across one side, a half-drunk martini with the olives still in it resting on top. On another side, a screen hangs from the pergola. An old movie plays without sound. The picture comes from a projector a little way across the yard on a stand under a white birch tree. Doris Day is clearly flustered by whatever Rock Hudson's smirking face is saying over the phone. The backyard scene would be a '50s tiki revival paradise, if not for the body.

And all the blood.

The victim is about mid-fifties. Strawberry blond hair streaked with gray pulled up and secured with a jade hair stick. She is slumped forward. Her vintage nautical bathing suit, once navy and white striped, is now a gruesomely patriotic red, white, and blue.

Anders slips in beside me, giving her report.

"The victim is Michelle Green. Impaled by a metal projectile, about a foot long."

Where the victim's torso meets the water, a glint of silver shines among the red. I glance at the dried bloodstains on Anders's latex gloves, then over at her underwater camera, streaked in gore. I can't imagine what it took to get those shots. To see what was going on beneath the surface.

"There's a mechanism in the jet. Shot it straight into her."

"Must've been a hell of a lucky shot to kill her so fast." With an ordinary shot to the torso, usually a person has some time. Can maybe crawl to a phone and dial for help as they bleed out. But this victim didn't move from where she'd been impacted.

"Cause of death was electrocution," Anders adds. "The rod was wired."

"How horrible," Mary whispers, crossing herself. "Poor thing."

Electrocution makes more sense, though. Hard to move when you're being cooked alive.

"Don't worry," Anders says. "Power's out. The jolt tripped the breaker."

"Why impale and electrocute?" I murmur, half to myself. "The blood must be for show."

I take a step closer, half crouching, getting a look at the victim's face. She is wearing full makcup. Perfectly arched eyebrows, her cheekbones angled a bit like Meryl Streep's.

Michelle Green.

She looks so familiar, but I can't place why, and the name isn't ringing any bells. I scan the rest of the tub, pulling on my latex gloves.

A voice carries into the backyard. The distinct accent of Detective Dennis "Jersey" Spiers, who is talking loudly. No doubt at his partner, Levi Weisz.

"That's the worst joke I ever heard," Jersey says as the two of them round the corner. Jersey's about five-ten, but he towers over the much shorter and thinner Weisz. While Jersey is muscular with a skin tone that can only be described as spray tan pumpkin spice, Weisz is gangly and so pale he is nearly translucent.

Jersey preens his spiked black hair with his fingers. "Eh!" he says, arms outstretched as he spies us. "Listen to this awful joke."

"—Damn," Weisz says, taking in the victim.

Jersey's eyes wander to where Weisz is looking, and even he goes quiet.

"I take it Price assigned you to her case?" I say.

"Yeah." Jersey regains some of his composure. "Said you were busy kissing the governor's ass."

I fill Jersey and Weisz in on what we know about the victim

and the circumstances surrounding her death, then say, "All right, Mary, let's roll."

Mary and I are about to leave when a label outside the hot tub catches my eye.

"What's this?" I say, pointing.

"The hot tub pump label?" Mary says.

"Look at the barcode. There is a QR code sticker stuck over it." Where it would usually say *scan me*, there is a pair of black wings.

"Good spot," Anders says. "It blends in almost perfectly."

I yank my phone out of my pocket and scan it. A URL for a social media site pops up. I click the link.

7

JENA

Monday, 8:28 a.m.

A FACE STARES back at me, a macabre grin with rotted teeth and sulfur yellow eyes that sear into my mind as I try to look away. I can't look away, though. I stare at this profile image, taking in dark lesions, boils, and sores that bubble from waxy flesh. Everything about it is grotesque and nauseating. The black nose partially eaten away. The hellish halo floating above. Demonic wings unfurl. Razor sharp feathers drip with darkness I can almost feel sliding down my throat, curdling in my stomach.

It is a new account created yesterday. No followers. The account isn't following anyone either. I spot the account name.

@azrael

"That name is biblical, right?" I say to Mary, who looms over my shoulder.

Mary nods. A devout Maronite Catholic, Mary's up on religious stuff. Way more than me, the agnostic who can't be bothered with faith unless it relates to a case.

That the person behind this avatar could be our killer makes me shudder. Killers like this, with delusions of religious grandeur, are the worst kind. They don't do straightforward torture. They rend flesh into a bloody pulp, throwing stone after stone in the name of The Almighty.

He had fiery red hair. Teeth glinting in puddles of blood among the rocks. A caved in cheek from a shattered occipital bone. Face forever stretched in a final agonizing scream.

I force the image of Silas's victim from my old case out of my head. There is a video on the page's feed, paused on a silhouette-darkened figure, the background alive with flames. I press *play* and jump as an anguished scream shreds my speakers. Grainy images flash across the screen. Blood. A woman bludgeoned to death, lifeless eyes turned up to the sky.

The shadow figure speaks in a deep tenor, distorted by a voice modulator. "Hello, Pittsburgh. Are you ready for a Second Coming?"

The voice is warped, but the venom is clear. Chills crawl up my neck, and I squeeze the phone.

"I'm about to slaughter nine of the twelve members of the jury who convicted the legendary Leviticus Killer until he is free."

My stomach drops at the mention of Silas.

His scalp ripped away. Dirt caked beneath his fingernails. A purple gemstone.

"Who will they be?" the phantom presses on. "And who will be the lucky spared three? Don't want to find out? My terms are clear. Leviticus free. Now. Or else prepare for a river of blood."

An atom bomb detonates on the green screen, blowing up the courthouse where Silas was convicted. A rolling mushroom cloud towers over the rubble. The image freezes.

My stomach turns sour as I ask, "Do you know anything biblical about killing nine people?"

"Um." Mary swallows, collecting herself. "No. Nine's not a very holy number."

"Michelle Green," I say, fumbling through my memories.

"You okay?"

I meet her gaze, responding in a whisper. "That's why I recognize her. She was the jury member who delivered Silas's verdict." I clear my throat, shifting my weight before I speak again, but my voice still shakes. "This guy is going to kill again."

I head for the Explorer, calling Captain Price. When he doesn't answer, I leave a message explaining what we've found. The victim. The social media video. "I want Green's case," I say before hanging up and sending him the video.

I get inside the car.

"What are we doing?" Mary says.

"Wait here a minute."

Mary shrugs and drinks her cold coffee.

Five minutes pass, my mind on Michelle Green, who sat in that courtroom and declared Silas guilty, before I call Price again.

"Captain, call me back."

"Ready to roll?" Mary says.

I shake my head. Wait two minutes. I'm about to dial a third time, convinced he is avoiding me, but then my cell rings with "Glory Days," and the corner of Mary's lip tugs up in an almost smile, the joke working its magic.

I answer the phone, putting it on speaker.

"Campbell," Captain Price barks, *"Stop leaving messages."*

"I want this case," I fire back. "Let the Odd Couple handle the disappearance of the governor's son. We have a budding serial killer on our hands. I'm the best person for the job, and you know it."

"Look," Price says. *"I appreciate your skills, but we don't know what we're dealing with yet. We don't know whoever posted that killed the victim. And if they did, there's no reason to think this is a serial killer, unless they kill again. Right now, this social media video is only a threat. Just in case, I'm putting surveillance on the rest of the jurors' houses. But the past is haunting you, and, if I'm honest, I don't think that case would be good for you. Find the governor's kid. End of story."*

"We've barely started. It's an easy switch," I protest.

"Let it go, Campbell. That's an order."

"At least tell me if Collins pulls anything from the social media account," I demand, but I'm yelling at silence. Price cut me off.

I throw the phone into the cupholder, then punch the steering wheel.

Mary gently touches my arm, as if she thinks I might spontaneously combust. "Sorry," she says. "I'm sure Jersey and Weisz will keep us updated. You know Jersey can't keep his mouth shut, right? Right?"

I nod, not trusting myself to speak.

"If it's more than just the one target, they'll tell us." Mary pats my arm. "Let's find the kid, huh?"

8

JACK

Tuesday, 9:09 a.m.

JACK WETS HIMSELF. A full stream that pours out of him for a long time. He knows that is what is happening, but the urine is whisked away. Hanging in the air, he stays completely dry.

A catheter? he thinks. But he has little sensation down there. Cut off from his own body. He is not sure if it is lack of circulation or something worse. Panic surges through his chest, making it hard to breathe. He swallows hard, his throat working and his Adam's apple bobbing.

When was the last time he ate? Or drank. His mouth is parched, his tongue thick and swollen. A foulness clings to the back of his throat. His mind races, heart pounding against his rib cage. Cold liquid trickles into his arm.

An IV?

Dread knots his stomach. Blinking is agony. Like gallons of sand have been poured into his eyes. Heat radiates from his cheek and temple, the skin raw and tender.

Infection?

Fear gnaws his insides, every beat of his heart a bass drum

in his ears as he fights to make sense of the situation. He wants to go home. Not this home. Not this fake place of pain and cold where the shadow monster lurks, waiting to hurt him. He scans the darkened room, heart thrumming, head pounding, palms sweating. But he can't wipe his hands because they're full of some nothingness he can't see.

Jack starts to cry, the tears welling in pools on his cheeks, unable to escape. He tries to wipe them away, but his hands don't reach his face. Snot drips from his nostrils. He is hyperventilating, blowing mucus bubbles that pop and cling to the skin outside his nose.

A wave of nausea hits him.

"Shadow," he croaks, not recognizing his own voice, so hoarse and weak.

He doesn't want to bring Shadow's attention. But it'll be so much worse for him if he makes a mess.

He gathers his strength, and cries out again, "Shadow? I'm going to throw up."

He dry heaves, leaning forward in that weird floating motion, his body flailing in the restraints.

A firm hand presses down on his shoulder, holding him in place. There is a metallic scrape of a bucket handle against plastic. It is surreal, something happening outside the world he is in.

"Don't miss," Shadow's warped voice says.

Images flash through his head.

A car.

A skeleton face.

A taser.

He remembers pain. Metal on skin. The shock of electricity ripping through his body.

"Don't hurt me," he says, peering into the darkness.

And then he throws up. Liquid sloshes inside a bucket. The vomit is thin and pungent as he doubles over, his body hanging in its suspension apparatus. He has no idea how to get out of this rig, this harness, whatever is imprisoning him. But he has to. He needs to get away.

A flood of liquid assaults his mouth. Water. The abruptness of it makes him choke. He wants to gulp it down, but swishes and spits, rinsing thc foul bile from his mouth. Then he waits, desperate for more. But no more water comes.

He wants out. Out! And then he is coughing, hacking. On the verge of throwing up again, but his stomach is completely empty.

He loses it. Swinging at the air, then clawing at himself. Tearing, determined to rip himself out of his prison. His hands won't close, so he batters the useless lumps at his chest. Again and again, dull thuds strike his body. Then he blindly bangs his hands together. There is a thump of hard plastic colliding against hard plastic that echoes through the room. VR controllers, he realizes. He smashes his hands together again and again, trying to bust loose.

And then pain. Liquid fire coursing through him as his muscles contract. Cramping so hard his calves are about to rip free of his body.

"Stop, stop!!" he wails, throat burning, teeth going hot.

The fire extinguishes. His whole body is left aching.

"What have we talked about?" The voice sounds far away.

"Follow the rules," Jack pants.

"This is a two-player game, Jack. You've got to do your part."

"Yes, yes. I'm sorry."

"Better."

"I'm sorry. I'm sorry."

"You're forgiven. This time. And now's your chance to make it up to me. You killed the last game. Murdered it. Time for the next one. Isn't that wonderful?"

Jack nods, biting down on his tongue. A distraction from the deep, raw ache in his muscles. He can't play a game. Not now. He is so sore. Exhausted.

His fake room morphs into a carnival scene, a cheery slide-whistle tune piping into his headset. The sun shines in a perfect blue sky, and Jack senses the wrongness of it. The sick perversion of reality.

There is pressure on his face from the VR headset, dried sweat caking on his cheeks. *I'm trapped in a dark room. I'm a hostage. A torture victim.*

Vivid red-and-white striped awnings cover booths constructed of wooden frames, each enclosure containing various games of chance and skill. Toss the ping-pong ball into the fishbowl. Throw a dart and burst balloons. Catch a rubber duck with a magnetic fishing pole. Everywhere he looks, barkers call out to come over and play, win a prize, three chances for five dollars. He can almost smell the sweet cotton candy and yeasty hot pretzels in the air, his dry mouth watering.

I'm so hungry. When was the last time I ate?

The booth in front of him is eye-catching, its back wall filled with dozens of colorful cats perched atop stacked shelves. Each metal face is painted in bright yellows and pinks and blues. Their gaping mouths are stretched wide as if waiting for a treat.

Or screaming.

There is a row of stools running along the front of the booth. Every seat is equipped with a stylized water gun like something out of a '50s sci-fi movie.

"Take a seat," Shadow commands.

Jack glides up to the booth and plops down. He is more crouching than sitting on a stool. His hands shake so badly.

"Shoot the treats into the cats' mouths. When one of the collars lights up, shoot it. Ring the little bell, and the game is over. You win, and dear old Dad gets his message."

"I already told you. He won't answer."

Panic takes over, his body trembling.

"He'll leave me to rot. Might as well kill me now." The bile is creeping up again. Jack heaves.

"Don't you dare. There are worse things than death. I could sever your spine, hmm? You don't need your legs for the games. Or maybe an amputation? What do you think about that?"

Jack whimpers, chomping down hard on his lip to keep in the scream. *No more pain. No more pain.*

"Settle down, Jack. As long as you behave and keep playing, you have nothing to worry about. Remember?"

"Okay," he manages. *Have to be good. Have to be good.*

"That a boy. Get ready. Set."

He grips the water gun—or treat gun, he supposes—concentrating on keeping his aim steady.

You can do this. You're a pro gamer. Get it together.

An alarm sounds, red lights whirling from the apex of the awning, announcing the start of the game.

He shoots the treat gun, his steady pull of the trigger sending out little triangle cat treats in a constant stream. He is doing it. Body sore, hands shaking, and still he is doing it. A little thrill runs through him, the adrenaline that comes with crushing a game. His brain is fuzzy, but he remembers Shadow's instructions and targets the cats' mouths. Fires the morsels in. Soon, one of the collar bells lights up, flashing a vibrant firefly yellow.

He takes aim and hits it dead-on. The bell rings.

9

JENA

Tuesday, 11:07 a.m.

BACK IN THE conference room, I'm on social media, scrolling through @azrael's profile. There are no new updates. Just that one video. I want another. Dread it, but want it.

"Azrael got over a thousand followers in four hours," I say to Mary. All of them no doubt also craving an update. That happened fast. And I have the sinking premonition @azrael's cancer is going to spread.

"What do you know about Azrael? Biblically, I mean."

"In the Quran, Azrael is the Angel of Death," Mary says.

"I thought Azrael was a Christian angel."

Mary shakes her head. "Common misconception. The idea of angels as individuals isn't really part of Hebrew scripture. That's the source material for modern Christian versions of the Bible."

"I'd protest you explaining it to me like a two-year-old, but yeah, I have no idea about this stuff."

"I know. Anyway, in the Bible, angels are referred to as

servants or messengers of God. They aren't usually given proper names."

"Huh," I say as Azrael's demonic avatar stares back at me. "You learn something new every day."

"We need to focus on Jack." Mary jabs the smart board with a digital stylus.

Of course, she is right. There is more at stake than Price's wrath because the governor is breathing down his neck. If we don't find Jack quickly, he'll most likely end up dead. But all I can think about is the call that went out to Weisz and Jersey this morning. It plays on loop inside my mind—another homicide.

This time it is Lisa Bell, also a past member of Silas's jury. Victim number two. I'm sick to my stomach and scared stupid for the other jurors. Not having any details about the crime scene is only making it worse, eating away at me. And the putrefying egg smell from my healthy breakfast platter is almost tipping me over the edge.

I watched Jersey and Weisz head out to notify Bell's family. Watched a team Price assembled scurrying around to keep this out of the press. A while ago, Anders hurried past the conference room headed for the lab with evidence bags in hand. I gripped the sides of my chair and stayed rooted in my seat.

"Is there any family who would hide Jack?"

Mary's words come at me like I'm listening to them underwater, muffled and distorted. My leg shakes, my heel hammering against the floor. I don't answer her. I shoot out of my office chair and sprint down the hall to the lab.

I swing the door open to find Anders leaning over a microscope. Her eyes widen when they land on me. She grins beneath her goggles and nitrile gloves, her long, open lab coat revealing a crop top beneath it. Wheels from a motorcycle tattoo peek out below the edge, covering her bottom rib. Pink ribbons hold her power puffs in place.

"Hey," she says.

"Hey. How's it going?"

"I'm about to find out."

She walks over to a monitor, reading a report generated in real time as it scrolls across the screen. A few minutes pass, the silence clawing at me until I can't stand it anymore.

I clear my throat. "Anything in the results?"

"Huh. Yeah." She scrunches one of her puffs with her fingertips, chewing her lip. "I've got a match."

"A match for what?"

"The poison."

My stomach tightens. "What poison?"

Anders narrows suspicious eyes at me. "Oh, right. This isn't your case." Her lips are a thin line, and I can almost hear her debating how to proceed. "Bell was found on her kitchen floor. Respiratory failure and cardiac arrest. Should I even be telling you this? I don't want Weisz and Jersey mad at me. Jersey's big on loyalty."

"I'm not going to interfere with their investigation. Please, Anders. I need to know."

"Okay, but you'll owe me one," she says with a smirk. "That fine DoJ boyfriend of yours have an attractive sister?"

"Sorry. Mason's an only."

"A girl can dream. Moving on, the poison's batrachotoxin. Found in three types of poison dart frogs, four types of beetles, and a couple of birds from New Guinea."

"Like the stuff they use in blow darts?"

"Yeah."

"I thought she had a surveillance car on the street. How did someone get close enough?"

Anders shakes her head. "Bell wasn't shot. She had a lot of animals. Two Pekinese dogs, five Ragdolls and one Russian Blue, plus an African Grey parrot."

Mary bursts into the lab. "Thought I'd find you here."

I shrug. "I'm that predictable?"

"A million percent. You already accosted Collins this morning about the social media account. Don't look at me like that. I knew where you were."

"Guilty," I say.

"Did Collins find anything?"

"Nope." I rub the back of my neck. "He says this Azrael is a hell of a hacker. Collins has never seen anyone so clean at covering their tracks." I look back to Anders. "Please, continue."

"One of the cats brought the poison into the house from outside. We found it on Fluffy's collar. We think the poison must have transferred to Bell when she petted or picked up the cat." Anders leans closer to the monitor. "Or when she tried to figure out what was wrong with Fluffy. Both Bell and the cat didn't survive."

Mary's face falls. "Poor woman."

"At least her passing would've been quick," Anders says. "And there's no antidote, nothing anyone could've done even if we'd known what it was."

This is bullshit. I should be on this case, protecting them. I can't have another string of people dying on me. Like with Silas. But I need to shove my feelings aside right now and think with my head. When you let emotions take over, more people die.

My brain works to piece together the circumstances of the two former jurors' deaths and the video on @azrael's page.

My gaze locks with Mary's. "What do you make of this? First water to blood…then poison, possibly from a frog. Ring any bells?"

Mary's face lights up with recognition, and she confirms my suspicions.

"He's enacting the plagues. Nine's not a holy number. But ten's a different story."

"Thanks for the help, Anders."

We rush out of the lab, discussing the implications. We're back in the conference room maybe thirty minutes, when Captain Price barrels in, the door banging shut behind him like he is a wild gunslinger entering a saloon instead of a dismal excuse for a professional meeting space. He stiffly places himself at the head of the table, standing up straighter than his brush cut. He squints, scrutinizing me as he smooths his well-groomed mustache, which ends in clean lines before it hits the corners of his mouth.

He raises a finger before he gruffly declares, "I'm going to say something, and before I do, I need it understood that you will not say one word of *I told you so*."

I respond with a subtle salute. "I wouldn't dream of it."

Price raises a skeptical eyebrow but continues. "It looks like we may have a serial killer on our hands. We need to take serious action on his threat to kill nine of the twelve former jurors."

I clear my throat, then add, "Plus one more."

Price's blue eyes pierce me. "What do you mean one more?"

Mary's chewing her bubble gum as she chirps, "It's the ten plagues."

She gestures toward the smart board. If Price had read our notes before he started barking, he would have known we were brainstorming on Azrael's case as well as our own. Mary neatly outlined the ten plagues with accompanying cartoon illustrations. The bursting boils are my particular favorite. One looks like it has an eerie smile, but Mary swears she was just drawing pus.

"But the threat was for nine jurors." The crease between Price's his eyebrows could swallow a baby.

"Because the tenth victim won't be a juror. We've already figured it out."

"Don't sit there looking smug. Out with it!" Patience isn't one of Price's virtues.

"Azrael is demanding Silas's release. And who has the power to pardon Silas or grant clemency and declare his sentence served?"

"The governor." Price nods. "Good work. We'll put out so much security, it will be up the governor's ass."

"Not the governor," I say, my voice dropping. "The tenth plague is the killing of the firstborn son."

"His son, Jack?" Price's stony face drains of color, his mouth slack for a moment before his composure returns in full force. He examines me, lips drawn into a tight line. "Fine," he barks, pointing at me. "You're on the case."

I open my mouth to say *thank you*, but Price makes a gesture to shut it.

"*With* Weisz and Jersey," he says. "I want you working together on this one. Now tell me you have a lead on that kid's whereabouts."

My face falls before I turn away, unable to meet his penetrating stare.

10

JENA

Tuesday, 8:26 p.m.

I WANT TO be comfortable in Mason's house, but I never am. Maybe because of its uncanny resemblance to the home where I grew up in Pittsburgh's East End. A few stairs lead up to the joint living room and dining room, separated from the cramped kitchen, which has a newer cut-out in the plaster dividing wall to make it less claustrophobic. It all hits too close to home.

My thoughts spiral toward a past life I've buried beneath layers of competency and sarcasm as I sit at the kitchen table with Mason, a half-drunk bottle of cabernet sauvignon between us.

"Earth to Jena," Mason says. "Where'd you go just now?"

"I'm sorry. It's this case, and Silas's five-year incarceration anniversary is coming up. It doesn't seem like a coincidence."

Mason furrows his brows, concern flashing across his face. "Maybe let Silas go. Just for tonight, huh?"

"What's that supposed to mean?"

Mason takes my hands, holding me like I'm a frightened bird, like he thinks if I get loose, I'm going to fly around and hurt myself. My back is immediately up as he looks into my eyes.

"You've just been a little obsessed with him lately. Well, not just lately."

I pull my hands back, his touch scalding. "What the hell?"

"I just… I want you to relax, that's all. How long have we been together, and it's like you're never fully yourself? You don't drop your guard. Even for a second. And it makes me wonder, if this is enough for you. If I'm enough."

I angle my body away from him, my fingers curling into fists.

"You know what? Never mind. Forget I said anything. I didn't mean to make this about us. I get that you're under a lot of stress at work, but maybe take a step back. That's all. Let your subconscious work on the problem for a while."

"What? You think my judgement's clouded. That I'm letting my emotions take over? And here I thought you knew me better than anyone." My nostrils flare, my blood pressure shooting up.

"I'm not saying that at all. I'm just worried about where your mind is at. It's like you're always somewhere else."

"Well, I'm sorry for having feelings, Mr. Cold and Calculated."

Mason looks as if I've stuck him in the gut. "That's not fair, and you know it."

I want to blow a raspberry at him, but choose venomous insults over childish actions. "Mr. Perfect. Mr. I-never-let-emotions-govern-my-decisions. Maybe if you got a little more emotional sometimes, you wouldn't still be alone."

That is completely out of line, but I don't care. If my coworkers could see me now, they'd all nod their heads, confirming their suspicions that lie beneath the comedic attempts. I'm that callous bitch they all knew I was. I can't look at the hurt blooming in Mason's eyes. I've put that expression there so many times. Caused this pain far too often to this man who has never been anything but patient with me. And that is my problem. I expect the worst of him, as if he will transform into my father, yelling and screaming and demanding whatever he wants, to hell with the consequences. But I'm the one who does the yelling and screaming.

This relationship is fucked up. I'm fucked up. And I'm not sure if I care as much about that, about repairing the damage between us, the damage within me, as I do about nailing Azrael. I'm a goddamn mess. In life and love. In everything. I should be grateful for Mason sticking with me this long and recant the things I just said, but I've started the freight train rolling now, and I've never been good at pulling the brakes.

I bolt from the table, the kitchen chair squealing against the tile.

"Jena, wait." Mason shoots to his feet, reaching for me, but I keep my arms firmly at my side, my eyes coldly assessing him.

"You know what? You can forget asking me to move in again. We're done."

I'm doing him a favor, I tell myself for the hundredth time. I'm doing us both a favor.

I flash a frigid smile. "Don't call," I say, and storm off.

Mason's pleas float after me, begging me to be reasonable and all the things he usually says when I get this way, but I don't listen, don't process them.

I fly down the few stairs to the landing, and out the front door.

A few hours later, I'm huddled up in my bed with my laptop perched on a pillow, but I'm still seething over my breakup with

Mason. How dare he suggest I have an unhealthy obsession with Silas? It is my goddamn job. He should understand better than anyone what it's like to bring your work home with you.

I push Mason from my mind and go back to scouring every detail. Too many windows open, I pore over the files for Jack, Green, and Bell. I've reopened Silas Halvard's records as well, although Mason would say I never closed them. Screw him. My gut tells me there is some connection, if only I could see it.

My phone dings and I glance over at the nightstand, expecting a message from Mason looking to reconcile, but instead a social media notification banner pops up on my screen.

intentionallyblank—that is my profile name.

Azrael (@azrael) started following you.

My stomach flips, and I pull my covers up to my neck. How the hell does he know this is my account? I only use it for work to covertly stalk criminals. There is nothing on my page. A little cartoon star for an avatar. A nearly empty bio that says, *This space intentionally left blank*. No posts whatsoever. No one I follow or any followers. Nothing.

Another notification appears.

[intentionallyblank] Azrael

Wants to send you a message

I scoop up my phone. Thumb hovering over the button, I try to pretend I'm not trembling. I scold myself for being a baby. I wanted this. Pushed this wish out into the universe, and the request manifested. It is not the way I wanted. I'd hoped for a public post. But I'll take any information I can get. However I can get it.

He probably has some hacker bot tracking accounts that look at his profile. That is the rational explanation. No way he knows it is me. Maybe he is trying to recruit followers and I'll learn something useful. I quickly check my phone's Settings to make sure the app's access to my camera and microphone are still disabled. They are.

I click the notification.

Hello, Detective Campbell,

I nearly throw my phone across the room, squeezing the sides, which causes it to take an accidental photo of the screen.

He knows who I am. How the hell does he know?

My breathing quickens, and I jerk up in my bed. Is he in my room? In the closet? In the bathroom? Peering at me through the slits in my blinds? The air vents? The crack beneath the door?

Stop freaking out, I tell myself. There is no way he can know it is me. It makes no sense. Unless…

Was he watching? At Green's crime scene? He could've been there, lurking. It is not uncommon for serial killers to revel in the aftermath of their actions.

If he saw me there, saw me scan the QR code, he would've got an alert right away. Known someone had accessed his profile. He could've had a direct visual of who it was.

Of course, he would recognize me from Silas's case. That makes sense. He connected the dots and knew this account, my account, viewed his profile. That is all the access he has to me. My DMs. Not my address or my private information. Nothing else.

The thought calms me a little, and I slump back down in my bed. I continue to read.

> *You probably think I'm evil, right? But you're not innocent either, are you? You could confess, little bird, and all this would be over. Leviticus would finally be free. Or maybe you could take a more unconventional path, hmm? Pay a hacker to find me through less than legal channels. Although I doubt anyone is talented enough. I'm very good at covering my tracks, as you'll come to find out. But what do you say? Will you make the same mistake?*
>
> *Seven more days to confess…*
>
> *~ Azrael*

My palms are slick with sweat, my heart thrashing in my ears. This time I do hurl my phone, right down onto the bed.

Azrael knows more than he should. So much more than he would through a casual observation of me at a crime scene. He can't know what I did to put Silas away. How the hell would he know that? No one does. No. He doesn't. Suspects, maybe. He must be phishing for information. If he knew what I did, had any proof, he would've come forward and had Silas out of jail. I need to pull back and use logic, think about it from Azrael's perspective.

But while Azrael may not know what he is suggesting, he has a lot of intel. Is he investigating me as hard as I'm investigating him? Already, he is winning because he knows who I am. That's more than I have on him.

What if he is tracking me? I reach for my phone again, my instinct to call Mason, but he probably won't even pick up. Not after our latest fight. Maybe I should get my phone to Collins.

See if he can trace the message. But the content will put me under scrutiny by my own department. I can't risk investigation.

I snatch my phone from the covers and turn it off. I have everything I need to protect me right here. I pull open the nightstand's drawer and pull out the Sig P320, my personal gun. I tuck the weapon beneath my pillow, and then something hits me.

Azrael called me *little bird.* There is only one person who calls me that.

Silas.

Azrael and Silas have been in contact.

Transcript of Recorded Conversation – Silas Halvard

Detective J. Campbell, January 22, 2018. 1:20 P.M

[JC's handwritten note: Silas isn't at all what I expected of a theology professor. Mid-forties. About six feet. Muscular, but slender. Shiny medium brown hair. Blue-gray eyes. Missing his left ring finger. A clean cut, many years old.]

JC: Professor Halvard. Thanks so much for taking the time to meet with me.

SH: My pleasure. I am so sorry it took me a while to get back to you. Things have been a tad wild. But I am glad you're here. I don't often get folks with such a keen interest in biblical studies. My students could pick up a thing or two from you. Not that I hold it against them. Back in my college days, all I cared about was acing the exams, too.

JC: I can imagine. It's a fascinating subject, but I have something more pressing to discuss with you.

SH: Well now, that sounds like a change of pace. I am all ears. What is stirring your thoughts, Detective?

JC: I'm knee-deep in an investigation, Professor. A series of murders. The victims are buried up to their chests before they're stoned to death.

SH: I did catch wind of that in the newspapers. Sounds like a heap of nasty business.

JC: We've had ten victims. Each one given a different gemstone to hold post-mortem. So far, the stones are...

[JC's handwritten note: The pause in the audio is me referring to my notes.]

...diamond, emerald, agate, turquoise, carnelian, chrysolite, beryl, topaz, ruby, garnet. They sort of match up with birthstones, but some of them aren't birthstones. Does that mean anything to you?

SH: Well, surely. Stoning is a brutal old form of punishing, rooted in biblical history. Used to correct various wrongdoings, like blasphemy, adultery, and such. It was a means for the community to cleanse itself, to cast out the wicked from its fold. As for the gemstones, they might bear a symbolic tie. In the Book of Revelation, those are ten of the twelve foundation stones of the heavenly Jerusalem. They stand for the twelve apostles and the twelve tribes of Israel.

JC: I'm not familiar with what foundation stones are. I've searched religious texts for references to these stones and come up empty. Can you tell me more about that?

SH: Certainly. The stones don't get called by name in the Bible itself. But they sure hold powerful meaning in the biblical lore if you know where to look. In older texts. Different tongues. Hebrew. Aramaic...

JC: You read those languages?

SC: I do. And ancient Greek and Sanskrit.

[JC's handwritten note: Silas's office at Geneva University is stacked with books and papers, both on the shelves and floor. Some are open as if recently used for research. I'm shocked by all the paper when digital is so much easier and quicker to access. Silas is the old-school type of scholar.]

JC: The first victim was holding a diamond. Any thoughts on that?

SH: Those gemstones are the bedrock of celestial purity. No purer stone than a diamond. The executioner was likely aiming to declare their mission to cleanse wickedness. Maybe by vanquishing that which is soiled, they aim to lay the foundation to usher in the heavenly city to our world.

JC: So, by getting rid of sinners, the killer is hoping to bring on the rapture or something?

SH: The rapture? Nothing as dramatic as that, I wager.

JC: Any speculations on what the killer might want?

SH: Maybe the executioner is trying to show others that the kingdom of heaven is at their doorstep.

JC: That's a quote from Jesus, right? The kingdom of heaven is at hand.

SH: Just as Matthew and Mark wrote it, yes. Churchgoing is not your forte, is it Detective Campbell?

JC: Sad to say, my partner, Detective Sarkis, is the religious one. My grandmother tried taking me to service, but I'm no good at sitting still.

SH: Ha! Can't say that comes as a surprise.

[JC's handwritten note: At this point, I spot several calluses on Silas's right hand. They are notably similar to pitching calluses, like the ones I had when I pitched college softball. Silas has nothing in his office to indicate a history of coaching or playing baseball, or any other activity that would cause recent sores. Those new calluses, along with his biblical expertise, are too coincidental. Suspect? Worth looking into.]

JC: I appreciate your insights, Professor. They've been enlightening. If you remember anything else that could help my investigation, please don't hesitate to reach out.

[JC's handwritten note: Audio delay here because I pass him my business card.]

SH: A card! Well, what a treat. I do cherish the old-style courtesies. And sure thing, Detective Campbell. I will keep you in my thoughts. Good luck unraveling those mysteries, now.

[JC's handwritten note: When I set up this interview to shed light onto the religious significance behind the gemstones, I hadn't expected to find a possible suspect. Not only does he have deep knowledge of the stones, those calluses stick out in my mind. They're consistent with what would form after repeatedly throwing rocks at a victim. Further investigation into Silas and his past in New Orleans is needed. Uncertain flight risk. Proceed with caution.]

11

JENA

Wednesday, 8:00 a.m.

GRAY MIST STRETCHES across the yard of State Correction Institute Fayette, otherwise known as SCI Fayette. A double row of twenty-foot fences topped with coiled razor wire surrounds thin grass and mud. A guard buzzes me through the mechanized entrance, the front door opens with a click. Another guard serves as my escort. I catch a brief glance of his name tag, which says Kyle something, before he turns his back to me.

"This way," Kyle says.

We venture down a long, wide corridor. That hideous mosaic of beige, white, jade, and burgundy linoleum runs its length, reeking of bleach. We travel about a hundred feet before we reach the first junction. To the right is the first of two blocks made up of cells and dormitory-style living laid out in the shape of a giant iron cross. Each block houses one thousand inmates, two hundred and fifty in each arm of the cross under maximum security conditions. But there are no iron bars here. The prison is all modern rooms with solid walls and doors and stainless-steel furniture.

Down the left hallway is a license plate press. SCI Fayette is the only penitentiary in Pennsylvania to make them. The sweat shop is exactly like the stereotypical prison scene you see in the movies. The hum of machinery pulsing in perfect rhythm, the clattering of metal plates falling into place, the intermittent hiss of steam. At the heart of the room stands the gigantic printing press, its sleek frame gleaming under the harsh industrial lights. Giant rollers spin with calculated precision, transforming blank metal sheets into plates bearing the states' seal. The volume of stacked plates is like an army waiting for deployment.

Beyond that is the Special Needs Unit for those who require, or have convinced the court they require, accommodations due to mental or physical health challenges. The common room is reminiscent of a themed restaurant for kids. A few years back, a mural project turned the cinderblock into a landscape that looks as if a jungle threw up fake foliage and cartoonish big cats. And right off that common room is where the prison built the add-on expansion for Silas's chapel.

Kyle turns to his left.

"Silas isn't in his cell?" I say.

The guard shifts, his face unreadable as he looks over his shoulder and grunts, "No. He's in his chapel. Spends as much time there as he can."

I get the impression Kyle isn't my biggest fan, and that his distaste has something to do with Silas. Maybe he volunteered to escort me so he could keep a close eye on me.

Since direct is my preferred mode of communication, I say, "You don't like me, do you?"

Kyle grunts again. "I really don't know you."

The corner of my mouth twitches up. "But you don't like me. Why?"

Kyle slows, his gaze locking with mine. "It's not about you. I don't think Silas did what he was convicted of. That's all."

"Who told you that? Him?"

Kyle's eyes narrow further, but his feet keep moving forward.

"Kyle, how long have you been working here?"

"Going on six years, now."

"Long enough to know, then, that everyone in here says they're innocent."

"I don't expect you to understand," he mumbles before turning back around and picking up his pace.

Heat rises in my cheeks at the thought that Silas has this guard fooled, just like the regular citizens who've devoted themselves to be his disciples. A prison guard should know better. But maybe that is unreasonable of me. I swallow my contempt. Going in to visit Silas wearing my emotions on my sleeve is the last thing I need. He'll grab on to them and twist, using whatever he can to manipulate me. I sink the flash of anger way down into the pit of my stomach, into the abyss where I shove emotions when I need to focus. The rage will stay there like a peaceful dragon sleeping on a golden hoard inside a dark cave. Until something provokes the beast again.

Still, I can't help firing off at Kyle, "Why do you think Silas has me on his approved visitors list?"

Kyle shrugs and keeps walking.

I want to tell him that it is because Silas enjoys manipulating and toying with people. In particular, those who see through his innocent Southern gentleman act. And ever since our first conversation, Silas has delighted in messing with me. Speculating on the killer's motivations when he *was* the killer. That I'm not the bad guy here. Or maybe I should appeal to Kyle's delusions, saying that if Silas believes I'm redeemable, shouldn't he give me a chance? Who is he to question the Almighty Silas? But it wouldn't make any difference, so I keep silent.

We come to a heavy wooden door that looks Gothic. A shapely pointed arch adorned with ornate carvings. Fluorescent lights reflect off high-gloss varnish.

With a swipe of Kyle's card, the massive door creaks open. He slips inside, taking his place against the back wall where he'll wait in the shadows until I finish my visit. On the other side, two towering guards flank the door: the most fit and surliest looking guards I've seen at Fayette. I can see why they were chosen as Silas's watchdogs. They stand at attention, their eyes riveted forward. Two more guards of similar build and disposition are positioned at the front of the chapel, also keeping a watchful eye. Four guards on one. Five with Kyle. Guess Warden Papich takes his duty to keep prisoners confined seriously.

Natural light filters in through a beautiful stained-glass window at the front of the chapel. A rainbow of colors is broken up by a white dove hovering over a crucifix inscribed with *INRI.* I remember Mary telling me the initials stood for Latin words that translate to something like *Jesus is king.*

The rising sun sends sparkling fractals of light across the chapel's interior. There is a modest pulpit and altar with rows of pews stretching across the space. Shelves on the back of each seat are stocked with Bibles. The smoky sweet aroma of incense lingers in the air.

A solitary figure kneels in prayer, head bowed, inside a pew at the front of the chapel. Silas. Without looking up, he says, "Hey there, little bird," with a hint of accent that sounds almost Brooklyn even though he is from New Orleans. His words echo inside the arched space.

My blood chills at the nickname and its connection to

Azrael's DM. I take a deep breath. I can't give anything away. Not to him. I march down the aisle, every step resonating like the tick of a clock as I move closer.

When I'm ten feet away, Silas slowly turns his head around, looking up and back at me. Red light slices across his handsome face. I stop, keeping some distance between us. The air turns heavy as time freezes. Silas is chained to the floor, his manacles secured with a thick iron chain. The chain is short, allowing him little movement. I repeat this fact in my mind.

"Silas." My voice sounds steady to me, but I doubt it is.

He flashes a striking grin that is awash in crimson from the stained glass. Like his teeth are smeared with blood. "Where are you at?" he says, his eyes burning through me. "I haven't laid eyes on you in a spell. How is my chapel treating you?"

"They just give you free rein over this place?"

Silas rises in his deliberate, unhurried style, the chain fastening him to the floor rattling in an unsettling way.

Silas's eyes dance in the ruby light. "Not quite free."

I'm not the only one he draws attention from. The guards adjust their position, maintaining line of sight. Silas is so tall, his hands and arms so well-muscled, that it takes everything in me not to flinch. He holds my eyes with his red gaze, his pupils penetrating. He raises his hands, the left one missing the ring finger. These are the same hands that hurled the rocks surrounding Joseph Burton's body.

My mind flashes back to the first time I saw those hands, a blister on the pad of his right middle finger filled with blood. Friction, tension, repetition—the painful ingredients for forming a callous.

Blood soaking the ground. Rocks scattered around the corpse, no bigger than tangerines. Stained red from their bludgeoning. Victim eleven. I couldn't let there be a twelfth.

Silas takes a step toward me, and I snap out of my flashback. The guard closest to Silas takes a step forward before stopping and maintaining his adjusted position. Standing my ground, I refuse to back off, but my skin mottles into goose bumps. His hands are cuffed, and his legs are in irons. The chain that shackles his manacles to a metal loop in the floor jingles as he moves, and I again remind myself he can't reach me.

I take a seat in the pew on the opposite side of the aisle. Silas lowers himself down where he is. He cocks his head to the side, sizing me up.

"Well, aren't you a sight. Strutting even while sitting down."

I refuse to let him get a rise, plastering on a polite smile.

Silas leans back into the pew rolling his shoulders like a panther. A predator. And I'm his prey. "What brings you to my humble abode? Maybe you have come to chit-chat about clemency, hmm?"

I remain a stony statue, waiting for him to talk. Because Silas sure likes to talk.

"No? Well, then. What about a pardon?"

I keep myself carefully composed. There is so much beneath his words. So much that he'll try to use to toy with me. I let a beat of silence pass, then say, "I received an interesting message from someone calling themselves Azrael. Want to tell me who he is?"

"Awful name. Not even Christian. But you have to admire his handiwork."

"So you do know him?"

Oh, he knows him. Silas tries to keep careful control of his face, but it is there—a slight wrinkling of the nose, a pull of the upper lip—makes me wonder if he finds Azrael's "work" beneath him.

"Azrael addressed me as *little bird.* Other than you, nobody has ever called me that."

"I find that surprising. Jena in Arabic means *small bird.* Mix it with Campbell, Gaelic for crooked mouth, and there you have it: a little bird who lies with a sugary tune. Seems rather obvious to me."

I peer at him from under my eyebrows, denying him the satisfaction of a response.

Silas raises his handcuffs and pinches his chin. "Hmm, now let me see. Might be I have a bit more to share. Perhaps you can sweet-talk Warden Papich into giving me a dorm instead of a cell. Maybe that will jog my memory."

My eyes narrow. "You know I can't do that."

Silas drops his hands, cuffs clanging into his lap. "I am an exemplary prisoner. I have walked the straight and narrow for the past five years."

"It's not five years of incarceration yet. And you know why you're isolated. You still need a twelfth victim to complete your whole twelve gemstone, twelve killings project."

Silas's eyes flash. "There is no concrete proof I committed those murders." He's trying hard to keep the venom from his words, but there is a poisonous edge to them. "Not a single shred."

My rage dragon's awake now and spitting fire at his denial, at his taunting about my competence. "You killed eleven people. Just because they only linked you to one—"

"Oh, little bird, don't you go insulting me. I'm clean as a whistle. Everything I do is above board. And you are well aware the Leviticus Killer can't claim another soul without his stone. Jasper, little bird. Beautiful, iron red jasper stone."

The insinuation is plain, but he doesn't know what I did. He suspects because I was the one who came knocking on his door. But he's only fishing for information. Just like Azrael. Somehow, they're working together to try to reel me in. "I'm pretty sure you'd make an exception."

Silas gives me the side eye. "Still trying to hang something on me that is not my doing, huh? But I get it. Sometimes you have to do what is right even when it is wrong."

Always smoke and mirrors with Silas. "What's that supposed to mean?"

"What is this Azrael of yours after?"

"Your release. But you already knew that."

"Seems to me, you have the power to make that happen. Both you and I know what you did, little bird. What say you? Ready to spare some lives? Confession heals the soul." His eyes reflect the red light like burning coals.

"How does this Azrael know your *little bird* nickname for me? I don't buy the 'he figured it out' explanation. He doesn't strike me as a scholar. Not studied enough to come up with the Arabic meaning of my name."

"Appealing to my ego, huh? I regret to say I can't unravel more than I already have."

"Unless…?"

"That's right. Unless. And Azrael might not be a scholar, but that doesn't make him any less vicious. If I were you, little bird, I would be quaking in my boots. Really, really scared."

I swallow hard and force myself to stand. I don't say another word to him. Walking down the aisle toward the exit in slow, measured steps, I refuse to flee. The posted guards track my every movement, their eyes flicking back and forth between me and Silas. It is comforting that they're ready to intervene, if necessary, I guess. Not so comforting that they're this vigilant over a shackled man.

As I go, anger roils at my failure to get anything out of Silas. Maybe I should confess to him. In private, as an exchange for more info that will help me catch Azrael. Nobody would ever know—it would be my word against his. I shake that thought out of my head, the stupidest idea I've ever had.

When I stride up to the door, Kyle, the guard who escorted me in, regards me with cold eyes. His stare penetrates me, like he can see into the depths inside of me, before he swipes his card to let me out.

Case notes – Tuesday, February 13, 2018

Detective J. Campbell

INITIAL SCENE INFORMATION

On Tuesday, February 13, 2018, we maintained surveillance on Silas Halvard, the primary suspect in the ongoing Leviticus Killer investigation. Throughout the night, there were no sightings of Silas leaving or returning to his residence.

The following morning, at approximately 07:15 AM, we received a report of a disturbing discovery in the Windgap neighborhood. I arrived at the scene, where Officer Tom Dale had already secured the area. In an isolated field, we found a body, buried up to mid-chest.

Decedent is male, fully clothed, small build, red hair. Appearance of heavy bruising and bleeding. Shattered front teeth. Scalp partially flayed. Right cheekbone concave. Appears to have been deceased less than 8 hours prior to discovery. No rigor mortis. Upon excavation, his hands were closed, the right one clutching an amethyst gemstone.

Decedent is wearing a white t-shirt and 22" gold chain. No weapons found. The scene was consistent with that of the Leviticus Killer's signature style. The decedent was removed from the field and transported to the Allegheny Medical Examiner for autopsy.

MEDICAL EXAMINER INFORMATION

ME, Rowan O'Reilly, identified the decedent as Joseph Burton, age 34. Cause of death was reported as blunt force trauma to the skull.

INVESTIGATION NOTES

- Joseph Burton is the eleventh stoning victim. He has previous multiple arrests for possession of child pornography.
- Gemstones found in order are diamond, emerald, agate, turquoise, carnelian, chrysolite, beryl, topaz, ruby, garnet, amethyst. Based on my previous conversation with Silas Halvard, these are the twelve foundations stones from the Book of Revelation, and one more stone is expected to complete the sequence.

NEXT STEPS

- I have coordinated with the relevant departments to allocate additional resources and forensic support, expediting the processing of evidence gathered from the crime scene.
- It is clear that determining how the gemstones were acquired could provide the vital information needed in this case to obtain a search warrant.
- Our surveillance efforts on Silas will be intensified, with a heightened focus on monitoring his activities, connections, and any potential leads that may lead to his arrest.
- The urgency to arrest the perpetrator is critical knowing that the Leviticus Killer plans to claim a twelfth and final victim.

12

JENA

Wednesday, 9:00 a.m.

I STAND OUTSIDE Warden Duko Papich's office, watching as he keeps an impressive beat to the machine gun rhythm of Metallica's "One," drumming along on his extra wide desk. His office is a shrine to heavy metal and alt rock, covered in concert posters with shelves filled with CDs. He is old school like that. A serious collector who swears mp3s sound filtered through robotic vocal cords. Don't even get him started on auto-tune.

When Papich spies me loitering outside his door, he scoops up a remote and lowers the volume. Waving me in, he shakes his head, long hair sweeping across the shoulders of his collared dress shirt. Epic hair is a metal thing, I guess. His white shirt is unbuttoned enough to show the Black Sabbath t-shirt beneath it. The cuffs are rolled up, revealing the tattoo sleeves on both arms with red-eyed skulls piled before a cemetery of crosses, the graveyard's crimson sky split open by lightning. The art is as if he was going for Metallica's *Master of Puppets* album cover but trying not to be too obvious.

Papich sighs as I take a seat. "Metallica just dropped a badass box set, loaded with rare bootlegs. But can a regular dude like me afford that on a civil servant's salary?"

I know better than to dare suggest the digital download. Those don't come with cover art and liner notes. What serious music aficionado would debase themselves that way?

"And inflation's a bitch," I add.

He slaps the desk. "Hell yeah. We've been waiting for a raise like forever. Can't even keep up with the damn cost of living. *Jebiga*," he curses in Croatian.

I nod my head empathically, letting him know we're in this together. Comrades in shitty government pay. Two people who have each other's backs when one of them needs help.

"But I'll quit bitching about my wallet. What can I do for you, Detective Campbell?"

"I had a very interesting conversation with Silas."

"Aren't they all just?"

"Half-truths and insinuations. Holding what he may or may not know over my head."

"Business as usual for him, then, I guess."

It is all I can do not to show my relief that Papich hasn't been ensnared by Silas's charm. "Something he said makes me think he's had outside contact with someone not on his usual visitors list. Have you noticed anyone new come to see him? Anything out of the ordinary?"

"No new faces, but he yaks with everyone—both cons and guards. Prayers and whatever. Maybe he's got someone on the inside relaying his messages." Papich crosses inked arms over his chest. A skull on his forearm sneers up at me with a ghastly smile. "I'll have my techs snag video feeds of his gabfests and recordings of the other inmates' yammerings. But man, it's a fricking mountain. Sifting through that stuff requires authorization and paperwork. Going to take us a bit to sort it out."

I understand there is a big labor cost involved in that process, but also that Papich is known to have his people work faster for the right price. I give him a grateful smile. "I really appreciate you looking into it. Thank you. One more question, if you're not too busy."

"No sweat. What's on your mind?"

"Silas mentioned clemency. Heard anything about that?"

Papich shakes his head with more emphasis than necessary, showing off his glossy mane. He uses more hair product than I do. Which I suppose isn't hard to accomplish since I use none.

"Nah," he says. "I haven't heard jack about that. Governor Taylor's not one to mellow out the heavy riffs. Shaving down first-degree murder sentences? That's not his style. Don't get me wrong, he's all about pleasing his crowd. But he's never pulled the trigger on releasing an inmate early from the slam. Still, I guess even he might change his tune."

My stomach churns and I'm nauseous. No way Governor Taylor would grant clemency to Silas. That is something I need to make sure we're both absolutely on the same page about.

"Thanks for your thoughts. And thanks again for having your people look into the visitation recordings," I say, getting up from my seat.

"Anytime. I'll give you a buzz if I unearth anything." He sighs again. "Killer tunes make this gig more bearable. But I can't score until the next payday, which is a couple of weeks away."

Before I can answer, he has got the remote in his hand again, cranking up …*And Justice for All.*

The acid keeps eating away at my insides, creeping up my throat. I need to get what Papich has on Silas. Fast.

As soon as I exit Fayette, I have my cell phone out, punching in a number.

A young man answers, his tone more nonchalant than professional. *"Dr. Disc."*

"Hi. I need a rush delivery on the new Metallica box set."

13

JACK

Wednesday, 10:18 a.m.

SHADOW IS IRRITATED. When Shadow gets like this, Jack doesn't speak unless spoken to. He has learned to stay quiet. Oh, how he has learned.

Jack waits for the next game like a good submissive. He is barely shaking at all. But he is so tired. The exhaustion almost drowns out the soreness of his body, the deep ache of his muscles. Almost. Maybe when this game is over, Shadow will let him sleep.

Jack floats above the bed while Shadow skates around the darkened room. *"We should've started by now,"* Shadow roars. *"We're going to be late because of these damn officers."*

"Officers?" Jack doesn't realize he has spoken until the word spills out. He tries to clamp his hands over his mouth, but they're restrained.

"I said officials. Race officials. Stop talking."

Jack breathes a sigh of relief. No pain. Not this time. Because Shadow is so distracted. Jack's pretty sure he said *officers*. Maybe there is something going on in the outside world that Jack can't see. Officers… Like police officers? Jack holds his breath, not daring to hope. They'd be looking for him, right? His dad would have the whole force looking for him. Maybe they've found Shadow. Maybe help is on the way. He tries to hold on to the thought of rescue as he hangs in his restraints, the room swirling and surging around him. His legs tingle, numb from lack of circulation.

Without warning, he defecates. Hot, thin liquid pours out of him into his poop bag, burning where the diarrhea touches the raw skin of his butt cheeks. A revolting odor erupts into the air.

Shadow's pacing stutters and he fixes his void-face on Jack. He can almost see eyes, two darker pits inside the dark silhouette, pulsing with unwavering rage. Jack recoils, scrambling, trying to get away. There is nowhere to go.

"That's disgusting, innit? You think you've thought through every detail, but you forget one small thing and it all goes to shit. In the literal sense of the word… Ah well, best laid plans…" He snarls like a wild animal, then adds, *"I should've given you a colostomy, but hell, I'm no surgeon. Can't risk you going septic. Yet."*

His bum hurts. Jack squirms, all gross and sore. His lip trembles, and a soft whimper slips out.

"Shut up," Shadow says, his voice reverberating as he stares out the window overlooking Pittsburgh. *"Finally. Here we go."*

The room dissolves, and Jack finds himself perched on a steel platform suspended high above an asphalt racing track, legs dangling down. He is really up high. Looking down gives him vertigo. He pitches forward, clutching the platform to keep from diving off and smashing his skull on the pavement below.

But this isn't real. This is VR. He is in no danger in here. No, the danger lurks in the outside world. He gulps air as he gets his bearings.

An upbeat chiptune song pipes into his headset. The tune is fast tempo. The high-octane musical equivalent of zooming. In the distance, there is a starting line with a checkered flag, the track's boundaries lined with trees and tall grass. He examines what he is sitting on, although not really sitting because the bag holding his diarrhea isn't squished against him. He is dangling in his restraints. Bending at the waist and hanging his head upside down, he reads the words "Safety Crew" painted in bright red letters. A conveyor belt carrying a row of sleek black helmets churns in front of him.

"Help the motorcycle drivers," Shadow's disembodied voice booms. *"They need helmets, but aim carefully. You don't want to miss your mark. Safety first."*

"Oh, yes," Jack cries. "You have to be safe. I'll do a great job. You can count on me."

Shadow says nothing. Has he overdone the enthusiasm? Sometimes he tries to be so so perfect, and that pisses Shadow off, too.

But then a gunshot echoes through the air and the checkered flag waves. He has to play the game. He has to win. If he loses, he doesn't know what Shadow will do to him.

Bikes rumble toward him. He reaches out to pick up a helmet, but his coordination is off, his muscles too tense. He misses snatching up the first helmet that trundles by. Heart racing, palms damp, he breaks out in a cold sweat, but manages to grab the next one.

He holds the helmet with outstretched arms, ready to drop it on a rider's head when the bike passes beneath him and then…

…He jolts upright as he opens his eyes, vision hazy and

unfocused. There is a helmet clutched in his hands. What was he doing? The game. Shit, shit, shit. He has to play the game no matter what. He has to win. Or else pain. So much pain.

A bike roars below him, and Jack releases the helmet. It arcs through the air, and he watches the black sphere hurtle toward the target. The helmet plops onto the driver's head, and elation sweeps through him. An amazing shot! A lucky shot!

He…

…Shudders awake. Where is he? What is that roaring in his ear?

Shadow is screaming, "*Wake up, Jack!*"

"I'm awake!" Oh, God. The motorcycle game. He has to play. Has to win.

"Stay with it, Jack. Or else I'll need to hurt you to keep you awake. But I don't want to do that. You don't want me to hurt you again, either, do you? Or do you need a few hundred volts straight to the tits?"

"No, no." His hands tremble. "I won't fall asleep. I'm wide awake. Honest. See." He blinks hard and forces a smile, giving Shadow his best imitation of jazz hands with restricted ability to spread his fingers.

"I need you to concentrate, Jack. The bonus level is here. Now! Don't let me down."

A diamond-studded helmet glides down the conveyor belt as the music speeds up. At the same time, he spots a driver with a flaming head in the distance. He knows what to do. He won't fail. *No more pain. No more pain.* He chants the words to himself. He is a superstar gamer. An absolute ace.

As soon as the glistening helmet reaches him, he uses all his might to scoop it up. Then he holds his breath as the motorcycle accelerates toward him before releasing the helmet.

He waited too long. The motorcycle will zip past before the helmet completes its fall, diamonds smashing on asphalt. Shadow's going to kill him. He is going to die. Or maybe Shadow will lop off his leg. He is not sure which is worse. His stomach contracts and he gags up hot acid.

But then something miraculous happens. The bike slows, and the helmet plops onto the driver's head. Magic. Almost as if he can't lose. That can't be right? But he doesn't think too hard on that fact, reveling in his luck. He won't be getting electric shock to the nipples.

Jack exhales as the motorcycle rider speeds off in his new jeweled hat.

"Shadow," he breathes. "I did it."

The music cuts off, and Jack's back in his room, the walls strobing, throbbing, breathing.

Shadow materializes like a ghost from the ether, nodding approval. *"Good job. Very good job. Your dad got the message."*

Jack's glad Shadow won't hurt him, but he can't keep his eyes open. He tries to flop down on his bed but is suspended in midair. Because this isn't real. Jack stares at his bedspread, the owl faces dancing below him. When he squints, he can almost see the artificial light glowing off the fabric, the virtual reality that makes up this fake world he is trapped in. But there is an outside world, too. He repeats that to himself like a mantra. Remember there is an outside world. One where Dad, Mom, and Jude are waiting for him.

His eyes search the boundaries of where he imagines the VR headset to be, looking for the tiniest shred of outside light. The tiniest crack. But there is only darkness. He strains, listening. There is no passing traffic, or the TVs of next-door neighbors, or even a fan or air vent blowing in a comforting whisper. Only the artificial stillness of the headphones covering his ears. Emptiness.

He is crying, but his eyes are too dry for tears to fall. And then his bottom flares up with a searing burn.

Jack howls.

"What?!" Shadow shouts.

"It's nothing. Just my butt. It's raw."

"I should leave you in it. But since I can't have you getting an infection…"

Velcro rips apart as the bag strapped to his butt tears away. He imagines the setup like those poop bags they put on carriage horses. And then comes the sting of alcohol against open wounds. Shadow grinds the rough wipe into Jack's flesh, flooding his senses with pain.

Jack howls, and he can't stop howling like a mad wolf baying at the moon.

14

JENA

Wednesday, 10:24 a.m.

I PULL UP to former juror Matt Butler's house in record time. The home is a new build in the Jefferson Hills area. Gray siding and a dirt yard waiting for sod. A PBP Ford Interceptor and a Dodge Charger already fill the gravel driveway. The garage is draped in a solid yellow plastic sheeting sealed up with red biohazard tape.

The weather is chilly, and there is a mist hanging in the air that is not quite rain but is trying to be. I walk in the front door, the damp clinging to my clothes. The walls are painted neutral eggshell and still give off a hint of fresh paint. Mary's waiting for me in the foyer. With a grim nod, she ushers me to a door leading into the garage. A dim bulb illuminates the space in a sickly yellow glow, making the officer inside look jaundiced. Shelves crowded with tools and old cans of paint line the walls. Hooks mounted at various points hold two bicycles, jump ropes, boxing gloves, a skateboard, a snowboard, tennis rackets. A grinder, hammer, and punch awl lay scattered on the dirty concrete.

Right in the middle of the garage, next to a glimmering, burnished gold Harley Heritage Classic, lays Butler's body. He is sprawled on the garage floor, legs bent as if ready to spring up for a fight, hands clutching an all-black helmet. A wet, dark stain stretches across the crotch of his jeans, a puddle of urine pooled beneath him. The smell of piss hangs acrid in the air.

My gaze shifts to Mary, then to the attending officer. "What the hell happened?"

The officer jolts like I've startled him. Even under the yellow light, I can tell his face is pale. "At first, we didn't notice anything out of the ordinary. Before he went into the garage, we'd searched the house and given him the all clear. We were waiting in our cars, about to escort him to work. Then he starts yanking on his helmet, swaying around the garage in circles like a drunk. That's when we knew something was wrong. I rushed out of my car and tried to help him get the helmet off. It wouldn't budge."

Kneeling down beside the body, I see bruising where the helmet is clamped around his neck. No way was that coming off by trying to shuck him out of it.

"It wasn't like we could get through the helmet. Do you know how much pressure it takes to crack a helmet? It could've killed him, us swinging at him with a force of a hundred or so pounds. So we tried taking off the faceplate, but couldn't get it loose."

"It won't open?"

"Right, so we tried to break in through the visor, but they're strong as hell, too. I once got hit in the faceplate by a rock when I was going one hundred miles per hour. Not a scratch. We tried his grinder." The officer points to the tool cast aside on the ground.

"I see that."

"But that didn't work either. Then I figured maybe a puncture, you know?" the officer continues, half-rambling now. "We got the punch awl and started hammering away. Better a bit of skull rattling than dying, but nothing. Not a nick. That's not a normal visor, if you ask me. Polycarbonate would have at least dented. But even if we had managed to put a hole in it, I still don't know."

"Know what?"

"What killed him? Strangulation, suffocation, or the bugs."

I lean closer and peer into the faceplate, covering my mouth with my sleeve. "What the..."

Mary bends down next to me, crossing herself.

I shine my phone's flashlight on Butler's face, tiny lice swarming beneath the mask. Lice. The third plague.

They're crawling in and out of his nostrils, his eyes. Butler doesn't have any hair, his scalp shaved clean. A perfect victim for lice because no one would suspect the bald guy. Pinching my phone under my arms, I pull out my nitrile gloves and snap them on. Pointing the spotlight on Butler again, I examine him more closely.

His mouth is wide open, letting the bugs crawl in. Because he couldn't breathe. If he was breathing fine, he would've pressed his lips together. Poor bastard. Asphyxiation is a horrible way to go. Nothing to do for him now but wait for Anders to process the scene.

"How long?" I say.

"For what?" the officer asks.

"For him to die?"

"About seven minutes."

I hope he passed out long before then. Seven minutes of hell. I can't let this happen again to someone else. I can't have another

Silas on my hands. The thought starts me hyperventilating, and I take small sips of air, getting myself under control. I want to cry, scream, stomp my feet. I won't have this happen on my watch. I won't have people dying. Families weeping. The whole city again afraid to go outside. But I squish the devastation down and let my training take over, thinking about actionable steps. We need more protection, more resources. But even then, I don't know how to stop a phantom high-tech killer.

15

JENA

Wednesday, 1:46 p.m.

THREE HOURS LATER when I pull into the medical examiner's lot on Penn Avenue, Matt Butler's violent death still lingers between Mary and me. An invisible wall shutting down communication. I push through the division, saying what is rattling around in my mind.

"This one was so brutal."

Azrael is escalating. Each death is worse than the last.

"We know who he's targeting," Mary says. "We have the order of the plagues. Flies are next. We'll stop that one."

I wish I shared Mary's confidence. I give her a half-smile, wanting to believe her.

"Where'd you go this morning? Before Butler's?"

I've been expecting her to ask, but hoped I could avoid the question. "Checking out a hunch."

"By yourself?"

I get what she is hinting at, and maybe she is right. That I can't handle this alone, and I should let her in on this. On everything. My visit to Silas. Azrael's message. Not handing my phone over to Collins. All of my secrets weigh on me. I want to trust Mary, but as I look into her warm, brown eyes, I see risk. Bringing her with me on my visit to Silas would've been stupid. He would've said all the right things about me to plant doubt in her mind. Assuming he even would have approved her as a visitor.

My gaze lingers too long, and she squirms under my stare, shifting, and clearing her throat. I give her an innocent smile, hoping it doesn't look guilty.

"It was no big deal," I say, brushing it off. "Really."

"Ok," she says, and I'm grateful she doesn't push further. "But did this hunch of yours turn up anything?"

"Not yet. But I set some possibilities in motion. I'm not giving up on it."

I park on the street in front of the stubby, beige building that stretches across the whole block. Surrounded by a sandstone façade, two sliding glass doors with the Allegheny Medical Examiner's seal adorn the front entrance. If you don't look too closely, you might think the structure housed corporate offices or an urgent care facility. But this wasn't a place that saved lives. This was where they preserved bodies with chemicals and frigid temperatures. Corpses of those whose lives came to a premature end by gun or knife or pills or rope or suffocation by motorcycle helmet and vermin.

I step out of the Explorer, angling my body away from the front doors of the ME's office. I need a minute to get it together, steeling myself for what lays inside. But the horde of lice crawling out of Butler's gaping mouth haunts me. Taking a deep breath, I head up the stairs. When the automatic doors slide open, I stop, heart pounding. My mind shoves another image at me from when I entered these doors five years ago.

Joseph Burton, lying on the ME's table. His skin waxy white against purple contusions. Fiery red hair a shock of color, bright under the harsh lights. The precise Y incision dissecting the middle of his chest that I couldn't look away from. As if the cut was done to mimic the last words Joseph screamed with tortured lips. Why?

I've been through these doors too many times since, but Matt Butler's making me relive the past.

"I'll go first if it helps," Mary says softly. "Come on. I'm here if you need a hand to squeeze. I've got you."

Mary passes me, leaving behind her scent of warm sugar as she heads inside. I look up at the gray sky, taking a deep, bracing breath before resigning myself to crossing into the claustrophobic space that awaits me in the basement. I march inside, catching up with Mary. I don't need someone to hold my hand. I need a perp to nail to the wall.

We flash our badges at the desk jockey and give him the victim's name.

A haunted look flashes across his broad face before he returns to professional mode. His eyes still show too much white. He has never heard of anything like the body that rolled past him earlier, I'm sure. Welcome to the club.

"They're treating it as a biohazard," he says. "You need to suit up."

He directs us to a changing room where we don baggy white biohazard suits. My faceplate fogs with each breath. And I'm back in the garage. I'm Butler suffocating inside a motorcycle helmet, my last exhale condensing against the plastic. I gasp and shake my head clear. Then I join Mary as we march to the autopsy room.

Inside, it is sixty-five degrees at best. The room is ripe with formaldehyde and Vick's VapoRub, which the ME, Rowan

O'Reilly, still uses liberally, never able to get used to the smell of death. Maybe that is healthy. Habituating to rot and decay probably isn't something to strive for. Although O'Reilly says he loves his job. Or maybe he loves the epic movie soundtracks he blasts all day. Powerful pieces that speak to the beauty of life and death, and maybe hope for an afterlife. John Williams's score to *Jurassic Park* pours out from the speakers. The music transforms the cold and depressing tiles the color of gravestones into another world far away from this one.

An isolation chamber stands in the middle of the room. Inflated tubes of alternating yellow and black hold up a transparent foil cube. Inside, I can make out two figures in biohazard suits. One of them photographs two black halves of a motorcycle helmet inside a large ziplock bag on a metal table.

I walk up to the isolation cube, gently rattling its walls. Faces warped beneath plastic faceplates turn toward me. The closest one, O'Reilly, waves us in. I quickly unzip the seal and step inside, zipping the foil back up after Mary joins me.

O'Reilly peers at me behind round glasses, the top of his collared shirt and trademark bowtie visible where the faceplate meets the suit's fabric. Anders stands beside him, looking like she could rock a biohazard suit on a fashion runway.

"Nothing to worry about here," O'Reilly says, shouting to be heard over the *Jurassic Park* music and the muffling of his suit. "The critters are all dead. Fumigated them." He taps his suit. "These are probably unnecessary now. No trace of disease or anything else in them. Probably better not to inhale insecticide, though."

"You work fast," Mary says.

O'Reilly beams. "Made this one a priority. I hope it helps."

"We really appreciate it." My eyes are trained on Butler. The white sheet covering him leaves a bit of his scalp exposed, the skin marred with red insect bites.

O'Reilly nods. "Cause of death, asphyxiation, as you probably guessed. Restriction to the trachea from external pressure. Plus lack of an oxygen source."

O'Reilly puts knuckles to his lower back and arches before tilting left, then right, releasing the tension. Looking at the bagged up motorcycle helmet, sliced in half by whatever instrument he used—maybe a bone saw?—it must have been a hell of a chore. Little white dots that look like seeds cling to the foam, turning my stomach at the sight. Stark ovals of a dead lice infestation against the midnight black.

"That's one high-tech helmet. An extra ring of solid polycarbonate around the throat that popped out. The faceplate kept shut by super magnets."

"Looks like the mechanism was activated by a remote," Anders adds.

O'Reilly shrugs. "You'd know about that better than me. My specialty is biochemistry, not technology. Anyway, there's a compartment in the back of the helmet that opened up. Filled with lice with their very own blood supply system to keep them alive. Analysis says it's rabbit's blood."

"Pretty ingenious," Anders cuts in. "For that level of alteration, I don't think there's any way that was Butler's original helmet. Azrael must have switched them. Collins is already on it. No footage from Butler's house, of course. Collins is looking for anyone who messed with or exchanged Butler's helmet at work where it would've been easily accessible. Nothing on the work cameras so far."

"Nice work," Mary says, and I realize she is chewing her gum inside the biohazard suit.

"Come on," I sigh. "Let's go notify the family. After that, we meet with Weisz and Jersey, run down the details. Both of the cases so far and the next possible victims. There must be something we're missing."

SMART BOARD

Victims

1. Michelle Green
   Plague #1 – Water to Blood
   COD – electrocuted
2. Lisa Bell
   Plague #2 – Frogs
   COD – golden dart frog poison
3. Matt Butler
   Plague #3 – Lice
   COD – asphyxiation

NEXT PLAGUE – #4 Flies

Targets / Jurors

1. Michael "Mickey" Hughes (50 yo male)
   Notables: Football coach. Four years Army service.
2. James Cox (46 yo male)
   Notables: Digital archivist. Into crypto. Family owns dairy farm.
3. Norma Littlejohn (53 yo female)
   Notables: Social justice warrior. Top fundraiser for a summer camp for kids with Type 1 Diabetes.
4. Charles "Chuck" Gomez (70 yo male)
   Notables: Likes Formula 1. Golden Retriever.

5. David Bacco (64 yo male)
   Notables: Into nature, tourism, and books. Multiple Sclerosis.
6. Kent Baker (42 yo male)
   Notables: Flemish rabbit. Teaches high school tech.
7. Avi Spieler (29 yo NB)
   Notables: Multimedia artist. Kosher.
8. Earl Rogers (76 yo male)
   Notables: Director of a nonprofit specializing in drug and alcohol treatment. Glaucoma.
9. Chris Brown (33 yo male)
   Notables: Mechanic. Bartends at night. Raynaud's disease.
10. Jack Taylor (17 yo male)
    Notables: Governor's son. Suspected to be a hostage in Azrael's custody, who has declared Jack will be the tenth and final victim.

Leads

~~Jack's laptop~~

~~Jack's phone~~

~~Azrael's social media account~~

~~Footage from Matt Butler's work cameras~~

16

JENA

Wednesday, 4:02 p.m.

I LEAN BACK in the rolling office chair, resting my feet on top of the conference table as I study the smart board.

"Baker has a rabbit, and Gomez has a dog?" Weisz says. "Is this the kind of information we need? How does that help us?"

"You never know what could be important," I say, defending Mary's work. "Bell's cat delivered the poison that killed her." I sit up in my chair, plopping my elbows on the conference table. "Anyone see a pattern or have any thoughts on who's next?"

"The next plague is flies?" Weisz mutters. "There are flies everywhere."

"Um." Mary snaps her gum. "David Bacco likes nature. A trail would be a great spot to kill someone. Lots of flies."

"He has MS. Probably not a big hiker," Jersey says as he doodles a picture of a wrench. "My money's on the high school teacher. Shop class is a dangerous place. All those blades and machines. Not sure about flies, though."

"We're keeping them all on home lockdown for now," I say. "We've searched every inch of their homes and we've got guards posted. Video surveillance too. Nothing goes in or out without our say so. Price is securing safe houses as we speak. We'll move them all in the next day or so."

Weisz nods. "That's the smartest thing I've heard said in this room. What about…"

I miss Weisz's next thought because a notification pops up on my phone.

[intentionallyblank] Azrael

Hello little bird,

My heart hammers so fiercely, I marvel that the others don't stop their conversation mid-sentence and stare at me. I dip the phone below the table and click on the message.

How are you enjoying my work? Three days in and already you pigs are squealing. How many more lives will you sacrifice before you set Leviticus free?

Six days to confess…

- Azrael

My stomach drops, and I press my free hand to my belly, eyes glued to the message. I should turn my phone over to Collins. Tell him Azrael's accusations against me are nonsense. That he is making up lies. I should walk down the hall to Collins's office right now and—

"Whatcha looking at?" Mary asks.

I quickly flick the message away. "It's nothing important, just…"

All eyes lock on me. Heat blooms in my cheeks. They know something is up.

"Mason and I had a fight," I blurt.

Mary's face falls with disappointment and concern. "Again?" she says so softly it is nearly a whisper.

"It was all me, being neurotic and losing my shit. Again."

"Well, I hope you patch it up," Jersey interjects. "Mason's one of the good ones."

"He is." I give Jersey a forced smile as my phone vibrates in my palm. I hold Jersey's gaze, not wanting to look down. Because I know what the message is going to be. Another *little bird* taunt from Azrael.

"Maybe James Cox's dairy farm would be a good place for flies," Mary says.

She is well aware Cox doesn't live on his family's farm. As the group starts chatting among themselves about the case, I'm grateful for the redirection.

I mouth *thank you* at her, then muster up the courage to check the new notification.

It is an e-mail from Warden Duko Papich. I contain the relieved sigh that wants to spill out and click on the message.

> *Yo Detective Campbell,*
>
> *Listening to banging Metallica tunes right now. I've got some visual gold for you to check out. Stop by.*
>
> *~ D* 🤘

Did he really put a devil's horns emoji after his initial? Maybe the gesture is another reference to my gift, but that doesn't matter right now. Mary rescuing me from Jersey and Weisz's scrutiny has put me in a soft mood. Time to bring Mary in on my little excursion.

"Mary," I say. "Time to go. My mystery trip may have produced something."

Mary shoots up from her chair, beaming as we leave the conference room. "Bye, boys," she chirps.

"You going to tell us what you've got?" Jersey calls after us.

I give a dismissive wave. "If it turns up anything. Keep working on what we already have."

"Unbelievable," Jersey protests, but not hard enough that I think he minds.

I swing the door shut as they start to banter.

"Where are we headed?" Mary says with an extra dose of perky.

"SCI Fayette."

"I had a hunch that's where you went."

"You know me too well."

I drape an arm around her shoulder as we march toward the Explorer.

Case notes - Tuesday, March 5, 2018

Detective J. Campbell

INITIAL SCENE INFORMATION

On Tuesday, March 5, 2018, based on the evidence obtained thus far, a search warrant was approved for the residence of Silas Halvard, the primary suspect in the Leviticus Killer investigation. The warrant was issued based on a pawn shop receipt found in Silas's garbage for the purchase of twelve gemstones, eleven of which matched the stones found in the possession of the eleven victims.

Detective Mary Sarkis and I proceeded to Silas's residence, a Tudor Revival home. Silas was at home, and refused our entry until a printed warrant was produced. After Detective Sarkis presented the warrant for his inspection, he cooperated, but remained nearby during the investigation. Starting on the ground floor, we systematically worked our way through each room, following the protocols and procedures of a search warrant. As we searched, Silas made several comments, noted here for future reference:

"They say the devil lurks in the details. But you won't stumble upon him holed up in my attic."

"It's like a grand treasure quest, isn't it? Embarking on a hunt for hidden gems."

"If your aim is to uncover skeletons in my closet, well, prepare for a letdown."

As we approached the basement, we encountered a locked door secured with a dead bolt. Silas claimed to be unaware of the key's location. We informed Silas that we would force the door if the key was not provided promptly and indicated to him the portion of the warrant which granted entry and access to all portions of his residence "through forceful entry if entry was not provided."

After clarifying details of the warrant, Silas obtained the key and granted us access to the basement, revealing a large, unfinished room that was a stark contrast to the rest of his pristine home. Silas informed both Detective Sarkis and I that the light switch to the basement was at the bottom of the stairs. After taking the key from Silas and assessing the risk, it was decided that Detective Sarkis would remain upstairs with the suspect while I proceeded into the basement alone. Primarily, this was to prevent Silas from locking us both in the basement with a spare key.

I proceeded down the stairs, using my flashlight. The basement was crammed with many items including canned goods, plastic jugs filled with water, stacks of newspapers and magazines, maps of Pittsburgh locales including City Hall and Ridge Limestone Quarry, blueprints of St. Anthony's chapel and PNC Park, and several bus schedules.

Among the items, I discovered a collection of religious paraphernalia, including crucifixes, candles, anointing oils, and religious texts. An ornately decorated open chest was also found, containing tiny bone fragments carefully arranged on velvet cushions. Each bone was neatly labeled with the names of saints and religious icons.

Of significant interest, I found a series of handwritten notes documenting Silas's surveillance of Joseph Burton's weekly routine before his murder, including locations and times. These notes, alongside newspaper clippings chronicling the past arrests of Joseph Burton, appear to connect Silas to Joseph Burton's murder.

INVESTIGATION NOTES

- The religious paraphernalia, newspaper clippings, and handwritten surveillance notes have been documented and collected as potential pieces of evidence linking Silas Halvard to the Leviticus Killer's crimes.
- Silas was placed under arrest for suspicion of first-degree murder and transported to the county detention center for further processing.
- Our investigation team will continue to analyze the collected evidence, conduct interviews, and pursue additional leads to strengthen the case against Silas Halvard.

17

JENA

Wednesday, 5:00 p.m.

WHEN WE ARRIVE at Papich's office, he is thrashing to Slayer's "Raining Blood" as he waves us in. The intentional guitar feedback gives me a headache, but Mary rocks on inside, shaking her shoulders in time with the cacophonous noise.

"Get it, girl," Papich cheers, and they share convulsive head-nods.

Mary giggles, and Papich lowers the volume. He is wearing an Iron Maiden shirt under his dress shirt today. There is also a very expensive Metallica box set perched on the corner of his expansive desk.

Papich catches me looking at the CDs as Mary and I take a seat. "Impressive gift, don't you think?"

Mary's eyes burrow into me, but I don't turn to meet her stare.

"It means a lot." Papich runs a loving finger across the top before spinning his laptop around to face us. "And I'm guessing this means a lot to you."

He nods in my direction. I click play as Mary and I huddle

closer to the screen. The grainy shot shows a figure dressed all in black in the parking lot outside the prison. Their face is entirely obscured by a skeleton gaiter and dark sunglasses. The skeleton approaches a guard with his back to the camera. They speak briefly. Then the skeleton hands him a piece of paper. The video stops, and I look up at Papich.

"He visited here a lot. Always decked out like that." He slides open his desk drawer and retrieves a thumb drive before handing it to me.

"And no one noticed?"

"Sorting through all the surveillance footage isn't practical unless we've got a reason. Also, he's been MIA for almost two weeks."

I lean away from the screen. "Because he already said everything he needed to say?"

Papich nods. "Could be."

Mary puts her elbows on the desk, tilting closer to Papich. "Where is this guard now? We'd like to have a quick word with him."

"He's all yours." Papich's eyes light up with hellfire, the lightning inked on his arm rippling as he squeezes the edge of the desk. "When you're done, send him my way, will you? We have some…matters to discuss."

Papich comes off all chill, but there is a reason he is the warden. He excels at discipline.

We leave Papich's office and another guard escorts us to the right room. I stand at the threshold, peering in. The space is a spot for guards to camp out—rust-pitted desks stenciled with D.O.C., the tang of burnt coffee in the air. One chastised guard waits inside, head in his hands, his fingers tangled in his dark hair.

It is the guard that escorted me to see Silas. This time I get a good look at his name tag: Kyle Mander.

He glances up and when he realizes it is me, his eyes narrow to slits.

"You okay there?" Mary asks.

His face softens as he takes in this tiny five-foot-nothing cop with the bright pink lips and manicure. "I didn't do anything wrong, I swear. I only wanted Silas's blessing. After what he did for me…"

I shut the door and lean on the desk in front of the one Kyle's hunkered down in. "What did he do for you?"

Kyle sighs, the tension melting out of his shoulders. "The wife and me, we were having horrible fertility issues. IUI. Then IVF. Miscarriage after miscarriage, draining our bank account and still, no baby. Silas, well…" His gaze flickers to Mary's gold chain as if he can see the outline of her cross beneath her shirt. "Silas prayed with me, told me to have faith."

"Faith is all we have," Mary agrees.

He nods at her, like he has found a kindred spirit. "I'm not real religious, you know? Or I didn't used to be. But I did what he said. Prayed the words he gave me every night. Two weeks later, we found out Cecilia was pregnant."

I roll my eyes on the inside. "And you don't credit the IVF?"

Kyle gives Mary a look like, can you believe your heathen partner? Mary makes a sympathetic noise, and Kyle turns his gaze back on me.

"It's okay that you don't believe me, but maybe you should try praying with Silas sometime. See if you still feel the same way afterward. It would be a blessing on your life if you did."

Over my dead body. That is probably the way Silas would prefer it, too.

Mary approaches, laying her hand on his forearm. "What messages did you pass?"

Kyle's wide-eyed, like a child, as he answers, "Bible verses. Nothing else, I swear."

"What Bible verses?" I say, stepping closer.

Kyle raises his hands as if I'm going to cuff him and he is ensuring me of his cooperation, which suits me just fine. "I can show you exactly which verses. I screenshotted them with my phone, so I'd remember them. A little extra divinity don't hurt, you know?"

He pulls his phone from his shirt pocket, and I retrieve mine, thrusting it toward him. He half-turns, as if he'd rather share the photos with Mary, but I insist, "Drop the pictures here."

"Sure thing," he says, and transfers the photos to my phone.

"And now for the grueling interrogation," I deadpan.

"If you don't mind," Mary adds.

Kyle's head jerks up. "Do I need a lawyer?"

"Not if you haven't done anything incriminating." Then deciding sarcasm probably isn't my best approach, I add, "We're not here for you, Kyle. Whatever you did is insignificant in comparison to the case we're on, and you're not in any trouble, okay? Not on our end, at least. I can't promise the same for Papich."

Kyle's eyes bulge, but then he narrows them, covering up his fear of Papich. That probably wasn't the right thing to say, either. I should probably let Mary do the talking. But she is the good cop and I'm the serious cop. So the grilling falls to me.

"Ask your questions. Then I'll decide."

"Please," Mary says. "We need your help, Kyle. You could save lives."

Kyle studies us both and then nods, resigned to the task. I fire my barrage of questions at him as Mary records his answers.

"Describe this skeleton, please, height and weight."

"About 5'9", maybe 170 pounds."

"Sex?"

"Looked male."

"Skin, hair, and eye color?"

He shrugged. "No idea, he was covered up."

"What can you tell me about his voice?"

"He used a distorter."

I raise an eyebrow. "You didn't think it strange that the guy was dressed up and disguising his voice?"

He glares back at me for a moment before replying. "I understand wanting anonymity. Associating with Silas is somewhat controversial, in case you haven't noticed."

I grunt and carry on. "What about his clothing? Brands?"

"Jeans, hoodie, sneakers. All black. Dark, wraparound sunglasses. Skeleton-face gaiter. I don't know anything about fashion labels. Can't help you there."

"Anything distinctive? Tattoos, jewelry, cologne?"

"No," he says with a shake of his head. "Nothing visible."

"Vehicle make and model."

"Never saw one, not in the lot, anyway. He must've parked somewhere else."

"How did he first approach you?"

"I was out on a smoke break."

"And you didn't find that odd? That he'd been watching the prison to target someone on their break?"

He tugs at his shirt collar and averts his gaze. "I didn't think too much on it, but now that you mention it, yeah, kind of weird. But like I said, he just wanted to give Bible verses to Silas. To show he was devout. He said he had some hard things going on in his life and hoped Silas might pray for him. No harm in that."

I drill Kyle with my coldest stare. "Is that absolutely everything you can tell us about the exchange between this stranger and Silas?"

"That's all, word of honor. You said lives are at stake. I take that seriously."

I nod curtly. "Thank you for your cooperation. Come on, Mary. We have what we need."

But Kyle clamps his hand over Mary's, his eyes pleading. "Silas is reformed. Even if I believed he hurt someone before, he wouldn't do anything to harm anyone anymore. He just wouldn't."

18

JENA

Wednesday, 7:15 p.m.

BACK IN THE conference room, Mary stifles a yawn. It has been a while since we worked late. She gets up at dawn with her kiddo and is usually in bed by 9 p.m. The coffee is long gone, and our dinner of convenience store tuna sandwiches was far from sustaining. I reach over and give her a consoling pat.

"Want me to brew another pot?"

She shakes her head. "I'm fine. Caffeine now will mess me up."

Collins uses the smart board to blow up Kyle's screenshotted Bible verses in a high-tech slide show. Collins is wearing a green t-shirt today, the sleeves barely reaching the tops of his biceps. I can count every single ab underneath the taut fabric.

"So, let me get this straight. Silas has the other inmates and prison staff under his spell?" Collins crosses his arms across his chest in a way that promotes voluntary and unnecessary flexing.

Mary smiles up at him from her chair and shrugs. "The inmates, for sure. How many of the guards, who knows? As for the higher-ups, Fayette is an underfunded prison suddenly receiving donations. I'm sure they're taking full advantage."

I open my mouth in mock surprise. "You're saying Papich is playing both sides for personal gain? I'm shocked, I tell you, shocked!"

"Still," Collins says. "I can't believe Silas has his own podcast spot on *PA Prisons and Parole.*"

"Going on four years now."

"Stupid to let him evangelize like that."

"If you're going to keep yapping about Silas, can you hand over the remote?"

"Yes, ma'am."

Collins tosses it over, and the remote slides across the table. Mary scoops it up and flips through the screenshots. The passages are all lengthy, but certain parts have been underlined.

"There's something about the order of the verses." Mary scrolls back to the first photo. "Leviticus 20 is first. Verse ten is underlined."

"That's the one about stoning," I say.

"Yep," Mary confirms. "If a man commits adultery with the wife of his neighbor, both the adulterer and the adulteress shall surely be put to death."

"Well," I scoff, "we know Silas agrees with that one."

Mary clicks ahead one photo. "Then Revelation 21. Verse nineteen is underlined. That's the one about the foundation stones."

"That was Silas's thing, right?" Collins says, raising an eyebrow.

"I'm envious you can forget," I say. To be fair, if it isn't on a computer screen, Collins couldn't care less about it.

"Remind me of the context."

Mary obliges. "The chapter is about a Holy City coming out of the clouds from heaven. Twelve angels, twelve gates, twelve precious stones decorating the walls. The Bible is big on twelve."

"Sounds fascinating," Collins mutters.

Mary's eyes dance. "You haven't lived until you've heard it recited in ancient Syriac in the middle of a two-hour service."

"So yeah," I continue, "you did a search for their acquisition, remember? The foundation stones are the gemstones Silas left in his victims' hands."

"Allegedly left," Collins says.

I roll my eyes. "Don't you start."

Collins smirks. "You interviewed him about those stones as research on his case, right?"

"Right, but before I knew he was actually the Leviticus Killer."

"Allegedly."

"Jesus Christ, Collins."

"Hey." Mary stabs a fuchsia fingernail at me. "Language."

"Sorry, Mary. I'll say some Hail Yous later."

Mary thwacks me on the arm with the back of her hand.

"Anyway," I say, directing my response to Collins. "Silas was the logical choice because he was a Professor of Biblical Studies at Geneva University. I thought he could help me better understand the Leviticus murders in relation to the theology behind stoning and the significance of the gemstones. And just like Mary explained, he said the gemstones would be used to build a gleaming city brought from heaven to a new earth after evil has been purged."

"And he was trying to speed up the purging," Collins says.

"Thank you," I say.

"For what?"

"For not saying *allegedly.*"

"Okay." Mary claps her hands. "Let's see if we can piece together some meaning from these verses."

She gets up and moves over to the smart board, flipping through the passages and making a sequential list of the underlined verses. She doesn't add any cartoons, probably figures that is irreverent. When she finishes, she stands back and scrutinizes her work:

BIBLE VERSES

Leviticus 20:10, If a man commits adultery with the wife of his neighbor, both the adulterer and the adulteress shall surely be put to death.

Revelation 21:19, And the foundations of the wall of the city were garnished with all manner of precious stones.

Proverbs 1:5, Let the wise hear and increase in learning, and the one who understands obtain guidance.

2 Chronicles 15:7, But you, take courage! Do not let your hands be weak, for your work shall be rewarded.

Luke 21:36, But stay awake at all times, praying that you may have strength to escape all these things that are going to take place.

Isaiah 40:40, Every valley shall be lifted up, and every mountain and hill be made low; the uneven ground shall become level, and the rough places a plain.

Isaiah 27:9, So in this way Jacob's sin will be forgiven, and this is how they will show they are finished sinning: They will make all the stones of the altars like crushed limestone, and the Asherah poles and the incense altars will no longer stand.

"There's something cut off at the bottom of the last screenshot," I say. "Handwritten. You see it?"

"Yes, ma'am," Collins says. "Sarkis, pass me the remote."

Mary zips it over and he fiddles with the settings, zooming in. All that is visible is the top of pen strokes. Impossible to decipher—

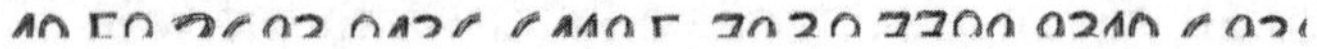

"The numbers for more Bible chapters and verses, maybe?" Mary suggests.

"Shit, we need those. But no way would Silas keep the evidence. Not for more than two weeks. He'd tell you himself, everything he does is clean. Probably swallowed the paper immediately."

"Let's go over what we do have, okay? Hopefully it's enough." Mary studies the smart board.

"Leviticus and Revelation must be Azrael letting Silas know he's familiar with his work," I say.

"We're sure the skeleton is Azrael?" Mary says.

"It has to be, but fair point, it could be a messenger. But I don't think Azrael would trust this task to anyone else."

"I agree with that."

"Proverbs and 2 Chronicles read like flattery. Azrael telling Silas how much he admires his work."

"Praising him like a mentor, saying Silas has been an inspiration for what Azrael is doing now."

"Right. Luke is about Azrael's plan to free Silas."

"Also agreed."

"What about the last two?" Collins says.

I glance at Mary, who looks as stumped as I am, her forehead wrinkled in confusion. "Um, maybe it's about his plans to lay waste to everything?"

"Like the jurors?"

"Could be." Mary chews her lip, bright pink lipstick smearing across her front tooth. "Could be something worse. Like his plans after he gets Silas out of prison."

"Then we'd better make sure Silas never gets free."

Pittsburgh Post-Gazette

Tuesday, March 5

Silas Halvard, Distinguished Professor, Arrested, Charged with First-Degree Murder

by Matt Burkhart

Silas Halvard, professor of Biblical Studies at Geneva University, was arrested this morning for the murder of Joseph Burton, the eleventh stoning victim within the last year. The arrest sent waves of both shock and relief through the city of Pittsburgh. Shock as residents grapple with the fact that a respected academic may be responsible for the gruesome string of murders that have plagued the area for months. Relief as they realize these killings may be over. Halvard's expertise in biblical studies adds a dark layer of significance to the crimes, which involved victims being buried up to their chests and stoned to death, with gemstones left as macabre calling cards.

Authorities apprehended Halvard following a meticulous investigation that pieced together evidence linking him to the death of Joseph Burton. The arrest came as a culmination of many months of tireless work by the Pittsburgh Bureau of Police, who had been relentless in their search for leads in the case.

In an exclusive interview with Detective Jena Campbell, the lead investigator in the case, she revealed, "We had been monitoring Professor Halvard's activities since my interview with him in January made him a person of interest. Certain elements began to align, and it became clear that he warranted further investigation. The evidence we gathered ultimately led to his arrest."

While the arrest of Silas Halvard provides a glimmer of hope for justice, it also raises a multitude of questions. How could a respected scholar be capable of such heinous acts? What drove him to commit these murders? The investigation is far from over, and the trial promises to be a lengthy and riveting affair.

Prosecutor Emily Sanchez, who will be leading the case against Halvard, stated, "We have substantial evidence linking the suspect to Joseph Burton's crime scene. The trial should shine a light on the motives behind these brutal acts, and we will seek justice for the victims and their families."

Patricia Burton, the sister of the victim, said, "As a devout Anglican, it's devastating to learn that a supposed man of God could be responsible for such cruelty. My brother was not perfect. He was flawed, as are all of us who are human. Maybe more flawed than some. But who are we to judge each other? My heart goes out to all the families affected by this nightmare."

As for Joseph Burton's "flaws," he had multiple arrests for possession of child pornography.

A former student of Halvard's reached out to the *Post-Gazette*, speaking on condition of anonymity. The student claimed, "Professor Halvard always had a dark aura about him. There was something unsettling behind his surface charisma, as if he had hidden secrets. But I never expected him to be capable of something like this."

As the city prepares for what is anticipated to be a high-profile trial, the focus now shifts to the courtroom, where the truth behind Silas Halvard's alleged crime will be examined in detail. The trial is expected to captivate the nation, as the prosecution and defense present their cases to the jury.

In the meantime, Pittsburgh residents are left to grapple with the chilling realization that evil can lurk in the most unexpected places. The arrest of Silas Halvard has shattered the illusion of safety, reminding us that the line between righteousness and darkness can be blurred. The city waits for justice to prevail and for closure to be brought to the victims and their grieving families.

837 Comments **ADD COMMENT** **Sort by: NEWEST**

*This conversation is moderated according to The Post-Gazette's community rules. Please **read the rules** before joining the discussion. If you're experiencing any technical problems, please **contact our customer care team**.*

Brutal-saurus Rex

Silas deserves the chair!

Tuesday, March 5 2018 @ 9:08 AM

> Kitteh38
>
> You live up to your name, don't you?
>
> Tuesday, March 5 2018 @ 9:10 AM
>
> Brutal-saurus Rex
>
> RAWR!
>
> Tuesday, March 5 2018 @ 9:12 AM

CarkMan

Took the PBP long enough.

Tuesday, March 5 2018 @ 9:08 AM

PrimantiBrosRestaurant

Detective Campbell is a hero. Detective, if you're reading this, free sandwiches for life anytime you stop in!

Tuesday, March 5 2018 @ 9:09 AM

ArtRooneyII

Agreed! Sending two box seats her way for the season. Here we go, PBP!

Tuesday, March 5 2018 @ 9:11 AM

LuvTrueCrime

Am I the only one who thinks all the victims were giant turds?

Tuesday, March 5 2018 @ 9:13 AM

CriticalBean

Someone needs to ban you. Your comments make me lose brain cells.

Tuesday, March 5 2018 @ 9:16 AM

LuvTrueCrime

I bet you're a lot of fun at parties.

Tuesday, March 5 2018 @ 9:17 AM

LupineScat

SILAS 4 PRESIDENT!

Tuesday, March 5 2018 @ 9:18 AM

RockStarGamer

Right?! Let's hope Leviticus levels up in the court room. This one's going down in the history books. I can only dream of achieving that status of game master. Legendary!!!!!!

Tuesday, March 5 2018 @ 9:21 AM

CriticalBean

You know what? Yep. After this comment, I'm taking a mental health break from this site.

Tuesday, March 5 2018 @ 9:23 AM

LOAD MORE

19

JENA

Wednesday, 8:00 p.m.

MARY AND I arrive at our last stop for the night, Governor Taylor's house. At the end of his rope with Mrs. Taylor's constant phone calls, Price has been nagging us to give the governor and his family an update on his son's case. I dragged my feet making a personal appearance, ashamed I have no notable progress to report.

"Maybe you should do the talking," I whisper to Mary as their bodyguard, Daniels, ushers us into the sitting room.

Mary nods, lips pressed together. I don't blame her for her reluctance. The governor will handle the situation like a politician, but Mrs. Taylor will handle it like a politician's wife—she'll take us apart piece by piece.

The family waits for us in the same arrangement as before, the governor in the armchair, his wife and Jude on the couch. Except this time, there are two officers in the room on guard detail, trying to blend into the wallpaper and appear unobtrusive.

"Four days," Mrs. Taylor says, her voice stony, hands folded in her lap. "Jack's been gone four days. And you send officers to guard our house without explanation. How do you think that makes us feel?"

"Frustrated, I'm sure," Mary says.

Mrs. Taylor's eyes snap to her. "Angry, it makes me angry."

"And scared," Jude adds.

"Forty-eight hours," Mrs. Taylor says. "That's the window to find a missing person alive. And that's what I tell your Captain Price every time I call."

And raise hell, I silently add.

"And do you know what he tells me? He'll update me when there's something to update me with. And so, I just sit here, picking my nails, waiting for you to show up and tell me my baby is dead."

"I'm so sorry," Mary says. "But we do have an update."

Mrs. Taylor steels herself and says, "Let's have it, then."

Mary opens her mouth, and I said I'd let her do the talking, but I need to interject. My eyes flick to Jude. "I need to be very clear this cannot leak to the public. No social media. No private messages. It could put Jack's life at risk. Is that understood?"

Jude swallows hard and nods.

Mrs. Taylor's shoulders loosen a fraction. "You're saying Jack's alive?"

"The evidence suggests he's a hostage," Mary says.

"What do they want?" Mrs. Taylor demands. "Money?"

Mary moves to sit on the love seat, and I sink down next to her. Mary puts her elbows on her knees, hands clasped together. She leans forward. "I'm afraid it's not that simple."

"What do you mean?"

"Let the detective speak," the governor says. The look his wife throws him could raze cities.

Mary breaks down what has happened as gently as she can.

The deaths of three former jurors on Silas's case. Azrael's threat to kill six more unless Silas is released. That he is enacting the ten plagues.

Governor Taylor turns to the crucifix hanging on the wall. "And the tenth plague is the killing of the firstborn."

"Oh, my God," Jude blasts.

"So my son is alive, just not for long," Mrs. Taylor says.

The governor looks back at me. "But you're going to catch this Azrael, right?"

"We're doing everything possible," I say. "We have all our resources on it."

His expression is stoic, but all the color drains from his face. "I could never pardon Silas. Or grant clemency. Pittsburgh would lose their minds."

I struggle to keep the relief from my face. "Agreed. There's no need for that. We have the jurors and your family well protected. Having two killers on the loose would cost more lives than it would save."

"You don't know that," Jude says. "Silas was only charged with one murder. People say he's reformed."

His father gives him an incredulous look. "A small group of fanatics. They're not the majority. You should read the letters they send my office. The notes saying he was wrongfully accused are the tame ones. They claim all kinds of insanity about Silas. The court may not have had enough evidence to try him for the other murders, but I don't buy for a second that Silas isn't the Leviticus Killer."

"Of course he is," I say, sounding too eager to back the governor up. "He'll kill again."

The governor grips the arms of his chair and stares at me for a long time before saying, "I have faith in you. I have faith in your team. You put Silas away the first time, and I trust you to keep everyone safe and catch this maniac."

Jude's head rubbernecks between his dad and his mom. "Why aren't you saying anything?" he asks his mother.

"I hardly have faith in this…team," Mrs. Taylor says flatly. Jude looks vindicated, before she adds, "But Ted's right. Silas can't go free. I can't have the murders he'd commit on my conscience."

"What the hell?!" Jude shouts. "You both care more about Dad's career than Jack?"

"It's not that simple," the governor says as Jude curses under his breath. "We need to pray for Jack's safe return."

"Oh, fuck this." Jude shoots up from the couch and storms out of the room, an officer trailing after him.

"Language," Governor Taylor calls after him half-heartedly.

Tense silence accompanies Jude as he marches up the stairs and slams a door.

We've clearly overstayed our welcome, so I rise from the love seat. "We'll let you know when we have updates."

"Thank you," the governor says, the politician's smile pasted on his face.

I give Mary a soft nudge. Time to go. We say our good-byes and Daniels escorts us to the front door before returning to the family. We head for the car. It is dark out, but the mansion's exterior lights are on. I pause as I spot a flash of motion behind the hedges. Mary's gaze flicks to mine. I put a finger to my lips and a hand on my gun. If Azrael's skulking around, he is in for a surprise. Silently withdrawing my Glock, I creep closer on the balls of my feet, sticking to the pavement until the last moment. When I reach the end of the hedge, I spring, finger on the trigger, landing on the other side.

"Freeze!"

Hands shoot up in the air, and I'm met with a face wracked with terror. "Don't shoot!" It is only Jude.

I holster the Glock, throwing Jude a stern stare. "What the hell are you doing out here?"

"Leaving," he mumbles.

"Well, you almost got yourself shot. How the hell did you get past the guard?"

Mary slides in behind him, having gone around the other end of the hedge. Teamwork.

Jude folds his arms defiantly. "It wasn't hard. Out my bedroom window and down the drainpipe. So much for your security."

"We're more interested in keeping people out. The cameras would've picked you up."

"Yeah, but I would've been gone by then."

Mary moves to stand beside me. "Your house, your family, isn't under threat."

"Maybe not my house. But my family isn't all here, are they?"

Mary puts a comforting hand on his shoulder. "Running away isn't the answer."

"I want to help find him."

"And what's your plan?" I ask, locking his gaze with mine.

"I… I was just…"

"Right. You don't have a plan. Look, I know you're upset, but I'm going to be straight. Your leaving puts Jack at more risk. Because then we need to pull resources, putting some of the officers working to find him to find you instead. Understand?"

Jude nods sullenly.

"Good. Emotions aren't the best way to make good decisions."

"You and my parents certainly have that down."

I ignore the insult. He needs someone to take his anger out on. Might as well be me if venting keeps him from doing anything stupid. "Stay put. You're safe here. You and your parents are in no way a target. Your cooperation is what will help Jack the most, okay?"

"Okay," he mumbles.

"I'm serious."

"I said, okay!"

"Good. I'm glad we understand each other. Now can you sneak back in the way you came so I can get back to work on the case instead of dealing with your parents?"

Jude gives a mirthless smile. "Roger," he says, half-mockingly.

Mary and I stay where we are, watching Jude retreat and shimmy up the drainpipe.

"Get someone to secure that exit," I say.

Mary nods, grabbing her walkie. She relays instructions as we head back to the Explorer. I open the door, the car's interior lights coming on. I'm about to get in when I see something near the front wheel, half rolled under the car. I bend down to examine the object as Mary jabbers away.

A small plush bird, no bigger than a golf ball. Bloodred. My shoulders crawl up to my neck, my heartbeat too heavy, too sluggish. I forget to breathe in as I stare at the creature. The beady little button eyes stare up at me. This is a test. Azrael taunting me to see what I'll cover up and what I'll turn over. And he has won this round. With a sharp inhale, I palm the bird, evening out my breathing as I shove the toy in my pocket. When I stand up, Mary's looking at me.

"Damn shoelaces."

Before I climb into the driver's seat, I pause, looking up into the air.

"I just want to check the surveillance setup for a second," I say, doing a slow spin. "Easier to see the red camera lights at night."

"Okay." Without a hint of suspicion, Mary gets in the car.

That is when I spot what I was looking for. A speck moving across the sky in the distance, glinting in the moonlight. If that isn't a drone, I'll eat the stuffed bird.

20

JACK

Thursday, 8:07 a.m.

JACK STARTLES AWAKE. "Dad?"

Darkness answers him. Again. He repeats the same cycle. Blackout. Jolt awake. Forget where he is. Remember. Blackout. Wake up. Blackout. Wake up. Can't sleep. No sleep. Sleep is not allowed. He can't sleep anyway. Even when he is left alone for long stretches. The ice pumping into his arm is laced with what must be a stimulant. He is trembling. His whole body shaking as he hangs like a helpless sack of meat from a butcher's hook.

"Hello, Jack." The warped voice swirls around him.

Not his dad. Definitely not.

"Why are you doing this?" Jack wails, then wishes he hadn't. Shadow hates questions. He tenses his body, teeth clenched, bracing for pain.

But no pain comes.

"I'm so glad you asked."

Shadow's twisted voice almost sounds pleased.

"I'm doing this because I want what we all want. Deep down.

To be a legend. Think about it. Why did you come meet me in the first place?"

Jack swallows but can't muster the strength to answer.

"Because I'm a famous YouTuber, right, bro? You wanted to rub elbows, hoped some of my glory would shine down upon you."

That is not true. He only wanted a friend. One friend.

Okay, being friends with a popular streamer did seem kind of cool, but that wasn't the reason. Not the only reason. Jack starts to weep.

"*See? You're being honest with yourself now, aren't you? I'm a thousand percent right. There's no shame in it. That's what we all want. Status. Power. Legacy. For our name to last ten minutes in the history books after we're dead and buried deep in the ground, the worms crawling in and out of our eye sockets.*

But damn, there are so many popular YouTubers now, aren't there? So many reality celebs. It's really difficult to be a legend anymore. Back in the day, you could be a nobody and rise to infamy. Take Alexander Hamilton. Shit, when there are only thirteen colonies it's easy to get famous, am I right? Give that guy a fucking musical. You want to be known worldwide in the present day? You've got to do something massive. And violent. But even that's not enough. Shooting up a school will barely get you a footnote. You've got to be creative."

"You're hurting me so you can be famous?"

"*It's not about hurting you. What did I say? I don't want to hurt you."*

Bullshit. Shadow revels in any excuse to inflict pain.

"What kind of violence? I don't understand."

"You're not meant to. Yet. But wait for it. Trust me. When this is over, EVERYONE will know my name. By the way, how are you liking my games, Jack?"

Careful. Give the right answer. "The graphics are amazing. Top shelf."

"Damn right. I'm a fucking artist. I'll release the games when I'm done. For a steep price, of course. How much do you think I can charge people to indulge in their sick and twisted fantasies? To put themselves in your shoes? Oh, and they will know what you went through. The outcomes of the games you play. That must be some consolation, right? So many people have hostage fantasies. And... other desires I can't tell you about without spoiling the surprise. I can charge quite a lot, I bet. But the games have been tame so far, don't you think? Time to spice it up. Violence begets violence."

"Violence begets nothing," Jack whispers. Something his dad says. He holds onto that thought, praying his dad will answer Shadow's messages. Stop Shadow from inflicting more violence on him.

"It's time for the next game."

The darkness of his fake room dissolves into...more darkness. There is a long gun in his hand. A hunting rifle. He does a slow spin, his heartbeat thumping. Everything around him is black. But as his eyes adjust, there are jagged outlines hanging over him, leaves trembling in a nonexistent wind. Trees? There is music, if you can call it that. A low, thrumming bass like a heartbeat.

"Wha—what is this? Shadow?"

No answer. And then a blur rushes at him from the darkness, twenty feet away. Fifteen. Ten. Closing fast. His hands shake, the rifle jerking left and right. The shape is massive. Five feet away. Two wicked hooks rush him. Attached to a wild boar the size of a linebacker. He fumbles with his gun, his mouth so dry his lips stick together, his tongue rough sandpaper against the roof of his mouth. Too late to shoot. Too late.

A tusk strikes his right side, spinning him around. He cries out as the gun flies out of his hands. Pain flares in his side. He doubles over, trying to make sense of what just happened. The games aren't supposed to hurt. They're not real.

Shadow's laughter haunts the dark space. "*Careful, Jack. Remember what I told you.*"

"Violence begets violence," Jack whispers.

"*An eye for an eye. A bullet for a goring. The next pig's coming. Don't miss.*"

His gun. Where is it? Oh God, where? Jack bends over, crawling across the ground on all fours, sweeping with his hands. There. A glint of metal in the gloom. He scrambles, grabbing the gun. He stands up and turns around. Turns again. Scanning the darkness.

And then he spots the boar. A streak of motion barreling right at him. His muscles are spent, his coordination sluggish. Still, he cocks the gun. Fires. The boar hurtling toward him stops and topples. A horrible death squeal pierces his ears. He wants to cover them, but he has to stay vigilant. He keeps searching. Searching.

"*Shoot the prize boar. You'll know which one. The beastie is twice as big as the others, and three times as fast.*"

The boars keep coming from all directions. His arms wobble more and more with each shot, the gun getting heavier, sinking lower. But he fires every time, his breathing and heartbeat calming a little as he gets into the rhythm. And then…

…He startles awake. Another blackout. The boar's bearing down on him. Tusks like baseball bats. Aimed right at his head. If those scythes hit him, TKO. Lights out.

Jack cocks the gun, the boar ramming into the barrel as he pulls the trigger. *Boom!* Right between the eyes. Jack flies back, but then his invisible restraints swing him in the opposite direction. He stops hard in front of the massive beast, the creature is on its side, an enormous tongue protruding from hairy lips, sightless eyes staring at him with all-white sclera. Dead.

The beast dissolves, and Jack's back in his inky bedroom.

"Well done."

Jack smacks dry lips. Thirsty, so thirsty. His tongue heavy as he tries to speak. "Water. Please."

"Not yet. Today is a special day. You have two games to win. Do that, and you'll see how generous I can be. I'll give you a day off tomorrow. How does that sound?"

That sounds sus as hell, he wants to say. But Shadow wouldn't like that. He nods instead.

"Excellent. Round two."

A run-down hospital clinic materializes. The subway tile walls are a sickly green, and the fluorescent ceiling lights flicker intermittently. Rows and rows of gurneys filled with patients coughing and moaning stretch before him. A music box makes up the melody, which might be soothing if the tune wasn't off-key and accented by aggressive beats of industrial guitar.

"Time to play doctor. Inject each patient with the needles beside their beds. Stay sharp. Get it? Sharp! And be on the lookout. One patient has a craniotomy. That means part of his skull has been cut away. He's your bonus patient. Inject him in the brain."

"Okay," Jack says. "Okay."

"If you miss, you'll be the one getting a needle. In the same spot as the patient. A surprise stabbing!"

His hands are plagued with tremors. He doesn't want a needle to the brain. Keep it together a little longer. Grab the needles and hold them steady. Don't miss. Don't miss.

He snatches up the first syringe.

21

JENA

Thursday, 9:46 a.m.

A GUARD OPENS the chapel's Gothic door, and I slip inside, pressing myself against the back wall. The same spot where Kyle stood the last time I was at SCI Fayette. Except, today, the chapel is packed with inmates, burgundy jumpsuits filling the pews. Surrounded by a perimeter of guards. The sweet smoke of incense in the air doesn't cover up the stench of sweat from the bodies of hundreds of adult men.

At the pulpit is Silas. He is preaching, the acoustics lifting his voice to the rafters, but he pauses at the opened door. The inmates turn to look, a sea of faces glaring at me. Silas continues. My presence insignificant.

"I say we *all* have our skeletons."

His words ring with natural charisma. You can't help but listen. The other prisoners turn their attention back to the front of the chapel. I block Silas out, running through what I need to ask him about the latest victim. Mickey Hughes. The football coach. Five minutes away from leaving his home for the safe house before his murder. I also block out my devastation that we're doing everything we can but couldn't protect another target. Showing emotions to Silas is like presenting him with a wound he can jam his finger into.

But I need more than a devout Catholic like Mary to make sense of what happened. I need a theologian. Azrael's had us in the dark at every turn, and I don't trust the safe houses to provide enough protection. I need to anticipate what is coming next.

The inmates murmur, a susurrus punctuated with occasional affirmative shouts of "Amen!" and "Preach!" I think one of the Hallelujahs comes from a guard.

Silas's words snag my attention.

"God nudges us to inspect our own lives, to drop our heavy loads. *Honesty is the key, between the Almighty and us.*"

Silas's stare pierces me, and I imagine him picturing my demise. My mistake for looking at him. Now I can't look away.

The chapel becomes claustrophobic. So many inmates. Not enough guards. Perhaps some of them sympathetic to Silas. What if he commanded them to turn on me? I wouldn't stand a chance. I can't even open the door to make a run for it. My breath rushes in and out of my nose, nostrils flaring and contracting.

Silas folds his hands in prayer, ending his sermon. "Go in peace to love and serve the Lord."

"Thanks be to God," the inmates chorus.

His gaze never leaves mine as the inmates file out of their seats. I will them to leave quickly, but they shuffle up to him in their manacles. He finally breaks eye contact as he turns to talk to the first of them. A minister receiving his flock of sheep. Cuffed hands shake cuffed hands as small group after small group departs with a guard.

Silas offers words of encouragement. "Keep that strength." "You are a fine soul." "Peace, brother."

As the last of the inmates exit, I sigh in relief. Four guards for Silas and my escort remain behind.

"Go ahead, Detective," my escort says. "He's chained to the floor."

I march up to the front, the aisle stretching under Silas's penetrating gaze. I step up the last stair, putting myself on equal ground, but staying out of reach of those hands. His manacles are again secured to a metal loop in the floor.

He folds his arms as if he can sense my trepidation. "Well, look what the cat dragged in. A little bird. What brings you around?"

I straighten, refusing to be cowed. Best to get straight to the point. "I need your help. Understanding a bit of theology."

Silas raises a perfect eyebrow. "Latest victim?"

I nod, giving a stoic expression. "Impaled by one of his hunting trophies. A boar's head mounted on the wall. The tusk shot him like a bullet. Right through the throat."

Silas says nothing, but I'll be damned if his eyes don't sparkle.

"I don't understand. We'd been expecting flies. What the hell does a pig have to do with the plagues?"

He leans forward, an elbow on the pulpit, resting his head on one hand. The other hand flips through the pulpit Bible. "Another one claimed by remote control. Azrael sure isn't one for sweat, huh?"

But Silas is. The last victim of his labor relentlessly haunting me. And there it is again. The same micro-expression Silas made last time we discussed Azrael's "work." A slight wrinkling of the nose. A left pull of the upper lip. This time, I'm sure what I saw.

With this revelation, I may have an advantage. At the thought, bubbles fizz in my chest.

"What do you think about what happened? With the boar, I mean. What's the reason for the pig?"

"You keep knocking on my door for help, and I keep wondering why you think I would offer it."

Time to see if my inkling is correct. This hunch, coupled with the fact that Silas loves the sound of his own voice, should tip this conversation in my favor. "Azrael." I stretch the name out, making it as distasteful as possible. And wouldn't you know it, Silas's mouth tugs to the left. "Your victims—"

"—You want to tread this path again?"

I raise my hands in surrender. I need cooperation. I'll say whatever he wants. I start again, rephrasing my words. "The victims of the Leviticus Killer. They were all egregious sinners. The worst of the worst. But these victims. The ones Azrael has killed. The remaining targets include a decorated military veteran. A social justice warrior. A fundraiser for diabetic children. The founder of a treatment center for addicts. They don't deserve this. Not one of them. And Azrael is attaching your name to this. Is this really the legacy you want?"

There is a slight lifting of his eyebrows. I think I've done it. Made a moral appeal to a serial killer. The idea is almost laughable. But Silas is in love with his own idea of justice. And what Azrael's doing doesn't fit that definition. I feel it in my bones.

"Wild beasts."

I keep my face impassive, not wanting to betray my delight that I have him talking. "I don't follow. What's wild beasts?"

"The fourth plague. Not flies, but wild beasts. That's how the older interpretation goes, same as jasper being the earlier interpretation of the foundation stones."

I hold his stare, refusing to acknowledge the accusation.

"In Hebrew, the fourth plague is called *arov*, meaning a blend, a mixture," Silas pontificates. "But what is mixed, you wonder? After frogs, the scripture says Egypt was drowning in useless, stinking frog carcasses. But with the end of the *arov* plague, God removed the *arov* from Pharaoh until not one remained. Why? Well, dead critters have valuable hides, and God didn't want that mess lying around for the Egyptians. If the *arov* meant a swarm of flies, those corpses would have been left behind, just like the frogs."

"That makes sense. What doesn't make sense is how Azrael, someone who clearly doesn't understand enough about religion to even come up with a good pseudonym, would have that knowledge."

A slow smile creeps across Silas's face. "Sure is a riddle, isn't it? Quite the head-scratcher."

"Was that information something you and Azrael passed back and forth in your little notes?"

"I haven't the faintest clue what you are jabbering about, little bird."

"The Bible verses. The ones he passed to you through a guard."

"I don't have the headspace to recall every plea that lands on my doorstep."

"We have the meaning for most verses figured out."

"So you say."

"Don't suppose you want to enlighten me on Isaiah 40:40 and 27:9?"

"You hit it spot on." Silas's smile turns wicked. He flips through the pulpit Bible until he finds what he wants, opening the book to a certain page.

He is baiting me. Wants to draw me in close to him so while I'm looking at the page, trying to decipher his clue, he can wrap an arm around my throat. Disarm me. Shooting isn't Silas's style, but he could snap my neck in a heartbeat. I don't budge.

"What about the handwritten numbers?"

"Standing here is taking its toll on me, little bird. Your time is running out." Silas shuts the Bible. I can't help but mourn the loss of whatever clue he just snatched away.

"The next plague. Is pestilence the right interpretation?"

"I'll throw you a bone. It's not like you'll stop it, with or without my help. Pestilence is correct."

"And what is that? Pestilence? Exactly?"

"Oh, little bird. The name suits you, doesn't it? Helpless as a hatchling left out in a storm. Pestilence is a vicious disease, spreads like wildfire. Think the bubonic plague. Keep an eye out for rats."

"Oh, I'm already watching them."

"If you truly want my help, you could put an end to this now. Admit how you twisted the truth to get me sent away."

I swallow hard. I'll never acclimate to Silas's death stare. "I have no idea what you're talking about."

Silas rises from the pulpit with such liquid lethality I've never been more thankful he is shackled to the floor. "What do you have faith in, little bird?"

"Justice," I say without hesitation.

"Justice as defined by the law? Or your own idea of Justice?"

"I have faith in the law."

"Keep reassuring yourself. Maybe someday you will even walk the talk." Silas's intense stare burns through me. "Now tell me, how do you intend to halt a premeditated killer?"

I have no answer to give.

His powerful fingers curl up and retract, turning his hands into claws. "I could stop him dead, and you know it. But you'd need to flip your stance on laying down your burdens. Sounds like a path you won't be taking, though."

I want to beg for his help, but I stay silent.

"The church bells are done ringing, little bird. See you around."

He turns away from me, kneeling beneath the stained-glass window with the crucifix and white dove. Zero fear of having his back to me. I wish I felt the same about him.

Confidential Case Notes

Date: August 2, 2019

Location: Law Office of Thomas Jones

Participants:

Thomas Jones, Esq., Attorney for the Defendant

Silas Halvard, Defendant

Summary of Client Meeting:

Mr. Halvard expressed his plea of not guilty, and I started the meeting by stating that our first step was to address the arrest warrant, as Mr. Halvard requested. I confirmed that I examined the warrant and provided a summary of the warrant's contents and the basis for Mr. Halvard's arrest, which relied on a pawn shop receipt related to the gemstones found in the victims' hands.

Mr. Halvard expressed disbelief, asserting that he never made any such purchase at a pawn shop. He contended that the prosecution's claims were unfounded and the evidence against him was a result of planted evidence.

I explained that I intended to file a pretrial motion challenging the authenticity of the pawn shop receipt, which the warrant was based on. If successful, his trial would be dismissed. I explained the prosecution would write a counter-brief in response to my arguments, and then we would argue our positions in front of a judge without a jury present. However, if the pretrial motion fails, we will proceed to trial with jury. In that case, our defense strategy would shift to attacking the prosecution's case and establishing reasonable doubt. Mr. Halvard expressed satisfaction with this approach.

I outlined key steps to initiate the defense strategy, including case analysis, investigation, witness interviews, expert consultation, legal motions, witness preparation, and trial preparation. I reassured Mr. Halvard that every available avenue would be explored to demonstrate flaws or unreliability in the evidence against him.

I discussed the advantages of using a mitigation specialist report, explaining that it would provide a more comprehensive understanding of Mr. Halvard's background and personal history without undermining the defense's assertion of innocence. However, Mr. Halvard expressed disagreement, expressing discomfort with anyone delving into his past. I clarified that while we fight for the best outcome, we also prepare for the worst. The worst here being the death penalty. I discussed how the report was a strategic tool for a more favorable outcome if a guilty verdict were to be reached, while still maintaining the belief in Mr. Halvard's innocence. Mr. Halvard stated that he did not wish for a mitigation report to be used as part of the defense strategy. I again reiterated that his denial to use a mitigation report could be the difference between the death penalty if the jury were to reach a guilty verdict. Mr. Halvard stated that he understood but did not agree to using the mitigation report. I told him that I respected his wishes, but that we may revisit this discussion depending on the course of the trial. Mr. Halvard consented to discussion at a later date but stated that he wouldn't change his mind.

The meeting concluded, and I reiterated my commitment to Mr. Halvard's defense and the primary objective of proving his innocence throughout the trial. I assured Mr. Halvard that the defense team would pursue all available avenues to secure the best possible outcome.

22

JENA

Friday, 10:17 a.m.

MARY AND I are at the medical examiner's building in Rowan O'Reilly's office. The victim is David Bacco. The nature lover.

"Necrotizing fasciitis," O'Reilly says, giving us the rundown of the autopsy. "Bacco received a massive dose of flesh-eating bacteria."

"Damn it," I spit. "I can't believe this shit. How? We had so much security on him."

Mary nods. "And we moved him to a safe house."

O'Reilly opens the file folder on his desk. Inside is a stack of photos. The top one shows a hand, the skin bright red, a patch in the middle bloody and raw. I pick the glossy image up.

"What am I looking at?"

"Injection site."

I put the picture back on top of the others. "Bacco had MS. He had an infusion at the hospital clinic. Yesterday."

"Infusions take a few hours," O'Reilly says. "He had this deadly stuff dripping directly into him the whole time. And necrotizing fasciitis in this amount is a very fast actor. Sepsis. Shock. Organ failure. Death."

"Is it contagious?" Mary whispers.

"Don't worry. It rarely spreads. I have the body in isolation. I suited up and took a luxurious chemical shower after I finished."

I'm furious we lost another one, but I don't want to take it out on O'Reilly. I swallow my rage and say, "Thanks again for the quick work. Don't take this the wrong way, but I don't hope to see you soon."

"Same. I've seen enough of your interesting cases this week to last a lifetime."

By the time we exit his office, I have a realization. I grab Mary's arm, stopping her in the middle of the hallway. "He was injected *yesterday.* Azrael didn't give us a chance to release Silas after he killed Mickey Hughes."

"I guess he doesn't have much faith in us."

"He's not sticking to his own rules. Why do I think we're playing a losing game? What if we can't protect the jurors no matter what we do? What if Jack ..."

Mary grimaces, a wedge of bubble gum showing between her teeth. "Don't think that way. We'll tighten security. And Azrael is way smart, right?"

"A hell of a lot smarter than us at the moment."

"Hostages are valuable. If his plan goes wrong, he'll need Jack to negotiate."

"I sure hope you're right. If we can just figure out where he's holding Jack and nail this son of a bitch, everyone will be safe. But if Azrael kills Jack, he could disappear and keep killing, and we'll never stop him. We can't let that happen. But I'm scared. Terrified, actually. Both for the jurors' lives, and that we have less time to find Jack than we thought. However much time Azrael's giving us, it's running out."

My phone vibrates in my pocket. Three short buzzes, three long ones, then three short again. SOS. The pattern I programmed for notifications from my social media account after my last message from Azrael. No way was I going to be caught by him again unaware.

I pull out the key fob for the Explorer and toss it to Mary. "I need a quick bio break before we head out."

She gives me a double thumbs up and heads for the front of the building. I duck into the restroom and make a beeline for a stall. The air is toilet bowl cleaner fresh. A pleasant surprise. My male coworkers think women's bathrooms must be this oasis of perfume and fresh spring water, but the things women do in public restrooms are the stuff of nightmares.

Door locked behind me, I click on the message.

Hello, little bird,

I can't help the involuntary shiver at the nickname, imagining the words said in Silas's voice.

There's something I've been pondering. How do you plan to stop me when I've set everything up in advance? The only way is to set Leviticus free. Otherwise, I'll sit back and relax while you watch them die. It's up to you, really. I'm not even getting my hands dirty.

Four more days to confess…

~ Azrael

Yeah, right. I'm not betting for one minute anything I do will stop his killing. Not even Silas's release. If Silas is out, they'll both claim more victims. More than the jurors and Jack. I hate weighing lives. Deciding that stopping more deaths in the future takes priority over protecting the lives of the few remaining targets. But the only way to stop this murder spree is to capture Azrael. Arrest won't undo the damage Azrael's already done. But seeing him on death row would be a nice consolation prize.

There is a video at the bottom of the DM. I click play. A montage of clips rolls, a skeletal avatar hand pushing buttons and manipulating the thumbstick.

Not even getting my hands dirty, Azrael said.

I play the video again, pausing at different intervals. I can't see anything human beneath the computer-generated hand. The controller is black and nondescript. The video is a tight shot. No background. We won't pull anything useful from the images, I can already tell. Still. I really should get the video to Collins. Which means giving him access to my phone and all the previous messages. Shit, shit, shit. I wish I knew more about tech. How to scrub Azrael's messages with the accusations. But even then, Collins could probably tell the phone had been scrubbed.

I need to send this in. Without handing over my phone. I click the share option and select Collins's e-mail as the destination.

> *Hey, I write.*
>
> *I'm on the road, but just got this video in my social media DM. Wanted to get it to you asap.*
>
> *- Campbell*

Before I can convince myself this is a colossally bad idea, I hit send.

I'm shoving my phone in my pocket when it vibrates, giving me a heart attack. It is a message from Collins.

Hey, I need to clone your phone to monitor new messages. Sending you a link to an app. Download and follow the instructions. Will take 2-3 hours to sync. Thanks.

- Collins

Shit. Whatever taunts Azrael sends me, Collins will have access to, and I'll need to come up with a way to explain them.

I gulp and wait for the link. My phone buzzes, my finger hovering as I wait to click on the app. But then the ringtone kicks in. I'm so stupid sick of Bruce's peppy "Woo" at this point, I want to throw my phone. But I'll take a phone call from Captain Price to delay sharing my messages from Azrael with Collins.

"Detective Campbell," I answer.

"Campbell. Governor Taylor wants another update."

"I'm a little busy. I'll go later."

"You chasing down a lead?"

"Not at the moment, but the other jurors—"

"Don't need you right now. You're going."

"Understood. I'll go. Tonight."

"You'll go now," he says and hangs up right as the *share-your-personal-life-with-the-PBP* link pops up from Collins.

This day keeps getting better.

Confidential Case Notes

Date: September 9, 2019

Location: Law Office of Thomas Jones

Participants:

Thomas Jones, Esq., Attorney for the Defendant

Silas Halvard, Defendant

Summary of Client Meeting:

I started the meeting by discussing Judge Spadina's denial of the pretrial motion to examine the warrant's credibility. Mr. Halvard was visibly upset and voiced his frustration. I acknowledged his disappointment with Judge Spadina's ruling on the pretrial motion. Silas forcefully stated that he had rights that weren't being protected. I refocused him on the current situation, and the need to prepare for trial.

After a brief reminder of the process, I returned to the idea of a mitigation report. Mr. Halvard stated that he wouldn't allow his "life to be paraded in front of the court." I discussed the importance of humanizing him in the eyes of the jury and how that could impact sentencing. Mr. Halvard again stated he wouldn't allow it, and that his personal life would not be part of the defense strategy. I told him I respected his objections, but that I needed to do what was in his best interests as his attorney.

Mr. Halvard proposed finding new representation. I stated that if he believed that was right for him, then I would support his decision, but that my years of experience told me refusing to provide a mitigation report wouldn't be a good decision. Mr. Halvard then told me to do what was necessary, but that he didn't agree and wouldn't participate. I stated that I understood, and would proceed with the mitigation report, noting his objections and maintaining his distance from the process.

The meeting concluded with me stressing the importance of maintaining a strong attorney-client relationship throughout the trial.

23

JENA

Friday, 8:15 p.m.

BACK IN MY apartment, I'm sprawled out on my bed. I bought a new burner phone. I say burner, but it has all the bells and whistles of my original phone. Azrael and the plague killings are the worst case I've ever had. I need to talk to someone supportive without the PBP eavesdropping. So I call Mason.

He answers, and the comfort his voice brings washes over me. His presence, even over the phone, is like coming home. The colossal stupidity of my actions hits me, and I swallow my pride, knowing I need to make things right between us.

"Hey," I say.

"Hey," he responds, but then goes silent. Because this is on me.

"I wanted to talk to you."

"Yeah," he exhales. *"Me too."*

"I know I said things…things I didn't mean."

"You were stressed."

"Doesn't excuse it, though."

"No, it doesn't."

"Look, I'm sorry."

"Me too."

"I let my pride get in the way. Again. I don't know if you can forgive me this time."

"We've been through a lot together. I don't want to lose that."

"Neither do I."

"You've got to stop doing this, though. I understand it but I don't know how much more I can take."

"And what do you understand?" I'm heating up. This isn't where I wanted to go. I don't want to be angry at Mason. He doesn't deserve it.

Mason sighs. *"I'm going to be straight, because you need to hear it, and I think I need to get this off my chest for us to move forward. You're afraid. Afraid of being abandoned, so you bail first. Afraid you're not worthy of love, so you set out to prove it. It's self-sabotage. And it needs to stop."*

I want to yell, scream, rage at him for daring to play pseudo-psychotherapist. But hell. He is spot-on. Of course he is.

"Yeah," I say, the anger morphing into despair. I struggle to keep the tears back, to keep the tremble from my voice.

"I've missed you," he says, trying to soften the blow.

It works. I can't stop the tears from falling. "I've missed you, too."

"It's okay, Jena," he says. *"Don't cry. I forgive you."*

We sit in silence, and the longer it stretches, the more the hurt and anger start to lift. And it starts to sink in. He forgives me.

When my sniffling has stopped, Mason says, *"Do you want to talk about your case?"*

"If that's okay?"

"Go ahead."

I hear the smile in his voice. He already knew that is why I called. Of course he did. Because Mason understands me better than anyone else in the world. And he is a very patient listener. I'm grateful as I relay to him what has been going on.

"Governor Taylor agrees there's no reason to free Silas," I say.

"You're sure the governor is solid on that?"

"Yeah. He said releasing Silas would only send the message that anyone who goes on a killing spree can get an inmate released."

"Smart man. Why don't you sound as thrilled about that as you should?"

"It's a moral dilemma, isn't it? We know Azrael will kill more people, including the jurors and the governor's son, if we don't catch him. Jack's just a kid. I have nightmares about what Azrael's doing to him. On the other hand, we're speculating freeing Silas would up the death toll even higher."

"But the pardon is the governor's decision to make, so it's not your moral dilemma to wrestle with. No use worrying about decisions outside your control."

I sigh. "Can I confess something to you in confidence?"

"Of course."

"I have an option that could get Silas out. But it could get me in trouble. And if I can't use Silas as a lure to catch Azrael, things will be worse than if I'd done nothing at all. Jack and the other jurors could die anyway. I'm not sure whether to use it."

"Is this option legal?"

I pause, not sure how to phrase my answer.

"You know what, never mind. I don't want to know. So, you're saying this would be a huge gamble. A shot in the dark that Silas's freedom would save lives and help you catch Azrael. You want my advice? It doesn't sound worth jeopardizing yourself."

"But you don't even know what it is."

"Jena, you don't always want my opinion, but I'm going to give it to you. Both personal and professional. You have a sterling reputation. All of Pittsburgh looks up to you as a hero for putting Silas away. Don't risk all the wonderful things you've built. Don't solve this outside the law."

"I'm trying. I'm really, really trying."

"Listen to me. You're smart. You're experienced. You can do this. You've caught a serial killer before."

Not while staying inside the law, I think. Instead, I say, "You're right. Thanks. Look, I need to get some work done before I turn in, but let's see each other soon, okay?"

"Sounds good. I miss you."

"Miss you, too," I say, then hang up the phone.

Not two seconds later, my other phone vibrates on my nightstand. Morse code. S.O.S.

I shake off the chill creeping up my spine, swap phones, and open the DM.

> *Hello, little bird,*
>
> *And hello PBP cyberteam. What, did you think I wouldn't recognize a little phone cloning? I'm no amateur. But I don't mind you spying on this message. I don't have much to say, except…*
>
> *Four more days, little bird. Four more lives left. Will you let Leviticus fly free?*
>
> *~ Azrael*
>
> *P.S. Cute that you wear scrubs as pajamas. Those pants are a lovely shade of lavender.*

I nearly throw my phone at the wall.

He can see me.

He can fucking see me.

I power off my phone before leaping from the bed, my heart punching a speed bag inside my throat. Pressing myself against the wall, I creep over to the window, peeking out, showing as little of my face as possible. Don't want to give him a target. I scan the street, the parked cars, the apartment buildings. Is he looking through this window right now?

With a shaking hand, I reach out and grab the cord for the blinds, snapping them shut. Next, I go to my nightstand and grab my gun. I sweep the bedroom looking for cameras, opening drawers, moving artwork, crawling under the bed. Standing on the side table, I check the ceiling tiles. Then I grab a screwdriver and unscrew the vents. Nothing found, I leave the bedroom, giving every room the same treatment. It is all clear. Must've been peeping in the window then. Probably using a drone again. I wish believing his voyeurism was remote, that he is somewhere far away, made me more comfortable. It doesn't. He knows where I live.

I stand there, shuddering and shivering. This just turned into a Sig-under-the-pillow kind of night. I could ask to be moved to a safe house until this is over. The scared part of me is begging me to ask. But the badass part of me says there is no way I'm leaving. No way he'll see me running scared. That part hopes he'll march through that door. Give me an excuse to put a bullet in him.

My brain whispers that is not his style. If he is going to kill me, he'll do it without me ever seeing his face. Which is why I need to find him. So he can see mine when I come for him.

I have one more place I need to check. I rush to the front

door, looking out the peephole. The hallway is empty, but that doesn't mean someone isn't running down the front or back stairs. I punch the door open with a bang, sweeping my gun right and left. Nothing. I wait, listening. But I don't hear footsteps. Only the faint music from Dustin's apartment next door.

I'm nearly at the back stairs, my Sig still out, when Dustin cracks his door open. I shove the gun into my waistband, pull my shirt over it, and turn around. Dustin slips out, looking me up and down. What a sight I must be. Mascara streaking down my face, my hair plastered to my scalp with sweat.

His face softens with pity, and I want to curl in on myself and disappear.

"Do you want to come in?" he says. He runs a hand through his blond hair, which is sticking up in haphazard peaks of awful bedhead, and I wonder about the last time he brushed it.

I shake my head, declining his invitation. He waits for me to speak, but I don't. I can't. I refuse to break down in front of a gaming bro.

"Let me at least get you a tissue."

I'm almost tempted, but then he holds the door open wider, revealing a dark interior, the video game music blaring out into the hall, shaking me from my pathetic trance and driving home the point that I don't belong there.

"I'll be all right," I manage. "But thank you. I appreciate the offer."

My lip is trembling, and I bite it to get it to stop.

"Well, okay, but I'm only a door away if you change your mind. I don't mind going AFK for a while."

I have no idea what that means, but nod like I do.

He gives a silly little formal bow, saying, "My lady," then

he disappears inside, the door shutting behind him, leaving me standing in a vacant hallway like an idiot.

And then the intercom starts buzzing. *Bah dah bah bah-dah baaaahh daahh. "Take me out to the ball…game."*

I run back inside to answer.

"Hello?"

"Detective Campbell? It's Dale. Are you okay?"

"Yes. Yes, I'm fine."

"Can you buzz us in? We've been sent for guard duty. And Collins says to 'turn your damn phone back on.' That's a direct quote."

My face heats. Of course Collins dispatched someone after Azrael's message. Because I turned my phone off, cutting off Azrael, but cutting Collins off, too. He must have been as freaked out as I was by that message. Cheeks still burning, I buzz Dale in.

24

JENA

Saturday, 9:28 a.m.

NORMA LITTLEJOHN'S SAFE house is a hotel that is three stars at best. Mary and I take the elevator up to the seventh floor.

"You look good," Mary says. "Refreshed."

"Slept like a rock." Thanks to the PBP patrolling my apartment last night.

When we arrive, there is a team inside Littlejohn's room including Anders, Jersey, and Weisz. It is your standard depressing space. Two double beds with ugly floral quilts. Fake wood headboards nailed to the wall. Abstract art. Heavy curtains. Threadbare carpet.

"Big closet," Mary comments.

"I smell mold."

Anders is working at the desk, Weisz attached to her shoulder. Jersey's chilling in the armchair, feet up on the ottoman, a dingy lamp illuminating his smug face like he is the patriarch at a family Christmas party.

Jersey rises and saunters over to me, a big self-pleased grin on his face. "We found it!"

"Ms. Littlejohn found it," Weisz chimes in behind him.

Jersey's smile falters. "You believe this guy? Always gotta contradict me. The biggest killjoy."

"Tell me," I say.

"Ms. Littlejohn's perfume," Weisz says. "It was making her itch."

"Anders tested it," Jersey cuts in. "Staph."

Weisz nods. "Would've given her boils for sure."

"Good job, team!" Mary chirps.

I'm nowhere near as pleased. "How the hell did she have a personal effect with her? Those were supposed to be confiscated."

Jersey's face falls, and now I'm the killjoy, but I don't care if I've downpoured on his parade.

"She had it in her purse. Never took it out."

"That's no excuse. Where's Littlejohn now?"

"In the shower," Weisz says. "Washing off the staph."

"Did you let her take her personal bar of soap in with her, too?"

Jersey shakes his head. "No. Hotel products only. I double checked."

I glare, hands on hips.

"Triple checked. I swear."

I move further into the room, my eyes running over everything.

"I see the wheels turning," Mary says as she joins me. "What is it?"

"Something's wrong. Skin boils won't kill you."

"You think it's a distraction?"

"Yeah. Littlejohn might not even be the target."

Seconds later, Littlejohn's scream proves me wrong.

I rush for the bathroom, reaching for the doorknob. There is a pop like a gunshot. I yank the door open, and smoke billows out. My skin and eyes burn. I hack and sneeze. But the smoke can't hide what has happened. The splatter of red on the walls. Littlejohn's body lying on the floor, tangled up in the shower curtain. Her head is gone. Blood drips from the stump of her neck, spreading out across the tiled floor. The entire bathroom, turned into a horror movie within five seconds.

I freeze, wanting to look away. Unable to. I grab my throat, swallowing the shout creeping up. And then I retreat. Putting distance between myself and the sight of this slaughter straight out of *Psycho*, crashing into the closet behind me. My lungs are concrete. I can't take a breath. Can't wrap my head around the idea that what is in front of me was just a living, breathing person. My entire body shudders, and the cement shatters, replaced by a hard thudding in my chest. Smoke keeps pouring out of the bathroom.

The noise of the room sounds far away. Mary's yelling. Jersey's dry retching. Someone hauls me back. I can't make sense of where I am, stumbling over my own feet. The door to the hotel room opens and I'm thrust out with the others. Then the door slams shut behind us. I look back toward the room, smoke leaking beneath the room's door into the hallway.

"I don't understand." Jersey sounds on the verge of tears. "We checked everything."

Weisz puts a hand on his back, and Mary says, "It's not your fault."

"Isn't it, though? 'Cause it sure feels like it."

The group is moving further away, sharing their shame and disbelief. I follow them in a daze toward the stairs, sniffing back the tears threatening to stream down my face, wanting to escape the hell I've left behind. But something catches my eye outside the hallway window and I stop, turn, walk over to it. Head spinning,

I can barely make sense of it all. I think I might have glimpsed a drone before it disappeared behind a building, but I can't be sure.

Then my phone vibrates. S.O.S. As I stare at the screen, the S.O.S. buzzes again. And I snap out of my thoughts. Azrael.

My upper lip curls back. The last thing I want is to open one of his messages. I should be with my team. But it might help make some sense of what is going on. Of what happened to Norma Littlejohn. I duck into an alcove with a vending machine and icemaker, checking the notification. It is a video. I click play.

Azrael appears, again in silhouette against a green screen.

How's it going over there?

His voice sounds jovial despite the warping from the voice mod. Piece of shit. Crowing after his kill.

You know what you can learn on YouTube? Sodium reacts with violence in water. Boils it before it explodes. Makes a hell of a lot of smoke. You should check it out. There's one video where a family throws a chunk into a pond and boom! *For an extra good time, try the 1947 disposal of twenty-thousand pounds of sodium in water. An oldie, but a goodie!*

Anyway, when you process the scene, you'll find Norma's shampoo wasn't what it appeared to be! Powdered sodium and mineral oil look a lot like shampoo at first glance.

That shampoo was hotel stock. How the hell did he replace it? The smugness in his voice makes me want to pull my Glock and blow away the screen. Shattering his face would be so fucking satisfying.

Gosh, you look surprised!

A shot of me stumbling into the hall appears on the video, my face slack with shock as Mary drags me out of the room. The picture starts further away and zooms in. Like it was filmed by a drone. I fucking knew it. It takes everything in me not to smash my phone into smithereens.

Anyway, boils! Get it? I left you a little clue, too. And you found it. Staph! Does it tell you more about me? Catch me if you can, before I leave your next present!

Littlejohn's headless body screams inside my mind and I can't blink the image away. The vision morphs into Jack, and I can't bear that a seventeen-year-old kid could be next. Bile shoots up my throat. I clap a hand over my mouth, refusing to puke like a rookie.

I need to calm down. Freaking out won't bring Littlejohn back or save Jack. And it won't help me catch Azrael. I gulp air until my breathing slows and I can think with a shred of coherence.

I play the video again, noticing Azrael's less contrived. More natural. Like with each kill, he is enjoying himself more and more. Convinced he is unstoppable. God, I want to stop him, but I don't feel smart enough to solve this case.

I will myself to push Littlejohn from my mind. To forget all the impending awfulness that is waiting for me once I rejoin my team; notifying her family, keeping another death out of the press along with our failure to stop it. I force myself to push away the guilt and despair and concentrate. Listen to each word for any clues. Any hints Azrael dropped he didn't think we'd pick up on that he is laughing about right now. Except it isn't what I hear that gets my blood pumping, but what I see.

I pause the video, then blow the picture up. The green screen doesn't extend all the way to the edge of the frame. There is a small sliver where I can see a window. Ha. Take that, you cocky fuck. Who isn't smart enough now?

Collins's probably looking at the cloned video right now. I shoot him a quick message.

You see it, right? The window?

Collins replies with a thumbs up, and I hurry out of the alcove to join the others to face the aftermath of this horror.

SMART BOARD

Victims

1. Michelle Green
   Plague #1 – Water to Blood
   COD – electrocuted
2. Lisa Bell
   Plague #2 – Frogs
   COD – golden dart frog poison
3. Matt Butler
   Plague #3 – Lice
   COD – asphyxiation
4. Mickey Hughes
   Plague #4 – ~~Flies~~ Wild Beasts
   COD – impaled by taxidermy boar tusk
5. David Bacco
   Plague #5 – Pestilence
   COD – flesh-eating bacteria
6. Norma Littlejohn
   Plague #6 – Boils
   COD – reaction of sodium and water

<u>NEXT PLAGUE – #7 Hail</u>

Targets / Jurors

1. James Cox (46 yo male)
   Notables: Digital archivist. Into crypto. Family owns dairy farm.
2. Charles "Chuck" Gomez (70 yo male)
   Notables: Likes Formula 1. Golden Retriever.
3. Kent Baker (42 yo male)
   Notables: Flemish rabbit. Teaches high school tech.
4. Avi Spieler (29 yo NB)
   Notables: Multimedia artist. Kosher.
5. Earl Rogers (76 yo male)
   Notables: Director of a nonprofit specializing in drug and alcohol treatment. Glaucoma.
6. Chris Brown (33 yo male)
   Notables: Mechanic. Bartends at night. Raynaud's disease.
7. Jack Taylor (17 yo male)
   Notables: Governor's son. Suspected to be a hostage in Azrael's custody, who has declared Jack will be the tenth and final victim.

Leads

~~Jack's laptop~~
~~Jack's phone~~
~~Azrael's social media account~~
~~Footage from Matt Butler's work cameras~~
Bible verses sent to Silas

25

JENA

Saturday, 11:34 a.m.

"ROCINANTE, RANKED BEFORE all other horses."

Joe Torres, the SWAT team leader with a savant-like knowledge of literature, is talking about his hulking white van that he has apparently named after Don Quixote's horse. And I'm crammed into the front seat of the steel beast. Torres is in the driver's seat. I'm in the passenger's. And Mary is smushed between my bony hip and Torres's gladiator thighs. But she has got on her classic smile, not looking one bit uncomfortable being a Mary sandwich. In the back of the van, the SWAT team is in full riot gear, ready to go. Jersey and Weisz are in the car tailing us.

"And now, I believe I'm due a briefing on why we're racing to 632 Fort Duquesne Boulevard with a no-knock warrant in hand," Torres says. "Since we're all assembled here in my ready room."

Is that a *Star Trek* reference? Torres is all over the place today. Must be the adrenaline.

As soon as Mary and I got back to the station, Collins briefed us, then rushed us out again. We've barely had time to process what happened to Norma Littlejohn. My throat still burns from acrid smoke inhalation. I catch Torres up to speed.

"This serial killer, calls himself Azrael, enjoys taunting us with videos. He sent a montage of avatar hands working a VR controller. Collins got nothing from that one. But this last one..." I can feel the gleam in my eye as I pause, building the anticipation.

"Tarry forth, dear lady."

"Of course, Azrael's a master hacker. He's covered his tracks so Collins can't pull info by trying to track down an IP address or anything. But with the last video he sent, he fucked up."

I stretch across Mary and hold up my phone for Torres to see. He glances down, then back at the road. On my screen is the frozen image of a bright yellow bridge.

"The Andy Warhol Bridge?"

"Right. Azrael uses a green screen for his videos. But it didn't extend quite all the way to the end of the shot."

I swipe right. The same image is zoomed in a bit more. It shows a window with a red mark on it.

Torres's eyes flick down. "What am I looking at?"

"I'm so glad you asked. It's graffiti. The letter *V*, according to Collins."

"So this image is what's sent us driving to Fort Duquesne Boulevard?"

"Yep. Collins worked out that for the bridge to show up in the video at that angle, it had to be one of the apartment buildings there."

"But from my many years working with Collins, I know he

wouldn't just toss us out to scour for an apartment with a red *V* tagged on the window."

"Right. He used Google Earth. In his words, 'powerful stuff.' Found a building with the word revolt spray-painted across the front. 632 Fort Duquesne."

"Reason is a man's instrument for arriving at the truth."

I have no idea what the hell Torres is quoting now.

"Reason, and the Internet," Mary says.

"Touché."

Torres turns onto Fort Duquesne from 6th Street and slowly approaches the location. The GPS on the dash points southwest of the Andy Warhol Bridge and not that far east of Point State Park, where we found Jack's car.

Despite the hip neighborhood, there is something almost taunting about the site selection. My hackles rise, on high alert. Torres cruises by the Byham Theater, the façade painted with a Richard Haas mural that pays homage to Pittsburgh's steel industry. The images are hyperrealistic. An old-timey man in a flat cap looks out at you, away from the vats of molten steel. Torres keeps going, passing the target. A squat gray building with P.P.G. Co. chiseled into the stone, the historic Pittsburgh Plate Glass Company. Above the storefront on the ground floor, the word revolt is spray-painted across several windows in bright crimson. I glance at the *V*. The lights are out in the apartment. Either no one is home, or they're keeping a low profile. Jack could be in there right now. Alone, or with unwanted company. A hostage in the dark.

Torres turns right down an alley and pulls past the spots reserved for theater goers after 6 p.m. Jersey and Weisz park there alongside the building, while Torres takes the van around back.

Mary leans in close so only I can hear. "Why does your face look like that?"

I relax my pursed lips. "I don't like this at all. Feels like a trap."

"Good thing SWAT's going in first, then."

I give a subtle nod.

"It makes sense as a location," Mary says. "Azrael wouldn't have had to take Jack very far from Point State Park."

"Not a bad theory. You're such an optimist," I say, although my attention is on the building. Everything is quiet.

"Jack could be here," Mary says.

"Sure," I say, but I'm not convinced.

Torres has his phone out, dialing.

"Detective Spiers," Jersey answers, his voice faint and tinny through the phone's speaker.

"'Once more unto the breach, dear friends, once more,'" Torres says. He means get ready.

"Copy that," Jersey says and hangs up.

Torres turns to me and Mary. "Time to gear up. We'll clear the building. You follow behind."

We climb from the van and move to the back. The doors swing open, and we're handed two bulletproof vests and a large Maglite. Mary and I tug on the vests, then pull our Glocks. Weisz and Jersey move in behind us, giving a nod. We're ready to go.

We step aside as the SWAT team pours out the back doors of the van. The two SWAT in front carry a large black metal ram. The others hold ready AR-15 assault rifles. They move with liquid precision to the building's entrance.

I dart after them, Mary at my side, Jersey and Weisz at our heels. The back door to the apartment building is open, and the group disappears inside. We follow them, hoofing it up the stairs to the fourth floor. They're halfway down the hallway as we emerge, already trying the door. Looks like it is locked as the front two SWAT swing back the ram, then let it fly. The door splinters, falling inward with one hit. The two with the ram move aside as the team storms in. Then they drop the ram and grab their own rifles, taking up the rear.

There is a sonic boom and flash of light as a stun grenade detonates. My ears are ringing, but I still hear the shouts of "Police!" "Freeze!" and "Clear!" from inside the apartment. My grip tightens on my Glock as I approach the door.

Natural light shines in through the windows. There is nothing inside except SWAT sweeping the area. An empty apartment with bare light fixtures and a wood plank floor littered with debris. Cardboard moving boxes and crates. Pizza boxes and fast food wrappers. An old yellow mattress. Discarded knickknacks. My heart shrinks.

Joe Torres is next to me. "'Lose, and start again at your beginnings. And never breathe a word about your loss.'"

Frickin' Torres and his quotes. But I get his meaning.

"Spread out and search for any leads," I relay to Mary, Weisz, and Jersey. "This guy wouldn't bring us here without leaving some kind of fuck-you."

I make a beeline for the window with the red *V*. The letter from the video is like an arrow pointing me to the evidence. As I approach the windowsill, I see a bird's nest with a pop of red peeking out. I hustle over and look inside. A bloodstone rests in the cradle of twigs. Heart in my throat, I palm and pocket it before anyone can see.

26

JENA

Saturday, 3:19 p.m.

I'M BACK AT SCI Fayette. A guard escorts me to Silas's cell. Not Kyle, this time. I wonder how he fared with Papich and whether he has been fired or just reprimanded and assigned a crappy duty. I hope it's the former. Silas sympathizers are better outside the prison.

As I follow my escort down the corridor, I prepare for my meeting with Silas by running over the evidence my team has that could lead us to Azrael. He said staph was a clue, but how does that help? Running records on everyone who had staph in the area is an enormous and impossible task. Azrael would know that. So, another taunt, then. And then there is the bloodstone. Also has to be a taunt. Probably about his connection to Silas. Which is why I'm here. That and because I have no other leads.

I startle as the mechanical door to Silas's wing clashes shut behind me, the bolt locking with an electric buzz. The guard walks ahead of me, down the bleached corridor. We pass the dormitory-style living into the single cells. The windows are much smaller here, and there is more fluorescent light than natural.

The cell door is solid with a sliding window. The peephole reminds me of the prisoner partition in the Explorer.

"Don't get within grabbing distance," the guard says before unlocking the window.

He acts like Silas is an annoying gnat, and I'm glad he is not one of the guards sucked in by Silas's charm. He slides the glass open and leaves me to it.

I approach the window, stopping an arm's length away, and then Silas's face appears. I root myself to the ground, refusing to startle. His eyes, which looked crimson in the chapel, are now two black holes, absorbing all the light. His gaze sucks me in.

I should believe I'm more protected with a door between us, but I felt safer in the church, his manacles anchored to the floor with armed guards watching him. Despite the max security cell, Silas has too much freedom for my liking.

"Silas." My voice sounds steady to me. "Can I ask you a few questions? About Azrael?" He gave me a hint last time. I'm hoping he'll be generous enough to give me more.

Silas pinches his chin as if I'm a solicitor he might shoo away or might permit an audience for the purpose of taunting. "And what do you have to trade for my help? A room with a view, maybe? Or freedom itself?"

I move closer to the window to show I'm not afraid, but the rising hairs on my arms say otherwise. "Azrael killed the social justice warrior. Powdered sodium in her shampoo. I heard her scream as she died. The innocent scream of a righteous, God-fearing woman."

I worry I've pushed too hard for his sympathy, but the left side of his mouth tugs, so maybe I've hit my mark.

"The jurors might be innocent, but what about you? Maybe it ought to be you playing hostage, instead of the boy."

Or maybe my shot was too wide. I keep my composure and make another push. "Trying to intimidate me won't do either of us any good. But if you're opposed to what Azrael's doing while claiming it's for you, you can help me."

Silas lets out the smallest of sighs. "So you are curious to get more on Azrael, huh? Did he leave a souvenir to share with me? A rock, maybe?"

Odd that he called the bloodstone a rock. I've only ever heard him refer to the gems as stones. I file that away. Everything Silas does is deliberate.

"No words for me, little bird?"

"None. But if there's anything more you can—"

He stops me with an upraised hand. "'The port is near, the bells I hear, the people all exulting, While follow eyes the steady keel, the vessel grim and daring.'"

"What?"

Silas sighs. "You should try reading sometime. It will keep your brain from dying of loneliness."

"Well, that's helpful." I can't help the acerbic tone.

"Yes, it is. Look. I'll toss you a bone, little bird, if you are hungry enough to catch it. He is a fan of video games."

"And that somehow relates to the quote thing you just said?"

He regards me, then shakes his head, taking a step back from the window. "Unless you have come to set me free, we are done talking, aren't we? But maybe mull over what I laid out. If there is a death due, who should it be? You? Or the boy?"

His eyes stab through me, but I refuse to let him in my head. Refuse to consider his threat, knowing it would be my life he'd collect if he were free. I hold his stare.

Silas turns his back to me. Once again, showing how little of a threat he considers me. "I feel quite sure you know your way out."

Silas disappears inside the shadows of his cell, out of my view through the little window. His cot groans as he settles in, my presence already dismissed.

I'm beaten down, like a boxer trying to get up after being punched in the mouth, but I can't go another round. I wave to the guard, who is leaning against the wall a little way down the corridor. He leaves his post, coming to escort me out.

Silas's voice floats out of his cell, chasing after me. "'They will make all the stones of the altars like crushed limestone, and the Asherah poles and the incense altars will no longer stand.' What does it mean, little bird? What does it mean?"

Court Mitigation Specialist Report

Completed by [redacted]

Defendant: Silas Halvard

Case Number: 2019-0012

Charge: First-Degree Murder

Introduction:

This report serves as a comprehensive analysis of Mr. Silas Halvard, a defendant convicted of one count of first-degree murder in the case of Joseph Burton's death. As a court mitigation specialist, my objective is to provide a thorough understanding of Silas's background, personal history, and any factors that may provide insight into his actions. Silas agreed to the report but refused to participate in the process. Therefore, there is no first-hand information from Silas included in this report.

Background:

Silas Halvard, a native of New Orleans, Louisiana, is an educated and sophisticated individual. Holding a Ph.D. in Theology, he has pursued a successful career as a distinguished theology professor at Geneva University.

Family History and Upbringing:

The following information is gathered from other sources without Silas's input, such as colleagues, neighbors, friends, teachers, child protective services workers, and police reports.

Silas's childhood environment, filled with abuse and neglect, has had a profound impact on his life. Raised in New Orleans, he grew up in a devoutly religious household where his father, Samuel Halvard, held stringent beliefs and administered harsh discipline. Samuel, haunted by his own abusive past, became a religious zealot who resorted to extreme measures in the name of discipline and salvation.

According to child protective services and police reports, the abuse endured by Silas and his siblings was a blend of physical and psychological torment. Samuel's methods were unorthodox, subjecting his children to brutal beatings, forced fasting, and prolonged isolation. He believed that suffering and sacrifice were the pathways to enlightenment and salvation, and he imposed these beliefs on his children with unwavering intensity.

Silas's mother, Martha Halvard, played a passive role in this abusive environment, trapped between her loyalty to her husband and her responsibility to her children. She was paralyzed by fear and conditioned to believe that the abuse was necessary for their spiritual growth. Her passivity allowed the abuse to persist and promoted emotional neglect during Silas's formative years.

Silas's childhood experiences and the abusive environment in which he was raised played a significant role in shaping a distorted belief system. The relentless physical and psychological abuse inflicted by his father left lasting scars, both visible and invisible. The professed religious fervor of his father became intertwined with the trauma, creating a distorted understanding of discipline, sacrifice, and redemption.

Adult Life:

As Silas grew older, his religious studies and academic pursuits intensified his delusions of grandeur. His extensive knowledge of theology and scripture provided him with a veneer of sophistication, masking the depths of his religious fanaticism. When his colleagues were queried about Silas's religious philosophy, they reported that his beliefs revolve around the concept of atonement, the idea that individuals must pay for their sins to achieve redemption.

It was reported by a family member that Silas committed adultery, and that his difficulty accepting this sin led him to cut off his left ring finger. This act, however, was not enough to earn his wife's forgiveness. She committed suicide via pill overdose shortly afterward. Following this, Silas began to view himself as an agent of divine retribution, driven by a warped sense of righteousness to make others want to atone for their sins as well.

I'd also like to highlight Silas's isolation from societal norms. Despite his distinguished academic career, he became increasingly detached from social interactions, immersing himself in his religious studies and rituals. This isolation allowed his delusions to fester unchecked, leading him down a dark and self-destructive path.

Throughout his life, Silas grappled with feelings of guilt and shame, stemming from his father's abusive practices and his own transgressions. Both the loss of his previous job at Loyola University in New Orleans in the religious studies department, and the suicide of his wife following his infidelity, amplified his sense of failure and increased his religious zealotry.

Conclusion:

It is crucial to note that while this report provides insight into Silas's background, it does not absolve him of responsibility for any actions he may have committed. Rather, it aims to provide information about the complex web of factors that contributed to his actions.

Moving forward, it is recommended that Silas undergo a thorough psychiatric/psychological evaluation to better understand the extent of his psychological disturbances and to determine the appropriate course of treatment, rehabilitation, and assessment for future risk.

In conclusion, the case of Silas Halvard presents a multifaceted portrait of a man whose life was shaped by a traumatic upbringing, religious extremism, and a distorted sense of atonement. It is now the court's solemn duty to consider these mitigating factors and to make an informed decision regarding sentencing.

27

JACK

Sunday, 9:46 a.m.

WHEN JACK WAS six, Dad signed him up for the junior golf league. He couldn't hit the damn ball. Endless walking and fresh-cut grass igniting his allergies. A hornet's sting. Red-wing blackbirds dive-bombing his visor. Sand in his eyes hitting out of the bunker. Disappointment in his dad's eyes when he quit.

When he was eight, tennis lessons, barely able to lift the racket, hiding behind blue backdrop curtains. Unable to cut it. Again.

But then at nine, his first laptop, strings of code fitting together, making vibrant worlds to escape into. Friends chatting and laughing and making inside jokes. Belonging.

And now, abandonment, pain, whole body screaming—

Jack startles from his waking dream, flailing in his restraints, pins and needles spreading down his legs. He blinks dry eyes, looks around, orients himself to the dark room, this fake world.

He senses his presence. Shadow creeping around the periphery. The thought of what is coming next fills him with dread. He fears pain, fears the games, fears losing, fears Shadow's pain stick jammed into the base of his spine, electric shock searing through his body, limbs spasming. But as much as he fears Shadow's pain, he needs Shadow. Needs to get the next message to his dad and hope rescue comes.

He is not sure how much longer he can hold out. It has been...five days? Seven? He has tried to keep count, but there is no sunlight, no day or night, no sense of any time. Just one long stretch of darkness.

His mouth is desert dry, head spinning, dreams leaking over into reality. *Keep it together*, he scolds himself. But he can't stay with it much longer. Already there are cracks beneath the surface. The uncontrollable urge to laugh until the madness shatters him into a thousand pieces.

There is shuffling, equipment sliding across a desk in the outside world. A crackle in his headset. Shadow's here. He twists around, checking the room's corners. Holds his breath, listens.

And then: *"Jaa-aack."*

The distorted voice startles him. He tips forward, arms windmilling.

"Ready for the next game?"

The mad laughter brewing inside him threatens to bubble over. Of course he is not ready. But also: "I'm ready." His voice comes out in a bullfrog croak.

"Hang in there a little longer. A few more days."

"And then what?"

"The big finale."

He doesn't like the sound of that at all.

The room dissolves, and he is in a snowy field. The change makes him woozy, vertigo hitting him, like he is falling into a pit of eternal winter. He stretches his arms out to the side, trying to find balance.

A remote control materializes in his hands, a drone hovering before him. Snowmen emerge from the ground, rising up like winter zombies from a frozen grave. The music is a duo of violins. A cluster of discordant high notes, sharp and screeching.

"It's an icicle-firing drone. Isn't that fun? You know the drill. Hit the snow zombies. Pierce their frozen hearts before they rip you apart."

"And hit a bonus zombie?"

"Right you are. He'll be the one with the hellhound on a chain."

Jack tests out the remote, flying the drone left and right, the violins grating in his ears. His operation of the controller is sluggish, the response far slower than he'd like. But he can barely stay conscious, fighting to make his body do what he wants.

"On your mark. Get set… Go!"

The horde shuffles toward him, and Jack fires. Icicle missiles fly from the drone. Some of them miss, but most hit their mark. This is what he is good at, he reminds himself. Tired, in pain, hallucinating. He can still do this.

As he thins the horde, he spots him. A larger snow zombie with an ice sculpture dog trotting ahead of him. The violins crescendo to a hellish wail.

And then…

…the world stutters.

Instead of a snowy field, he spots the back of a house. Peeling yellow siding in need of paint. A man opens a sliding glass door. He is older. Probably close to seventy. His head is mostly bald and dotted with age spots, but he has a ring of white hair and a white goatee. A golden retriever trots out from inside the house, wearing a red sweater, tongue lolling out of a smiling mouth.

What the hell is this? This looks real. Like really real and not a VR replica. But it isn't real. It is more like watching video footage.

"Shit." The voice is muffled through Jack's headset. But it is the voice of a person. The voice of the YouTube streamer he'd befriended and come to meet. Young. Angry. Male. "Shit, shit, shit."

Frantic clicking in the outside world. Shadow pounding away on a keyboard.

And then the snowy field is back. A snow zombie and ice dog replace the old man and the golden retriever. And that is when Jack realizes…

…Shadow's games aren't just VR. He is using an AR/MR overlay.

That is why his fake bedroom looks so accurate. Shadow must've recorded it. Invaded his home with a camera. He shudders as the games he has played flash through his mind: harpoon the whale, target the cat, put a helmet on a motorcycle racer, shoot the wild boar. His actions were affecting the real world. But what was he doing?

He doesn't want to ask Shadow. But he needs to ask Shadow.

"What happens?" Jack whispers.

"What?"

"If I shoot that man. With an icicle. What happens in the real world? It won't hurt him, will it?"

Pain shoots through him, a live wire boiling his blood from the inside. Jack screams.

"No questions. Shoot the snowman. Unless you want more pain."

"I…can't."

"Do it!" Shadow screams. *"Now!"*

"I can't…not if it will hurt him…I won't. Will it hurt—"

Another jolt, his body alive and shaking with pain.

"Now! I said now!"

His head falls forward, his eyes pressed closed. No more pain. He can't take any more pain. The violins laugh maniacally as Jack fires and fires and fires and fires, refusing to look up and see what he has hit.

28

JENA
Sunday, 10:55 a.m.

CHUCK GOMEZ IS dead. And outside.

The outside the safe house part has woken up my rage dragon. I'm beyond pissed and barking at the other officers, but right now I don't care what they think of me. Call me a bitch all they want. This shouldn't have happened; he had no business being outside.

"What the hell happened?!" I shout at everyone, at the universe. But they're all hiding from me.

Gomez lies on a slab of concrete at the bottom of the back stairs. His head looks like it has taken multiple gunshot wounds. One between the eyes; a deep, circular laceration on his forehead. His left eye is red and swollen like the skin is about to turn black. A second shot to the cheek. A third where jaw meets throat.

Minimal bleeding to the face. But there is a pool congealed beneath his head where he would've smacked the pavement after his fall.

The wounds give me flashbacks to Silas's last victim. The

pattern so similar I'm hyperventilating, my hands sweating, heart hammering.

"I said, what the hell happened?"

Mary squeezes my shoulder. "Let's go inside and talk to Anders, huh?"

I nod and take deep breaths. I can't take my fury out on my team. I need them. Need to make progress on the case and catch this Azrael bastard.

I march up the steps and through the sliding glass door into a shared area between the kitchen and dining room. Anders is set up on the kitchen island.

Down the hall, there is whining and scratching behind a closed door.

"The dog?" I say.

Anders nods. "Poor thing was howling next to Gomez after the incident. Wearing a little red sweater like a Hallmark winter holiday card and everything. Heartbreaking. He's inconsolable."

The pitiful crying amps me up even more. "Was the dog hurt?"

"No," Anders says. "He didn't get hit. The security team assures me Gomez only opened the door for a second to let the dog out. And then it was over in a blink. You need to look at this."

She beckons Mary and me toward the fridge, then pulls out the bottom freezer drawer. Inside, there are three round ice balls, four or five inches across.

"We'll have to get the body over to O'Reilly, but my guess is the hit between the eyes shattered the left frontal orbital bone. The one to the throat could've collapsed his airway. Then he fell down the steps and faceplanted."

"That's our hail," Mary says forlornly.

"Hailstones." That is why the pattern looked like Silas's victims. Hurling fucking stones. Silas's rocks, now Azrael's ice.

The dog keens, and I sympathize. We've pulled out all the stops to protect the jurors. And it still isn't enough.

"These were fast shots. Similar impact to a .44 magnum if the bullet was a hell of a lot bigger."

I admire Anders's detachment. I wish I could say the same, but my blood is boiling.

"Do you have anything on the weapon that fired them?"

"Yep, a drone."

Of course it is a fucking drone. I think back to the drone that dropped off the stuffed bird at Governor Taylor's house. The one at my apartment I didn't see but saw me through my window. The one outside Littlejohn's hotel.

I open my mouth, but Anders cuts me off.

"Before you ask, Officer Dale was on watch duty. He saw the drone pretty quickly. Took a few shots at the drone, but it self-destructed instead of attempting to fly away. The pilot was probably afraid Dale would down the drone. He's a good shot. I've collected the pieces and shipped them off to Collins. I'm not hopeful. The biggest scrap I could find was no bigger than my thumbnail."

"I really, really hate this Azrael piece of shit."

"Me too," Mary says.

I pull out my cell and call Captain Price. When he picks up, I say, "It's Campbell. A motherfucking drone took out Gomez. We need air surveillance for the remaining five targets. And no one leaves their safe house. Not for a smoke. Not to let out a pet. I don't even want them cracking a window. Nothing. Not a goddamn one of them opens any exterior doors."

Yeah, I shouldn't speak to Captain Price like that, but it is done now.

"You need a break?" Price says.

"No, I don't need a goddamn break. I need this bastard's head on a platter."

"Copy that," Price says and hangs up.

If I set Silas free, it will cost more lives. And there is no guarantee it will help me find Jack, and that is what I need for this all to be over. I need to find Jack. If Jack's safe, there is no reason to kill more jurors, and everyone is safe. That is what I have to believe.

But what if I can't find him?

That is the question that keeps me up at night.

SMART BOARD

Victims

1. Michelle Green
   Plague #1 – Water to Blood
   COD – electrocuted
2. Lisa Bell
   Plague #2 – Frogs
   COD – golden dart frog poison
3. Matt Butler
   Plague #3 – Lice
   COD – asphyxiation
4. Mickey Hughes
   Plague #4 – ~~Flies~~ Wild Beasts
   COD – impaled by taxidermy boar tusk
5. David Bacco
   Plague #5 – Pestilence
   COD – flesh-eating bacteria
6. Norma Littlejohn
   Plague #6 – Boils
   COD – reaction of sodium and water
7. Chuck Gomez
   Plague # – Hail
   COD – shot with ice balls

NEXT PLAGUE – #8 Locusts

Targets / Jurors

1. James Cox (46 yo male)
   Notables: Digital archivist. Into crypto. Family owns dairy farm.
2. Avi Spieler (29 yo NB)
   Notables: Multimedia artist. Kosher.
3. Kent Baker (42 yo male)
   Notables: Flemish rabbit. Teaches high school tech.
4. Earl Rogers (76 yo male)
   Notables: Director of a nonprofit specializing in drug and alcohol treatment. Glaucoma.
5. Chris Brown (33 yo male)
   Notables: Mechanic. Bartends at night. Raynaud's disease.
6. Jack Taylor (17 yo male)
   Notables: Governor's son. Suspected to be a hostage in Azrael's custody, who has declared Jack will be the tenth and final victim.

Leads

~~Jack's laptop~~

~~Jack's phone~~

~~Azrael's social media account~~

~~Footage from Matt Butler's work cameras~~

Bible verses sent to Silas

Drone fragments

29

JENA

Sunday, 8:35 p.m.

"I'M BARELY KEEPING it together," I tell Mason.

We're lounging on my couch, a bottle of cab sauv half empty, our glasses half full. Despite the guise of unwinding, I'm anything but. My nerves on edge. A bomb inside of me ready to detonate.

I eye the message on my phone with disgust. Collins recovered nothing from the drone fragments. Not that I expected much. That along with the booming bass from next door accompanied by the ridiculous soundtrack to whatever video game my neighbor, Dustin, is playing doesn't help me relax.

I must be close to the edge, because I want to confess to Mason what I did to put Silas away. But I don't trust him to protect me. I don't trust anyone. That is my flaw.

"What is it?" Mason says, always too adept at reading me.

I open my mouth to spill my guts. Close it. Telling him would be a conflict of interest. He wouldn't be hearing the info as my boyfriend, but as a DoJ attorney. "It's all too much," I say instead. "Jurors keep dying no matter what safety protocols we put in place. I have no clue how we're going to stop Azrael. How we're going to find Jack. And to top it all off, the governor's youngest son is convinced I'm not even going to try."

"You gave him another update?"

I nod and drain the dregs of my wine. "Jude, the youngest, has determined I'm there to persuade his father to let Jack die. And I understand why. Governor Taylor's position seems like he doesn't care about his oldest son. But it's so much more complicated than that."

"So the governor's still not considering a pardon for Silas."

"No. And I don't think he ever will."

"But you're having a change of heart?"

"I don't know what the right thing to do is. What right do I have to play God? To gamble on who lives or dies?"

Mason's hand covers mine. "None. You're human. All you can do is your best."

"What if it isn't enough?"

Tears threaten to spill over, and I hate myself for showing weakness. But I need someone to trust. Someone to whom I can show vulnerability.

"Will you stay?" I ask. "I really need someone here tonight."

"Of course," Mason says.

Because he is the best human that ever existed. I wish I were him right now, instead of me. He pours the rest of the bottle into our glasses.

"Want me to open another?"

I nod. He retrieves another vintage from my small countertop wine rack, and we polish that off before turning in early. There is no intimacy. I'm not in the mood. But Mason holds me as I drift off.

Before I'm out, my phone rings. Bruce motherfucking

Springsteen. I want to hurl the mobile at the wall so the circuits shatter and the ringing stops.

I pick the phone up instead, my head swirling under the giddy oppression of wine.

"Detective Campbell," I heave.

"Campbell," Captain Price barks. *"Good news. The night shift found the next weapon and shut it down. We've stopped one."*

"What? Who?" I can't form an articulate sentence.

"James Cox."

Cox insisted on staying at his parents' dairy farm, while his wife and kids stayed in the safe house. He didn't want his family in harm's way. Noble as fuck, if you ask me.

"The riding mower was rigged to blow. Grasshopper brand."

Grasshopper. Azrael's pun on: "Locusts."

"Yup. Bomb squad's already detonated it."

"We stopped one?" My mind won't let me process the victory.

"We fucking stopped one! The teams are staying vigilant, but I'm hopeful this is the end of it now that we've messed up Azrael's plan."

"But he still has Jack. What if this just escalates him?"

"We can only worry about what we can control. Maybe we'll get a message Azrael's willing to negotiate now."

"Yeah, maybe." I'm not convinced at all. "I'll call Governor Taylor and let him know."

"Thanks. Then get some sleep, Detective. We'll see where we're at in the morning."

The morning. The day of the locusts.

I call Governor Taylor, but he doesn't answer. I leave a message, aiming for a bright tone as I deliver the "good news."

When I hang up, Price's suggestion to get some sleep doesn't take. I toss and turn all night, and no amount of soothing from Mason keeps the buzzing of wings from haunting my dreams.

30

JACK

Monday, 7:34 a.m.

JACK CAN'T HOLD on to the beast. He has no grip strength, hands slipping off the antennae he clutches like reins as he rides. The giant grasshopper soars over a farmer's field, shooting missiles from its mouth. A military modified insect. The soundtrack is bass, snares, and fifes. Very World War II.

Jack needs to keep the creature under control. Keep blowing up tractors. But his legs unlock from the torso, dangling, his balance precarious. What fresh pain will he endure if he falls?

He gulps air, forcing his eyes open. He leans forward, hoping a change in position will help him stay on.

"Just find the bonus tractor, and the game will end." His lips so dry, so stiff, it is as if he has marbles stuffed in his mouth. Maybe he should try to say, *Chubby bunny.* He almost laughs, but childhood games seem like another reality. Another life that was never his. A world far away. The same one where he saw the man with the dog. A person beneath the virtual snow and ice; the snowman he shot up with icicles.

The thought is too much, haunting him every minute since

he fired the drone. What were the results of his actions in the outside world? He doesn't want to think about what might have happened. Doesn't want to play another game, this game, that might hurt someone.

Besides, he can't stay upright another second. Water. He needs water. And sleep. Seven days? Maybe eight since he has got a full night's rest? The exhaustion overwhelms him. No sleep. Just one long nightmare.

Jack's strength is giving way, and he looks down at his hands. Virtual fingers thin and skeletal. Like he is already dead. He screams, cries, yells. Can't take it anymore. Lets go of the antennae. Stops playing the game, but the snare drums march on.

And then Shadow is there, a guttural whisper in his ear. *"What are you doing? Keep playing."*

"I can't. I'm so tired. What *am* I doing? I mean really doing? I can't. I'm done."

The whisper crescendos into a shout. *"Keep. Playing!"*

"No."

The expected pain assaults him. Convulsions rip through his body like an inmate shaking in the electric chair. He doesn't care. He won't do it anymore. If Shadow kills him, at least he'll get some rest.

"Keep. Playing!"

"Fuck. You."

Rough hands clamp over his, manipulating the controls. He is forced to grip the antennae again, still riding on the giant grasshopper's back despite giving up. The grasshopper changes direction, swooping through the air toward a golden tractor.

The grasshopper spits missiles from its mouth. A direct hit. Jack squints, not wanting to see the results, not wanting to think about the real world beneath this one. But he can't shut his eyes. He needs to see. He waits. Waits.

Nothing happens.

The tractor keeps on driving. Doesn't blow up in a ball of fire the way the others did.

"No. No, no, no, no, no."

Jack freezes as Shadow throws his tantrum, sitting on a grasshopper who hovers over the field.

"It's the goddamn remote. No signal. What the hell?!"

Shadow releases something tight off Jack's hand. A strap, maybe? Shadow tugs the controller out of his grip. Jack's hand is empty. He can't believe it. Tries to close his fingers, but the muscles are stiff from disuse. Too used to their current position, they protest the movement, shooting pain through his hand. But he doesn't care. He has experienced so much pain, what is a little more? He works the muscles, opening and closing, as Shadow pitches a fit.

"Going to have to do it by hand," Shadow growls.

Opens his fingers. Closes.

"Shit. Should've had a Plan B."

Open. Close. Open. Close.

The game dissolves, the drums fade away, and he is back in the gloom, hanging above his virtual bed. Then there are heavy footsteps. Shadow stomping away from him. A door slamming. Jack pauses his finger stretches. Shadow has left him alone. And his hand is free.

Jack holds his breath, listening. He is still trapped in this fake world of artificial silence. But the room outside is silent, too. He keeps working his hand. Open. Close. Open. Restrained, with limited movement, his sluggish mind struggles to come up with a plan. He can't reach his torso or his face. Can only reach his other hand.

What can he hope to do? Hungry. Thirsty. Weak. Exhausted. And cold. So cold. The cold envelops him. A side of beef hanging in a meat locker. Cold so thick it is like a blanket of snow covering his skin. But beneath that outer layer, an icy river, even colder, still flows into his full hand. He has become almost numb to it, but when he concentrates, really strains to connect with his body, he is aware of it.

He closes his eyes, gathering his wits and his strength, and starts to hum the theme from *The Legend of Zelda*. His throat is scratchy and raw, but the heroic bars give him courage. Jack's powerful as he reaches out with his free hand, searching for the cold spot on his other hand.

Maybe he should stop humming. Keep listening for Shadow's return. The creak of the door. Footsteps rushing toward him. Shock stick in hand. Ready to plunge the tip into his spine. But he has no control over when Shadow comes back. Wouldn't be able to stop him, anyway. He can only control his own actions. He keeps humming, louder and more epic.

His fingers slide over skin, raising goose bumps. He touches something rubber. Thin tubing. He wraps his hand around the plastic cord and attempts to grasp it. But his fingers won't close tight enough.

His humming turns into wordless singing, belting out the Zelda theme. "Bah-daaaah bah-dah-bah. Bah-daaaah bah-dah-bah." His fingers close a millimeter, followed by another, clasping onto the tubing.

There is pain as he tugs, his full hand erupting into one giant bruise. He doesn't care. He can't stop. Won't stop.

"It's dangerous to go it alone!" he cries. "Take this!"

With a shout, he rips the tubing free. Warmth spreads across the back of his full hand while cold liquid leaks into his free hand from the tube. He gathers up the slack, more and more of it filling his palm. It is attached somewhere high up. When the line is taut, he yanks. There is a sound of ripping plastic and then, *sploosh*. A deluge of salty, plastic-smelling liquid douses him, running from the top of his head down his face. Some drips onto his mouth. But as desperate with thirst as he is, it is too foul to attempt to drink. He shivers, wetness seeping in around the edges of the headset, trickling over his brow. He opens his eyes, blinking the wetness away. There is nothing. Darkness within darkness. The headset has shut off. His replica bedroom has vanished.

A little shout of victory. But it is not enough. He needs to get out. Get away. His father isn't coming. No one is coming. No friends to care about him. The person he thought a friend shattering his trust deeper than he has ever been wounded before, tying him up, starving him, freezing him, hurting him. He is alone. The only one who can save him is himself.

He takes a deep breath. Forces himself to stay calm and think. Assesses the new weight of the tubing in his hand. There is something attached to the other end.

He grips the tubing harder. Starts to swing it, his movement limited, but the plastic cord is long. It whips across the room. A lasso and he is a cowboy. He tilts forward in his hanging restraints. Hits nothing. Turns to the left side as much as he can. Empty. Turns to the right. Stretching until it seems his muscles will tear from his body under the stress. The restraints bite into his thighs, shooting bursts of pain down his legs. He ignores it, his thoughts on only one thing—escape.

He twists harder. Swings harder. Yells, "Yee haw!"

The heavier end of the tubing snags something. Pulling with all his strength, he uses his weight to yank it toward him.

There is the groan of metal right before it slams into his head. Stars explode across his vision. A whole galaxy of pain. New wetness spreads across his forehead, warm and metallic. Pulling him down into an abyss of blackness.

31

JENA

Monday, 10:46 a.m.

TWELVE HOURS SINCE the team found the bomb inside the riding mower. I'm in the living room of James Cox's parents' house in Oakdale, sunk down into the cushions of a Shaker couch. The wood frame is so substantial it must've taken an army to carry the furniture piece in here. The black iron pulls on the drawers of the coffee table look forged by a master blacksmith. The walls are rustic beige, but with expert painting technique. The floor is wide oak planks.

I'm a city girl. Even though the farmhouse is cozy—and there is obvious money here—I'm not comfortable. Mary doesn't look any more at ease in her mammoth armchair, and it is not just the oddness of city cops invading this country home. Doesn't matter that we found the bomb. We're still on high alert. Cox can't even piss without an officer pulling up the toilet seat for him. No way we're risking another attempt. Our air surveillance is on high alert for drones. And if Azrael shows up in person, I'll be waiting.

Cox is sitting in a massive armchair, looking rather gray. Cox's mother hands me a glass of water with a fresh slice of lemon in it. I thank her, and she nods before heading back to the kitchen to start lunch preparations. Old-time bluegrass music plays from an antique radio, punctuated with intermittent static. It is like I should be chewing tobacco, but I don't see a spittoon.

My phone rings, the electric guitar of the E Street Band profane against the fiddles and banjos.

"Detective Campbell," I answer.

"Kent Baker," Price says, frustration turning his usual bark into a growl.

"Fuck. How?!"

Price pauses. *"Rifle shot. Through the window."*

"On whose watch?"

"It doesn't matter."

"That's some fucking lax security, is what it is."

"I'm as pissed as you are, believe me. But now's not the time."

If Price is telling me to calm down, I should probably listen, but goddamn it, I wanted the bomb's disposal to mean this was all over. Or at least that Azrael's plans were smashed, hoping he'd negotiate with us for the kid. That the remaining jurors were safe.

"Roger that," I say. "We're on our way."

I pound the screen with two fingers, hanging up.

Mr. and Mrs. Cox stand off to the side, Mrs. Cox holding a tray of sandwiches, their mouths hanging open. I realize I just dropped multiple F-bombs. My cheeks redden at what they must be thinking about me. Boorish city cops and their terrible manners.

I paste a polite smile on my face. "Thank you for your hospitality." I dislodge myself from the chair, nodding to Mary. "We need to go. Don't worry. The other officers are staying."

Cox gives a feeble smile but says nothing.

Mary stands and smiles. "Would you mind if I took a sandwich?"

"Help yourself." Mr. Cox's voice is gruff, but Mary doesn't seem bothered as she grabs what looks like salmon salad with chopped up pickles on wheat.

She is so good at putting people at ease, even though she must be screaming on the inside.

I grab a turkey and tomato, not wanting to look rude. "Much appreciated."

We're crunching down the gravel pathway on our way back to the Explorer when Mary says, "Who is it?" She hasn't taken a bite of her sandwich.

"Kent Baker."

"I can't take this anymore."

"Same," I say as my phone vibrates. Morse code. S.O.S.

I stop and pull out my phone. Mary turns, staring at me with questioning eyebrows. I hold up a finger, asking her to wait. She nods, looking ruefully at her sandwich as I click on the message.

> *Whew, you guys almost had me there. I had to pivot. You made me get my hands dirty, but it was worth it! Crickett. Get it? Not as good of a pun on locust as a grasshopper, but close enough! Will you set Leviticus free? Or are we going to play this out until the final boss level?*
>
> *One more day…*

~ Azrael

Below is a gif of some guy in a black baseball cap and ear protection rapid firing a Crickett rifle. I thank my lucky stars for Azrael's message, knowing Collins is receiving this on the other end. I dial Collins's number.

When he answers, I say, "Collins, my favorite person. Did you see the gif?"

"Affirmative, ma'am."

"Great. I need a favor."

"Shoot."

"I need you to track down every Crickett rifle bought in the Pittsburgh area in the last twenty-four hours."

"Child's play, ma'am."

"Glad to hear it. Let me know what you get."

I hang up and head for the Explorer, crushing my turkey and tomato in my fist.

We have another body to examine.

SMART BOARD

Victims

1. Michelle Green
   Plague #1 – Water to Blood
   COD – electrocuted
2. Lisa Bell
   Plague #2 – Frogs
   COD – golden dart frog poison
3. Matt Butler
   Plague #3 – Lice
   COD – asphyxiation
4. Mickey Hughes
   Plague #4 – ~~Flies~~ Wild Beasts
   COD – impaled by taxidermy boar tusk
5. David Bacco
   Plague #5 – Pestilence
   COD – flesh-eating bacteria
6. Norma Littlejohn
   Plague #6 – Boils
   COD – reaction of sodium and water
7. Chuck Gomez
   Plague # – Hail
   COD – shot with ice balls
8. Kent Baker
   Plague #8 – Locusts
   COD – shot with Crickett rifle (improvisation)

<u>NEXT PLAGUE – #9 Darkness</u>

Targets / Jurors

1. James Cox (46 yo male) – failed target, but can't rule out another attempt
   Notables: Digital archivist. Into crypto. Family owns dairy farm.
2. Avi Spieler (29 yo NB)
   Notables: Multimedia artist. Kosher.
3. Earl Rogers (76 yo male)
   Notables: Director of a nonprofit specializing in drug and alcohol treatment. Glaucoma.
4. Chris Brown (33 yo male)
   Notables: Mechanic. Bartends at night. Raynaud's disease.
5. Jack Taylor (17 yo male)
   Notables: Governor's son. Suspected to be a hostage in Azrael's custody, who has declared Jack will be the tenth and final victim.

Leads

~~Jack's laptop~~

~~Jack's phone~~

~~Azrael's social media account~~

~~Footage from Matt Butler's work cameras~~

Bible verses sent to Silas

~~Drone fragments~~

Purchase of a Crickett rifle

32

JENA

Monday, 1:33 p.m.

"TELL ME YOU'VE got something good," I say as Collins walks into the conference room, joining Mary, Weisz, Jersey, and me.

"Yes, ma'am. Video footage from the store that sold a Crickett rifle this morning."

Collins marches over to the smart board and hooks up his laptop. He opens a video file and clicks the play icon as I lean back, taking in what I'm seeing. The storefront of a big box hunting and fishing store.

A man comes out the front door. Black Jeans. Black hoodie. Black baseball cap. Face covered by a skeleton gaiter and dark sunglasses. Carrying a big cardboard box with a picture of a cartoon cricket carrying a gun. The words on the front say: "My First Rifle."

"Cute," Mary says.

"It's the same kid from the footage Papich gave us. That's him. Azrael. Has to be."

Jersey makes a face. "Gotta love that you can buy a gun wearing a mask."

"They would've ID'd him," Weisz says. "Made him pull down his mask at the counter."

I turn to Weisz. "Doesn't mean his ID wasn't faked."

"It was," Collins confirms. "Already checked that out. Got a copy of the form 4473. The store does on-the-spot checks, and he passed because of course he's that good of a hacker. Made the license out in the name of Dallas Ravish."

"Well, he's got some big balls, doesn't he?"

Mary quirks an eyebrow at me. "What? What am I missing?"

"The ID. It's an anagram," Weisz says.

"Hey, wise guys," Jersey says. "Let Sarkis and me in on the joke. What do you mean, anagram?"

"Dallas Ravish. It's a scramble of Silas Halvard."

Comprehension spreads across Mary's face. "Wow. Yeah. Huge cajones for sure."

"He would've had to pull down his mask for the ID check. Find the clerk who sold the gun and send a sketch artist to the store. I want to see Azrael's face."

Collins salutes and scoops up his phone. He has the video running on loop on the smart board. Azrael repeatedly marches out of the store and walks off the screen. On the fifth pass, I notice something odd about his clothing.

"Hey. There are faded letters on that hoodie. The shirts he wore to the jail were solid. Can you enhance that?"

"Yes, ma'am."

With the kid's hoodie now three times the size, I can read the faint words: rock like a boss.

"That a brand anyone's familiar with?"

I get back a chorus of head shaking.

"I know a bit about fashion." Jersey says. "I'd bet money that's not a major clothing line."

Silas's question about Azrael from my last visit rockets into my mind: *"Did he leave you anything to share with me? A rock, maybe?"*

Rock. That wasn't the only strange thing he'd said. I pull out my phone and dial. Mary peeks over to see who I'm contacting.

"You're calling SWAT?"

I shake my head. "Not SWAT. Their brainy commander. Joe Torres."

"My dear Holmes," Torres answers. *"How may I assist you?"*

"I get it. Sherlock Holmes. Because I'm a detective. Funny."

"Witty," Torres replies.

Is he correcting my word usage? Whatever. I don't care. His literary mind is exactly why I called.

"And we all know what comprises the soul of wit, don't we?"

"Um, punchlines?" I venture.

"Brevity, Detective Campbell. Brevity. Hamlet. Act Two. Scene Two."

"Right. Of course. Must've slipped my mind. While we're on the subject, I have a quote I need your help with."

"Oh, please. Test me. I beg you."

"Something about a port and bells and a grim, daring vessel. Do you know what it's from?"

Torres clucks his tongue. *"Disappointingly easy. Walt Whitman. O Captain! My Captain!"*

"Thanks, Torres. Much appreciated."

"If that's all you require of my service. Adieu, Detective. Parting is such sweet sorrow."

I hang up first, not wanting to risk further monologue.

"Collins!"

He looks up from his phone. "At your service, ma'am."

"Can you do a people search on your laptop? Key phrases *rock like a boss* and *captain.*"

Collins has the list up before I've enunciated the last consonant.

Mary whistles. "Wouldn't you know it?"

The first hit at the top of the search engine. A video game streamer.

Captain Rock.

The first line of the website teaser reads: *This channel will change your life, no doubt. Like and subscribe. Official merch. Rock like a boss.*

"Click on it."

Collins does.

And there is Azrael's avatar face. All shadows and silhouettes against a green screen.

"That's him. That's our killer." I swipe a pointed finger across my team. "We're watching every single one of these videos until we get a lead. No one's flawless. We'll find somewhere he's slipped up. Something that gives him away."

"I'll get the popcorn," Jersey says.

"No salt," Weisz pipes up. "I'm watching my sodium."

"Zip it." I get comfortable in my seat as Collins plays the first video. Azrael speaks with vocal distortion. Just like in the videos he sent me. As the minutes tick by, watching this guy stream video games and make inane comments, I wish I had let Jersey get snacks. Twenty minutes. Forty. Stupid joke after stupid joke, bro. I'm expanding my acronym vocabulary, adding RDM, random death match, and 1337, gamer code for elite, to useless things in my head I wish I could forget.

Maybe it is the repetitive nature of the videos, but Azrael's cadence is starting to sound familiar to me. Like I've heard it somewhere before.

More minutes of streaming. I add XP, experience points, to my lexicon. I hadn't even noticed Mary got coffee until she shoved a steaming hot cup in my hands.

"Thanks," I say.

"You didn't miss anything," Jersey adds. "These videos are useless."

His attitude irks me. "We're not giving up."

Mary pats Jersey's shoulder. "Let's give it a few more, huh?"

I sip the coffee as we watch a first-person shooter game taking place on an ancient spaceship, then a game about joyriding a car through the California streets. Azrael slows down his car, which looks like a Dodge Viper and Chevy Camaro had a baby, pulling up to a red vendor's stand that says chili dogs. That's when I hear it.

Bah dah bah bah-dah baaaahh daahh. "Take me out to the ball...game."

It is the intercom. The intercom from *my* apartment building.

The video game music. Always floating through my wall from next door.

"Oh, God! It's Dustin. Azrael. It's fucking Dustin."

"That's great," Mary says at the same time Jersey says, "Who the hell is Dustin?"

But I'm too busy dialing Captain Price to explain.

"The sketch artist drawing is in," Collins announces, holding up the portrait on his phone.

And I see his harmless-looking face—wide-set, ice blue eyes and blond bedhead—at the same time Price answers the phone.

33

JACK

Monday, 2:02 p.m.

JACK OPENS HIS eyes but sees nothing. He raises his head, lifting his chin off his chest. With this small motion, pain erupts through his skull, so bad he thinks he'll pass out again. The copper stench of blood overwhelms him as he reaches for his head, but his arm movement is restricted. He is hanging, but it is like he is spinning. Dizzy. Nauseous. In danger of vomiting. And then he vomits. Inhales the acrid bile. Listens to it hit the floor.

Shadow won't like the mess. He won't like it at all. The fear sinks back in. He hasn't escaped. And when Shadow finds out how he has tried to flee…

Jack's not sure how long he has been out, but it seems more like hours than minutes. He looks toward the door, despite being unable to see. Thinks maybe there are faint footsteps. He reaches out, but there is nothing within his grasp. The tubing is gone, along with whatever it snagged that crashed into him. All he can grab onto is his other hand. He searches there until he finds a strap. He works on the fastener for a while with weak fingers, and eventually the strap comes loose. When it does, the controller in his left hand falls away. Both hands are free now. He searches the harness that is holding him, but there is no release, no clasps or anything he can find. There is nothing useful to do with his hands, so he flexes the newly liberated one, trying to get ready. When Shadow comes back, maybe he can surprise him. Grab him. Wrestle him into submission.

The idea is laughable, but Jack needs something to hope for. Without hope, it is game over.

The footsteps grow louder, and the door opens.

"Fuck!" Shadow says in his human voice. "You broke my green screen."

So that is what smashed into him. But he didn't break the green screen. It was the other way around. The green screen broke his head. He has a throbbing gash on top to show who won that fight.

"Is that the controller in a pile of puke? Jack. You are in so. Much. Shit."

There is the rustling of objects as Shadow rummages through whatever else is in the room. Then the rattling stops.

"Duct tape should fix it."

Jack nearly breathes a sigh of relief. If Shadow's busy fixing the green screen, he isn't busy breaking him. But then Shadow's steps approach, Shadow so close Jack can smell his pepperoni breath. Heartbeat drumming, he thrusts out his arms, hands flying in wild circles as he tries to grab Shadow.

There is the ripping sound of tape, and then his hands are clamped together.

"No, no, no," he moans as Shadow wraps duct tape around his hands.

"You think you're so fucking clever, don't you?"

"No, no, no," he continues to cry.

"The police think they're clever, too. But they're shit at covering their tracks."

Jack's hands are bound so tightly he can barely feel them. They're going numb with lack of circulation.

"You don't need your hands at this point, do you, since you won't play any more games?"

Jack wants to be brave again. Tell Shadow to go to hell. Dismember him. Kill him. He is past caring. But the pain in his hands, the thought of Shadow slowly hacking through his wrists, turns him weak.

"I'm sorry. So sorry. Let me play the last game. Give my dad one more chance."

Jack doesn't have much faith in his dad, but there is that hope again. He is desperate to cling to it.

"Oh, your daddy's going to get the message this time. Believe me. Just not from you. And whose fault is that, hmm? You broke the headset and controller. You leave me no choice."

"You have another one, though, right? You must. No pro-gamer has only one. I could use that."

"I do, but you can't be trusted."

He is sobbing now. Hates himself for sobbing but can't make it stop.

"God, you're annoying. I should knock you out."

Jack also hates that he'd love Shadow to knock him out right now. There is no pain or fear if you're unconscious.

"I won't, though. What I have planned is going to be so much more effective if you scream."

Jack presses his chin to his chest. Just like when he woke up. There is no more fight in him. And very little hope. He lets himself hang there, wondering how much longer it will be before he dies.

The monster's voice floods his ears. "Are you ready for some fun?"

34

JENA

Monday, 3:15 p.m.

NERVOUS ENERGY PUMPS through me as I wait inside the SWAT van. Last time, at the apartment on Fort Duquesne Boulevard, I was flooded with adrenaline, too. Because I knew something felt wrong. But this time, I'm sure we've got the right place. And I'm keyed up.

Even with the time it took to get the warrant, I haven't cooled off. Two years Dustin has been my next-door neighbor. Blasting video game music. Chatting me up in the hallway after his snack runs, arms full of cheese puffs and slushie drinks. I shudder to think what might've been going on behind the wall that separates our apartments while we joked and made small talk. I'm still struggling to believe it is true. Dustin has always been kind to me.

I remember once, after a bad fight with Mason, I came into the lobby soaking wet, the rain hammering down outside. I stumbled up the stairs, a dripping wet abomination. Dustin cracked his door open, took one look at me, and invited me in. Offered to get me a towel.

I declined his invitation, the way I always did. Now I wonder what he must've had inside. His whole streaming setup, no doubt. Probably drones. High-tech weapons. At this point, it wouldn't surprise me if he'd had dismembered body parts in his freezer.

He'd been toying with me. Betting I was the type of person who would never cross that boundary. And he was dead right. That he could profile me so well, knowing how I'd respond to his neighborly offers, while I'd failed so hard to judge his character, has my rage dragon spitting fire. I smother the flames. I hope Dustin is in a neighborly mood today, too. It is our best chance to get Jack out safely.

I hold in my hands the box for a brand new Xbox. Looks like I'm about to become a gamer. Mary sits beside me, smiling as she puts a calming hand on my knee.

"You've got this." She squeezes, her fuchsia nails tickling me before she lets go.

"Blinds are still drawn," a SWAT member watching the apartment says into my earpiece. *"I've seen no movement. Air surveillance hasn't picked up any drones."*

There has been no change in the apartment since we put surveillance on it. No one in or out. We're going in blind. But whether Dustin is home or not, we need to go now. Have to hope he is there. Hope Jack is there.

The white SWAT van I'm waiting in—The Rocinante—is parked in my designated spot in the underground lot of my apartment building as Joe Torres, the SWAT commander, briefs his team.

"Assume this guy is heavily armed," Torres says. "Possible explosives. Campbell goes up the front stairs. We wait in the back stairwell. Go on the word *slushie*. Keep a sharp eye for the kid. We need him alive. Best thing we can do is drive Dustin out. Get your tear gas ready. All right, everyone, let's move."

The rear doors of the truck pop open, and officers spill out into the parking lot, grabbing their equipment. I lead Mary and the SWAT team to the emergency stairs and swipe them in. No need to make a racket by busting down doors. Yet.

Once inside, all eyes are on Torres, but his eyes are on me. I'm waiting for him to quote some pretentious text, but instead he says, "All you motherfuckers are going to pay."

"Now that's poetry," I say.

"Jay and Silent Bob Strike Back," Torres says. "Good luck to you, Holmes."

"You too, Shakespeare."

As the team starts their ascent, I hurry to the front stairs, cradling the Xbox packaging to my chest. I walk up the steps and into the hallway, stopping a little way out from my door. Epic video game music booms from Dustin's apartment, causing my breath to catch. He is home. I force myself to exhale and breathe regularly. Can't look suspicious. Good thing Dustin can't hear my racing heart. It would a thousand percent give away my intentions.

I make a show of inspecting the box and looking confused. Dustin has an uncanny way of appearing when I'm the hallway. If my hunch is correct, he can track when I'm there. I spend a short time pretending to read instructions while sighing, but Dustin doesn't appear. I've been here too long. If I wait any longer and Dustin is watching, he'll know I'm up to something for sure. No more time to delay.

I march up to his door and knock. "Dustin? Dustin, are you home?"

I step back from the peephole so if he looks out, he'll see the Xbox.

"Dustin? I could really use your help. I just got a video game system, and I don't know how to set it up."

The only answer is electronic music.

He is not coming. What if he is tracking what is happening in the back stairwell, too? Every second I waste could be the one he decides to kill Jack. Fuck. I wanted to be the one to put a bullet in his knee cap the minute he opened the door. But it is go time.

"Come on, Dustin," I yell. "I'll owe you one. I'll even buy you a giant SLUSHIE."

The emergency door swings open and bangs into the wall. SWAT swarms the hallway, all of them wearing gas masks. I drop the box I'm carrying and grab my gun, aiming it at the door with one hand, turning the knob with the other. Locked.

Grabbing my mask from inside the Xbox packaging, I move out of the way as a battering ram hurtles toward me. The front two officers swing and the ram breaches the door in one go. The guys behind them chuck two cannisters of tear gas inside.

"Police!" Torres shouts, his voice crackling in my earpiece. *"Come out with your hands up."*

Mary's at the back of the team, but I rush to the front of the pack, sweeping my gun left and right. SWAT fans out, searching, shouts of *"Clear!"* popping up here and there, muffled by the gas masks. But I don't leave the front room. It is empty. It is fucking empty. Not a couch or a table or even a goddamn bean bag chair. Nothing but a fucking speaker in the middle of the floor blaring that shitty music.

I want to scream. Want to punch holes in the dry wall. Want to empty my clip into the ceiling. There is nothing here. And I mean *nothing.* I can tell using my detective spidey-sense from so many years doing this job that he didn't recently clear it out. He never lived here in the first place.

Everything about this creeps me out. It is not just that the floor plan is exactly the same as my apartment. But that Dustin has pretended to live next to me for two years. Planned this entire plague killing spree for that long.

"Sick bastard!" I shout, the words echoing in my ears.

Torres approaches me from what, in my apartment, would be the bedroom. "'*When sorrows come, they come not single spies, but in battalions.*'"

"What is it?"

"Campbell, I'm so sorry. This isn't the end. We'll get him. We're mushroom-cloud-layin' motherfuckers."

"Samuel L. Jackson," I whisper. *"Pulp Fiction."*

My guts twist and I race toward the bedroom, images of Jack's lifeless corpse punching their way out from inside my brain. But when I enter, there is no body. No blood. No bones. Just a gaming chair. A garbage can full of food wrappers and empty slushie cups. And one entire wall covered in monitors. The hallway. Living room. Kitchen. Bathroom. Bedroom. My house. All of it. Up on the screens.

I checked every room when I thought he was watching me. Where the fuck are these cameras? And how the hell did he hide them?

I'm hyperventilating. Unable to suck any air through the inhalation valve of my gas mask. Squeezing my Glock so hard I'm afraid it'll go off. A moan echoes inside my mask, and I realize it's mine.

Two years. Not just how long he'd been planning this. How long he'd been watching me. Violating my privacy. Invading my life. I think of all the showers I've taken. All the times I've had Mason in my bed.

I lean over, hands on my knees, my vision spotting.

Mary comes in, takes one look at me, and rushes over.

"Are you okay?"

As an answer, I pull off my gas mask and throw up like a fucking rookie. All over her shoes.

35

JENA

Tuesday, 6:58 p.m.

I PACE THE length of the room of Earl Rogers's safe house. More than twenty hours since finding the Peeping Tom wall in Dustin's apartment, and my mind is still a mess. Humiliated. Furious. Sick to my stomach.

It doesn't matter that Collins tracked down the cameras. Retractable fiber optics. So when I went looking for them, Dustin reeled them in. Dustin's overplanning and tech abilities make me want to scream. I'm a rat in a maze, and he is the one opening and closing doors to lure me to the center.

No way is Dustin getting his hands on Earl Rogers while I'm on watch. There are four jurors left as targets. Besides Rogers, there is Avi Spieler, Chris Brown, and James Cox. I'm hoping Dustin's mark is Rogers. I want not only to stop this, but to get revenge for how Dustin violated me.

I stomp over to the window and peer out from behind the curtains. The sun is starting to sink below the horizon. I turn around, march back toward the sitting area. It is the second safe house we've moved this man to today; an apartment used by the PBP for surveillance. There is no place more secure.

"Hey," Mary says from the couch as I clomp closer. "I need you to look at this."

She holds out her phone and I hustle over, hoping she has got something good. I glance down at the screen. It says: *You're making Mr. Rogers nervous.*

I freeze in my tracks and glance at the elderly gentleman with his thinning cloud of gray hair that turns snow white at the temples. He is a sharp dresser. Paisley tie and tweed blazer. Matching leather belt and wingtip shoes. He looks up at me with rheumy eyes, giving me a brave smile that quivers. Shit. I'm spooking the hell out of him.

"Sorry," I say to Rogers.

He gives a shrug that doesn't look very nonchalant. "You're doing your job."

I force myself to sit in the armchair next to the couch he and Mary occupy. The room is filled with police-use electronic equipment. One monitor shows "Captain Rock's"—aka Dustin's—video game channel. There is no live streaming going on at the moment.

We've checked every inch of the apartment. Air surveillance. Cameras outside the building. Cameras inside every room. Checked the vents, in between the walls, the pipes, the gas lines, every appliance, every light switch. Every morsel of food, every drink, has been tested. Everything. Including Rogers's glaucoma eye drops, which tested fine. We confiscated them anyway in case Azrael magically replaces them with Sarin or something. One day without the medicine won't kill him.

"I'm thinking about cooking a pizza," Rogers says. "I'm quite hungry."

"I'll do it," Mary says.

"Thank you kindly."

Mary gets up and heads to the kitchen. Rogers rises as well.

"Just need to use the little boys' room," he says.

I nod. "Keep the door unlocked."

"Of course."

He is shuffling down the hallway when the lights go out. Oh God, this can't be happening. A second later, they pop back on again, but my heart is still in my throat.

"What the hell?"

I pull out my phone and dial.

"Collins at your service, ma'am."

"Hey, we had a power flicker. Are we on main? Or generator?"

"Main, but I'll check it out."

"Thanks."

I put in a call to Dale, who is on outside patrol. When he answers, I say, "Hey, can you go check on the generator? Make sure nothing is…"

The lights go out again. This time they don't come back on. I hold my breath. Wait for the generator to kick in. It doesn't. Shit. I hang up on Dale.

"Mr. Rogers?"

No answer.

"Earl?!!" Mary's frantic calling joins mine.

I turn on my phone's flashlight and check the time. 7:04 p.m. Sunset.

I rush to the bathroom, the phone's flashlight guiding me. The door is closed. And locked.

"Fuck!"

It isn't a hard lock to pick. A single hole that can be popped with a small Allen key. I pull my multi-tool from my bare-bones utility belt and get to work, my hand unsteady, heart pumping.

"Mr. Rogers?" I call as I punch the lock. Still no answer.

I swing the door open, my flashlight sweeping over the floor, sink, toilet, shower. No Rogers. I exhale and hurry out of the bathroom, finding Mary in the bedroom.

"Nothing," she says. "He wasn't in the kitchen. I've checked this room and the office."

"He couldn't have left."

I rush to the front door anyway and swing it open. My light shines into the faces of the two guards posted outside, who have their Maglites out and on.

"Did anyone leave?" I demand.

"No, Detective," the taller one answers.

I slam the door shut and continue my search inside. Where the hell could he be? There is no balcony. The ceilings are plaster. Mary's footsteps following behind me nearly make me jump out of my skin.

And then my light falls on the front walk-in closet. There is a faint creaking inside that sounds like the kickboxing bag at the gym when it is swinging. I swallow hard and reach out with a shaking hand, sliding the door open.

On the floor, the step stool is knocked over onto its side. Earl Rogers hangs from the light fixture by his belt, his dapper paisley tie wrapped around his eyes like a blindfold.

The ninth plague. Darkness.

36

JENA

Tuesday, 7:17 p.m.

"FUCK!"

This can't happen. I can't breathe.

Rogers's legs kick.

"Get him down! Now!" I bear hug his thighs, lifting him up, taking the pressure off his trachea.

Mary rights the stool, pushing it under his wingtips. His feet find purchase and I step up onto the stool, too, our limbs crowded together.

"Take him!" I shout.

Mary supports his weight as I unwrap the belt. Rough leather slides through my hand, hot on my skin as it loosens.

Rogers coughs and sputters.

He is alive. Thank fuck, he is alive.

"I've got him," I say. "Get medical."

Mary lets go. She grabs her phone and barks instructions.

I shudder and shake, face wet as I cradle Rogers, bringing him to the ground. The old man is light, frail, and unconscious, but his chest rises and falls. The breath goes in and out, in and out, and I refuse to take my eyes off him until the paramedics arrive.

Five minutes pass. Ten. A lifetime.

Finally two young guys carrying a stretcher burst through the door, buzzing around Rogers.

Agitated pacing consumes me as they work. I wait for news while they give him oxygen, check his vitals. I can't look at him, the bruise ringing his neck already in full bloom. My mind races. His hanging makes no sense. How did Azrael—Dustin, I chide myself, refusing to use that stupid nickname—how did Dustin hang Rogers? How does this fit with his pattern of rigging up high-tech contraptions, which he has used every time? Well, if you don't count the Crickett shooting, but that was an unplanned response to us detonating the mower rig. The only answer I can come up with is that he didn't hang Rogers. Earl Rogers hung himself. It is the why part I have no answer to. Maybe Dustin had something on him. But as the director of a nonprofit for drug and alcohol rehabilitation, I have a hard time believing that about the kind old gentleman I met. Sure. There are other people who've been a shining example on paper and monsters behind closed doors. Still. I don't buy that about Rogers. And it is the not knowing that is driving me mad.

"Oh, my gosh," Mary says, pointing to the monitor tuned to Captain Rock's channel. "He's starting a live stream."

I hurry over to join Mary while the paramedics continue to work. Captain Rock materializes, a shadowy silhouette in front of a green screen. The background is filled with the night sky dotted with infinite stars.

"Hello there, my favorite rockheads," Dustin says, using deep

voice distortion. *"I have a special guest today I'd like to introduce you to. Jack."*

The camera pans to Dustin's left, showing a close-up of Jack's face wearing a VR headset. Then the shot jerks right so only Dustin is visible. The glimpse of Jack was brief, the green screen's starry night filling the background. Nothing to give away where they're recording. But that is not my biggest concern. It doesn't look like Jack is moving. I'm not even sure he is breathing. I clutch the arm of the couch, and the frame groans in protest.

"Okay. Let's jump into the latest game."

The shot changes to picture-in-picture. To the right, comments from his army of subscribers scroll across the screen so fast I can't read a sentence before it moves on to the next one. Dustin's face is in a small box, bottom left, superimposed over a screen capture of the video game he is playing. It isn't a game I recognize, not that my gaming knowledge extends beyond the top few games advertising hits you over the head with. This looks like a game of hide-and-seek in the dark, with strobe lights flashing on and off to show where players are lurking. There is something that approximates music playing in the background. It sounds like the thumping of a racing heartbeat. Dustin's character is marked by the name floating on top of the avatar, "Captain Rock." The character is a paladin, a literal knight in shining armor. Metal breast plate and helmet. Gauntlets and greaves. Ironic iron.

"This game is wild when experienced through a headset. Don't let me jump scare you. You'll piss yourself."

Dustin's character lunges at another character that looks like a giant green blob. Reminds me of Slimer from *Ghostbusters*. When Dustin catches the blob, the lights strobe and you can see the blob character's insides like an X-ray, all rib cage and bones.

The blob glows with high-voltage sparks, the current flowing around the character making it look like electric shock.

There is screaming. And it isn't coming from the game.

"See, I told you it's scary. Jack here is freaking out. Look out, Jack!"

Jack's blob character now has Xs for eyes to show it is dead in game, I guess. As long as Jack's not dead out of game, that is all I care about. As much as the screaming shakes me, at least I know he is still alive.

"If you want to be next to die, subscribe to Tier 3. Want me to kill someone else? Gift them a Tier 3 sub!"

Sub notifications pour into the comments as Dustin moves away from Jack's dead character, chasing another player. He whispers something that sounds like my nickname, but I can't be sure. It could be gamer-speak nonsense. *"Little bird,"* he whispers again. *"Answer the phone."*

"Did he just…?" Mary's eyes are glued to the screen.

"Yeah. He did."

I hear a ringtone coming from somewhere in the apartment. "Feeling Good" by Nina Simone. Mary looks at me.

"You monitor the video," I say. "I'll find the ringing."

Nina's a cappella powerhouse voice keeps soaring as I follow the sound. Closer and closer to Rogers. Each step heavier, my movements more sluggish as I draw near the hallway.

Nina may be feeling good, but I'm sick to my stomach. I shuffle up to the paramedics, and it is clear the ringing is coming from Rogers. I see light through the pocket of his blazer. We X-rayed the phone, screened the hell out of every inch for explosives, extra circuits, tampering, etc. I tell myself it is safe to answer as I approach.

"Sorry," I mutter to the paramedics. "Can I get that?"

The paramedic monitoring Rogers's vitals nods. "He's stable."

Thankful as I am for the news, I need to get that phone. I'll celebrate our success stopping Azrael from killing Rogers later.

I rummage through Rogers's pocket, but the opening is tight and he shifts at the disturbance. My gaze jerks upward to the ring of purple around his throat. I grab the phone and hurry away. The number calling the phone comes up private. I head into the kitchen and answer.

"Hello?"

A recording crackles on the other end.

"Four jurors left to pick from," vocally distorted Dustin says. *"Three young bucks with their whole lives ahead of them…and you, Earl. You all got close during Leviticus's trial, didn't you? Became more like family than friends. Still send each other holiday cards. Check up on everyone's kids."*

"What do you want?" Rogers's voice warbles, but his tone is firm.

"Tuesday. At sunset. Wear a nice leather belt. A fancy tie. Blindfold yourself with the tie. Hang yourself with the belt."

"And why exactly would I do that?"

"Because if you don't, I'll kill your cute little granddaughter in Florida. The one with the pigtails and missing front teeth. It's your life, or hers. Your choice."

I should be recording this. I pull out my phone, scrambling to find the voice recorder.

"How do I know you won't kill her anyway?"

I find the recording app and punch the red button.

Dustin sighs, the sound like a combo of white noise and a roaring waterfall. "*Because I have a plan, Earl. And you know what it is. Ten plagues. Ten people. And you're going to be number nine. Don't annoy me. You wouldn't like it. You know what? Too late. I'm annoyed already. If you don't crush your own airway with a belt, she's dead. Maybe your wife too, your daughter, your daughter's husband, and all three of your other grandbabies. How does that sound?"*

Silence. Then Rogers says, "That sounds like a deal."

The weight of what has happened hits me. Rogers tried to take his own life to save lives. I've held onto my secret too long. I could've prevented this. Guilt and shame wash over me and I struggle to force them down. Hindsight and second-guessing are the way to a mental health leave.

"Thought you'd see it my way," distorted Dustin continues. *"The lights will flicker when it's time for you to go make your preparations. When I cut the lights completely, that's your signal to go."*

The line goes dead. I hang up Rogers's phone, and a video pops up on the screen. The still image is frozen on a close-up of Jack wearing the VR headset. I switch my phone over to record the video as I hit play.

The camera pulls out from Jack's face to include his body. He is suspended in some type of harness. The shot scans down to also show his hands, working the VR controllers. Then it moves across the room to a monitor. On the screen is a view of the hot tub oasis. Michelle Green slips into the water in her nautical bathing suit, putting her martini on the counter. She is watching the Rock Hudson and Doris Day movie when a red target that looks like a rifle sight appears superimposed over her.

The camera shot pulls further back, going really wide, showing both Jack and the monitor with Michelle Green inside the target. Jack presses a button on his controller. The words *Direct Hit* appear on the screen as Green is electrocuted and blood fills the water.

This sick fucker had Jack kill a juror. My blood burns. If I ever see Dustin, he'd better hope he sees me coming first.

Direct Hit! flashes on the screen a few more times, then disappears.

The video moves on to an outdoor view of Lisa Bell letting her cat outside.

"What is it?"

Mary's voice makes me jump out of my skin before I recover and share the screen. We both watch with growing horror as the video shows Jack committing murder after murder. Remotely opening the panel on Butler's motorcycle helmet. Firing the boar tusk at Hughes. Operating a drone that injects Bacco's IV bag with flesh-eating bacteria.

Mary's eyebrows pinch together. "Do you think Jack realizes what he's doing?"

"I hope not. And for his sake, I hope he never finds out."

The video ends when *Direct Hit!* flashes following the shooting of ice balls at Chuck Gomez. A message pops up:

> *Did you enjoy the show? I'm excited to find out what Governor Taylor thinks about it. Maybe the threat of sending these to the media will be enough for him to pardon Leviticus. What do you think?*
>
> *Time's almost up!*
>
> *What? Were you afraid stopping Earl's death meant the game was over? No worries! Darkness, the ninth plague, will come soon. And it will be so much bigger and nastier next time. But I'll tell you what. I need a little more time to prepare now that you threw a wrench into my plague plans.*

So I'll give you until midnight tomorrow to secure Leviticus's release. Otherwise… RIP, Jack!

~ Azrael

The shred of hope I held that rescuing Rogers meant this was over just detonated. Azrael will never stop. This won't end until he ends it. But sinking into despair is pointless. And we have an immediate issue to deal with.

"He sent the video to the governor," I say. "We need to get to Governor Taylor's house. Now."

Pittsburgh Post-Gazette

Monday, December 9

Silas Halvard, Convicted of First-Degree Murder, Sentenced to Life Without Parole

by Matt Burkhart

The city was devastated by a chilling murder spree that came to be attributed in popular reference to the Leviticus Killer. Today, the verdict was delivered in the trial of Silas Halvard, a professor of Biblical Studies at Geneva University, who was convicted of first-degree murder in the case of Joseph Burton, the eleventh victim to be murdered in the same style as the supposed Leviticus Killer's reign of terror. Was Silas responsible for the other ten victims' deaths, or was this some type of copycat killing? The court decided there was only enough evidence to charge and convict Silas with one death. We may never discover the truth about the other ten.

Detective Jena Campbell, along with her partner Detective Mary Sarkis, played a pivotal role in Silas's arrest, whose conviction represents a significant milestone in the quest for closure and peace for the victims and their families.

In a recent interview, Detective Campbell shared her thoughts on the investigation and the trial. "The Leviticus Killer case was a true test of our abilities as detectives," she stated, her voice filled with raw emotion. "We knew we had to put an end to the horrors that were unfolding, and it's a relief to see justice being served today."

Amidst the public discourse surrounding the trial, there were individuals who rallied in support of Silas Halvard. One such person, Rebecca Thompson, a colleague of Silas's from Geneva University, shared her perspective. "I've known Silas for years, and I don't believe he's capable of these acts," Thompson expressed. "He's always been a pillar of our community, someone who inspired others through his teachings. I stand by him, believing that justice has most definitely not been served today."

The trial also highlighted Silas Halvard's secretive past and his denial of any form of abuse during his upbringing. These revelations raised questions about the underlying factors that might have influenced his actions, and his refusal to acknowledge these facts helped the prosecution paint him as an unreliable historian capable of deceit. Prosecutor Sanchez leveraged the fact that not one single family member had shown up to support Silas since his arrest and throughout his trial.

While the sentencing of Silas Halvard to life without parole brought closure to many, the crimes will leave a lasting impact on both the survivors and the city as a whole. Undoubtedly, the name Silas Halvard will forever be associated with the darkest chapter in Pittsburgh's history.

1042 Comments <u>**ADD COMMENT**</u> **Sort by: NEWEST**

This conversation is moderated according to The Post-Gazette's community rules. Please ***read the rules*** *before joining the discussion. If you're experiencing any technical problems, please* ***contact our customer care team****.*

SteelCityFan
Wow, what a spine-chilling case! Kudos to the detectives for bringing him to justice. Heroes! Stay safe out there, Pittsburgh!
Monday, December 9 2019 @ 8:03 AM

JusticeSeeker
Life without parole is too lenient for someone who committed such disturbing acts. I say death penalty now!
Monday, December 9 2019 @ 8:07 AM

> Eye4AnEye
> Sometimes a lifetime behind bars is a worse punishment than a quick death. Let him rot in prison, haunted by his actions.
> Monday, December 9 2019 @ 8:08 AM

PghSportsFan
Hey, Pittsburgh made the headlines again for all the wrong reasons. Can't say I'm proud of this one. Let's focus on the good stuff, like our sports teams!
Monday, December 9 2019 @ 8:10 AM

> BleedBlackNGold
> I feel you, buddy! Our teams will always be the pride of the city. Let's hope the Pirates win the World Series and wash the taste of this one out of our mouths.
> Monday, December 9 2019 @ 8:13 AM

LaughingLlama
You can't make this stuff up! Hollywood should be taking notes. Maybe we'll see a "Leviticus Killer" movie in the future. Who should play Silas Halvard?
Monday, December 9 2019 @ 8:16 AM

> 1MovieBuff
> Hmm, how about Joaquin Phoenix? He's great at playing complex and disturbed characters.
> Monday, December 9 2019 @ 8:19 AM

> OpinionsMyOwn
> Nah, man. Michael Fassbender or Jake Gyllenhaal for sure. Gyllenhaal even looks like Silas. Did you see him in Nightcrawler and Enemy? Creepy AF.
> Monday, December 9 2019 @ 8:21 AM

> 1MovieBuff
> If we're going by looks, Cillian Murphy's a dead ringer.
> Monday, December 9 2019 @ 8:22 AM

> DontCareWutUThink
> Resurrect Heath Ledger from the dead!
> Monday, December 9 2019 @ 8:23 AM

> RockStarGamer
> Sad that a movie will be the only way we see the final boss level to this masterfully played game.

Disconnected before achieving his final creep score. Forget Ledger. Resurrect Leviticus!
Monday, December 9 2019 @ 8:24 AM

CriticalBean
Was looking like a civil convo on here, so I thought I'd post. Looks like I waited too long.
Monday, December 9 2019 @ 8:26 AM

HumorUs
A theology professor turned serial killer? Talk about a career change! I wonder if he offers any online courses from his jail cell. "Murder 101: How to Stone Your Way to Success." Just kidding, folks!
Monday, December 9 2019 @ 8:23 AM

BlackComedy09
Haha! I can just picture the professor's PowerPoint presentation on stoning. Talk about a lecture that really hits home! Too bad his students won't be offered extra credit for that one.
Monday, December 9 2019 @ 8:27 AM

CriticalBean
I'm really starting to doubt that there is any actual moderation on this site. Wake up, Post-Gazette moderators!
Monday, December 9 2019 @ 8:31 AM

LOAD MORE

37

JENA

Tuesday, 8:05 p.m.

MARY TAPS ME on the shoulder. "Ready to go inside? Or are you going to keep strangling that steering wheel?"

I look down at my hands, my knuckles white and bloodless. I release my grip. "Sorry."

Mary points toward the window. "Our friend Mr. Daniels is waiting for us."

I nod and exit the Explorer, heading for the front door. It swings open. Daniels comes out, but he doesn't say anything. Doesn't look us in the eye. This is bad. Very bad. He motions for us to follow him, and we do. Instead of heading to the living room like I expect, Daniels says, "This way. They're in the sunroom."

We walk beyond the staircase through a galley kitchen, all stainless steel and granite. It is a straight shot to a glass-roofed room lit by moonlight and soft artificial lights. No sun in the sunroom at all. The furniture is new, but antique in style, all mohair and velvet. A baby grand piano is nestled in the far end, its lid lowered. I doubt anyone has played it in ages.

The room's stiffness is lightened by rows of floor-to-ceiling windows along three walls that look out onto a monstrous rectangular pool. The water is a black mirror, reflecting the stars above. Daniels drops us off and does his disappearing act.

Governor Taylor is in a velvet wingback chair. His wife is next to him in a matching chair, an empty wine glass on the side table between them. Jude is absent.

"Sit," the governor says with a half-hearted gesture toward the love seat. There are dark circles beneath his eyes, and he looks like he has aged a few years since I last saw him.

I lower myself onto the edge of the love seat. The mohair is stiff and itchy on my arms. Mary drops down next to me.

What is going on is obvious, but I still voice it. "You've seen the video."

He nods. "It came as a text to my phone."

"How could you?" Mrs. Taylor's glare bores into my skull. She is slurring a little, and I expect she has had more than just wine. But while substances may have softened her words, her anger is at full force. "How could you let him do this to my son? My baby boy. When he was born, he choked during his first feeding. Did you know that? Stopped breathing. He had a seizure. Then another. The doctor thought we were going to lose him. But he's tougher than he looks. He survived. But I don't know how he can survive this." Her rage segues into brimming tears, and she turns her head away from us. "Jude won't come out of his room, and I think maybe he has the right idea. Whatever you've come to say, it's too late. You've killed my son. He's already dead."

"Now Shannon—"

She cuts her husband off with a slice of her hand. "I'm done talking. And I'm done listening."

She rises and strides out of the room.

"I'll talk to her," Mary says, always playing equal parts social worker and cop. She follows after her.

"Apologies for the display," Governor Taylor says.

"No need to apologize. You've all been through hell. I should be the one apologizing for not catching this bastard. And also for having to talk business when I should be offering sympathy."

"You're just doing your job." The response sounds canned, like the man is on autopilot. He is worn out and worn down.

"The videos—"

"—Are intended as blackmail."

"What did Azrael say?"

"I release Silas, or these videos go to the press."

"And are you going to? Release Silas, I mean?"

"To keep the videos private?" He shakes his head. "The press will realize Jack did these things unwittingly. He's a hostage under threat."

I nod, but I don't believe the media won't villainize Jack.

"A pardon won't do what anyone hopes," he says with conviction. "It will only make things worse."

I want to say, *"Worse than allowing your son to die?"* but I don't.

As a police officer, I should be relieved. The harm Silas would cause as a free man is unthinkable. Still. The life of a seventeen-year-old innocent is on the line. And while I've been wrestling with the moral dilemma of which is worse, Silas's freedom or Jack's death, Jack's not the only reason I think maybe releasing Silas is the way to go after all. Dustin is the bigger threat in terms of potential body count. If he kills Jack, he could disappear. Continue killing. And there might be nothing I can do to stop him. If I can't figure out where Jack is, rescue him, and arrest Dustin, my confession might be my last shot to lure Dustin out of hiding.

"Are you 100 percent on that, sir? What if we set up a negotiation? A trade. Silas for Jack. We could use that to lure Azrael into a trap. Catch this bastard and give him the death sentence he deserves."

Governor Taylor folds his arms. "And what, in your estimation, Detective, are the chances something could go wrong? That Azrael doesn't show up at the site? Or that Azrael out plans us, as he's shown he can do, and we lose all three of them?"

I have no good answer. "A hostage exchange can be risky, of course. But I'm confident we can pull it off."

"You've had eight jurors murdered right under your nose. How do you think you could outwit Azrael in a hostage exchange?"

"It's day ten," I say. "It could be our only shot to rescue Jack." My plea sounds so weak I cringe.

The governor pushes his tongue into his cheek, thinking. "No," he finally says. "Any risk is too much. The exchange goes wrong, and it will be all over the papers. We'll be in an even bigger mess."

His career is what would be in the bigger mess. By which I mean it would be over.

"I know you're trying, but no," the governor says. "I have trust in the Lord. Often, He knows the path, and it's only us who can't see it."

"It's your call, of course, Governor. And I respect your decision."

Respect it. But that doesn't mean I have to agree with it. Or accept the decision as my own. If he won't help me lure Azrael out of hiding, then I guess it is up to me.

I leave Governor Taylor to his thoughts and head for the Explorer to wait for Mary.

As I approach the vehicle, a voice whispers from beyond the hedge row, "Promise me."

It is Jude, standing in plain sight, illuminated under the mansion's outdoor spotlights. Looks like he learned from last time not to sneak up on me. I don't blame him. There isn't much more unsettling than having a Glock thrust in your face.

"I thought I had your escape window blocked off."

Jude stands with his arms across his chest. "I said, promise me."

"Promise what?"

"That you'll bring him home."

"I don't make promises I can't keep."

"So promise me and keep it, or I swear to God, I'm leaving right now to find him myself and there's nothing you can do to stop me."

"Believe me, there is."

"You won't shoot me."

"No, but maybe I'll handcuff you to whatever drainpipe you crawled down."

Jude's face twists, the skin bunching around his eyes, looking at me with a pained stare. I feel like shit about my callousness and reach out to him, but he flinches, his body jerking back.

I sigh, retracting my hand and running my fingers through my hair, wishing Mary were here. She is the one who is good at talking to people.

"I promise I'll do everything I can to bring Jack home, even if it means sacrificing myself. How's that?" I hold my hand out to him again.

Jude mulls over the words as if he can't process what I just said. Or maybe doesn't believe them. He searches my face, my eyes, then finally nods. "That's acceptable."

Jude thinks he has won something, unaware I already made the same promise to myself I just made to him. He shakes my hand, then turns around, sprinting back to the house. I make another promise to myself: that I won't let the kid down.

38

JENA

Tuesday, 9:42 p.m.

MASON IS ASLEEP in my bed. I try not to disturb him as I pull on an oversize shirt and tiptoe to the living room.

Since my phone is cloned, I go over to my laptop on the coffee table. Opening a private browser, I login to social media, using a new anonymous account. I click on the DMs for Dustin's *@azrael* account. My fingers hover for only a moment before I commit and start typing.

> *Dear Dustin, (no way am I calling him Azrael)*
>
> *I'm ready to confess, if you promise you won't kill Jack or anyone else. It will take some time to go through the legal red tape before they release Silas. What do you say? Do we have a deal?*
>
> *~ Little Bird*

I type the Little Bird nickname as a reclaiming, letting Dustin know I'm not afraid of him. A statement that he can't manipulate or intimidate me.

I wait, unable to focus on anything but the screen, reminding myself to take my next breath, then the next. The minutes pass, acid gurgling in my stomach. And then dots appear on the laptop.

...

Dustin is typing.

Dear little bird,

You have yourself a deal. The kid will live. No more deaths while I wait meekly as a little lamb. Let's shake on it, shall we?

Shake, shake,

- Azrael

I breathe out and close the laptop. My entire body is quivering with the adrenaline of what I just did as I slide back into bed and gently shake Mason.

"I need to tell you something," I whisper.

His arms close around me, and I rest my head on his bare chest.

"That was the greatest sex you've ever had, and you woke me up for round two?"

"I'm serious."

He extracts his arm and rolls onto his side, so we're nose to nose. A satisfied smile on his face, he studies me with those sparkling ebony eyes, like sunshine through a glass of porter.

"Shoot."

"I, um, you see, I couldn't—"

I take a gulp of air. Mason is going to leave me when I tell him. For good this time. His moral compass always points true north. He won't understand.

Mason puts two fingers to the side of my throat, just below my jaw. My pulse is fluttering faster than hummingbird wings.

"How is it you can fearlessly chase down killers, but talking to me gives you a heart attack?"

I raise an arm in surrender. "Remember when I first tried to get a warrant for Silas based on the calluses on his hand?"

His eyes narrow. "The judge denied it. Not enough evidence."

Breathe, Jena, breathe. My heart is hammering, but I need to do this. I need to tell him.

"And then we asked the sanitation worker who collected Silas's trash to deliver his bags to us?"

"Right."

I close my eyes because it is easier to say the next part when I don't have to look at the concern painted across Mason's face. "Leto's Pawn Shop had just closed. The owner, Leto, passed away, and he used generic receipts. No record of what was in the shop except in Leto's head."

"You didn't."

I open my eyes, refusing to chicken out of this part. "I did. I falsified a receipt for the twelve gemstones and planted it in Silas's garbage."

"Oh, Jena."

I feel like I'm going to vomit, but I need to get it all out now. The words. Not the vomit. Better out than in. "It gets worse. I wrote the wrong name for the twelfth gemstone. I put bloodstone, but apparently it's actually jasper. I couldn't even get that much right. Leto was a pawn guy and not a gemologist, so no one thought it weird he wouldn't know the difference. But Silas knows. Suspects it was me, even though another officer found it and wrote the affidavit for the warrant, and he has no proof. God, he was furious about that receipt during the trial. Venomous he couldn't get the warrant looked at. If his eyes could've stabbed me, I'd be dead fifty times over."

His brows squish together. Two parallel frown lines I've rarely seen except when he is in the courtroom. "I don't think—"

"I messaged Azrael."

"You what?"

"He's agreed not to kill Jack or anyone else if I can get Silas released."

"You can't trust him. Think, Jena. That's insane."

"I'm telling Captain Price. First thing in the morning."

"Like I was saying before, I'm glad you told me, but there's no way you should tell anyone else."

That isn't what I expected Mr. True North Moral Compass to say.

"Not because it would be the end of your career, which you're risking on the word of a madman—and I know how much your work matters to you, how much your putting Silas away mattered to this entire city—but you could be looking at criminal charges."

He is worried about me more than he is about the right thing to do, and it makes my heart ache. He looks down at me, warm eyes like richly polished leather. My breath catches, my skin tingling. I want to melt and do whatever he tells me. But it looks like I'm the one about to do the right thing.

"I know what it means. I'm going to tell Price anyway. But I need your help. Can you get your prosecutor friend who works for the city on it? Scott Gellman? I need an audience with a judge fast. Like, first thing tomorrow."

"This isn't as easy as you think. Even if I can get you squeezed in, and Gellman convinces the judge to see you, the judge might not believe you. If someone came to me saying they lied in the past, I'd ask what proves they're not lying now?"

"I thought you might say that."

I open my nightstand drawer and pull out a receipt pad, the yellow carbon copy of the receipt I forged right there on top. A bit crinkled and creased with black lines, but still legible.

"You kept it?"

"Yeah. In my gun locker."

"Why the hell would you do that?"

I shrug. "Guilt, I guess. It was too heavy of a thing to let go."

Mason squeezes my hand and slowly shakes his head.

"Will you help me?"

He bites his bottom lip, studying me.

"Jack's life depends on it. Future lives depend on in. If we can't catch Azrael while he has Jack, he might disappear. Start a new round of killing. There's no telling what the death toll could be. We need to nail him now, while I still have something to bargain with. Please."

Sighing, he gives a reluctant nod.

39

JENA

Wednesday, 8:01 a.m.

WHEN I ENTER Captain Price's office, he is already behind his maelstrom of a desk. He leans back in his chair, arms folded, eyeing me. "You have an update?"

I drop into the chair in front of him, putting my shoulder bag on my lap, unable to meet his stare knowing I'm about to break his heart. I pick the skin around my nails as a distraction, or coping mechanism, or whatever. "A ninth victim is still going to die. And Jack is going to die at midnight if I don't do something about it. Then that maniac, Dustin, will be out there in the free world doing whatever the hell he pleases. I can't let that happen."

"This doesn't sound like good news."

I bring my gaze up to meet his. "I thought maybe we could set up an exchange. Silas for Jack. Lure Dustin out into the open. But Governor Taylor won't hear it."

Price makes a face. "A pardon for Silas would be a disaster for the man's career. For the whole system. I don't blame him."

"Neither do I. But I can't let this go."

"And you don't have to. We'll keep working to track this Dustin down."

"Believe me, I'll never stop. But it will be too late for the ninth target and Jack." And I'm not confident we'll catch Dustin without bait. He could disappear. Or he could escalate his murder spree and leave the PBP looking like a bunch of bumbling idiots. More than we already do. I take a deep breath. "I have something to tell you. DA Scott Gellman is already waiting to meet with me, but I wanted to tell you first."

Price's eyebrows shoot up as Mason walks into the room and takes a seat beside me. I look to him, and he gives a reassuring nod.

"My escort." I shrug.

"Sorry I'm late," Mason says.

"You were saying?" Price gestures for me to continue.

"You know the warrant was a point of contention during Silas's trial." That is putting it mildly. "The receipt. I did it. I planted it in his trash."

After a moment of stunned silence, Price points at me. "If you're just saying that with some misguided belief that Silas will lead us to Dustin, you'd better take it back. Right now."

"I'm not." I pull the receipt pad, now in a plastic evidence bag, from my purse and put it on Price's desk.

Price glances down. "What the hell am I looking at?"

I say nothing. There is nothing to say.

"A fucking nightmare, that's what I'm looking at. How am I going to explain this? To the Chief? The press?" A knife sinks into my guts as his stare turns on me full force. "You were supposed to take over this desk when I retired." The knife sinks deeper and twists. "You really want to do this?"

"Yes."

"Well, I'm sure as hell not arresting you. Go self-report, then." He pushes the receipt pad back to me, his gaze looking past me, like I'm no longer there as I tuck it away.

"You're relieved of duty. Leave your badge. And your gun."

I turn over my star and my Glock, shaking as I plant them on top of a stack of folders.

Mason squeezes my hand and clears his throat, turning on professional mode. And I'm so grateful he takes over because I'm about to fall apart.

"Like Jena said, she has an appointment with prosecutor Gellman. Based on the new evidence, we're going to push for an emergency hearing with Judge Spadina. I can't see Spadina denying Silas a new hearing. They'll have to throw out any evidence they found in his house. Fruit of the poison tree. Silas will be out soon."

"Understood." Price's mouth forms a hard line as he turns his cold stare on me. "Dismissed."

I rise on weak legs and Mason joins me, leaning in close as we exit Price's office. His lips brush my ear as he whispers, "I know that was awful. You did so good. After you speak with Gellman, I'll do everything I can to prevent a felony charge, but it's out of my hands now."

I nod, but it is like I have a chicken bone caught in my throat. I've thrown away my career, reputation, and all the work I've done, that everyone has done, to get Silas locked up. Probably just put myself behind bars, too. I really hope I've done the right thing. That Silas's release will lead to Jack's safe return and my team will get something to help them catch Dustin. But right now, as I shuffle down the hall with Mason to go see the DA, I don't think so. What I think is, I fucked up. Again.

40

JENA

Wednesday, 8:30 a.m.

WHEN MASON AND I step into the District Attorney's office, it is buzzing with activity. Clerks and secretarial staff move purposefully about, their conversations a cacophony of overlapping voices. The air is heavy with the smell of stale coffee and Xerox toner, the too-close beige walls pressing in on me. I clutch my purse, an accessory I almost never carry, but I'm grateful for the bag acting like a security blanket right now.

Down the hall, Officer Dale is talking to a clerk. He gives a friendly wave, unaware I'm no longer PBP, no longer one of them. I don't have the strength to face him with an explanation right now if he asks what is wrong, so I smile and wave in return, nausea rolling in my stomach as I hide my shame. At that moment, it hits me. I have to let Mary in on what I'm doing. But I can't focus on anything except maintaining the courage to tell the DA.

Mason approaches the secretary at the front desk, an older woman named Marge with glasses perched on her nose. "We're here to speak with District Attorney Gellman immediately. He's expecting us."

Marge glances at me, her eyes narrowing. We've never gotten along. She once called me a "power-tripping shrew." In all fairness, I was being pretty unreasonable at the time.

"You'll have to wait," she says curtly, turning her attention back to her computer screen.

Mason leans in closer, lowering his voice. "This is urgent. A life depends on it. We need to see Gellman. Now."

The secretary's eyes widen, and she picks up the phone. Mason has that effect on people when his charisma turns from kind to demanding.

After a brief conversation, she hangs up and gestures down the hall. "He'll see you in his office."

"Thank you."

As we navigate the maze of cubicles and offices, I receive dozens of stares. I've worked with most of these people. I wonder if my dismissal from the force is already spreading, or if my guilt is oozing out so palpably, they can't help but draw their own conclusions. I'm exposed, vulnerable. I grip my purse tighter, my legs shaking with every step.

It takes forever to reach DA Gellman's office at the end of the hall, its frosted glass door displaying his name and title. Mason knocks, and a muffled voice invites us in. Gellman is a tall man in his late forties, with a receding hairline and a permanent frown etched on his face. His desk is overcrowded by three computer monitors, the smell of vanilla vape smoke lingering in the air.

My heart hammers, my gaze drifting to a baseball on the far corner of his desk, aged and slightly faded despite being under glass. It is signed. By Roberto Clemente, probably the greatest outfielder in the history of baseball. Eighteen years he played for the Pirates. An outstanding career. And then when he tried to help others by delivering supplies to earthquake victims, his plane crashed. I'm trying not to take the baseball as an omen.

"What's so urgent it couldn't wait?" Gellman asks, his voice gruff.

I keep staring at the baseball as images rush at me. Pirates' games with Mason. My own days pitching softball. Silas's days "pitching." I catch my own reflection in the glass, stiff-necked, shoulders hiked to my ears. I grip the sides of my purse as I take a big gulp of air and recount my confession.

"Five years ago, when I was working on the case against Silas Halvard, I falsified a pawn shop receipt to obtain a warrant for his arrest. At the time, I didn't have any concrete evidence linking him to the murders, but I believed he was guilty. I couldn't risk the possibility of him killing again."

As my confession hangs in the air, the silence in the room is suffocating. Gellman stares at me, blinking as he tries to process what he has just heard.

I open my purse and pull out the bagged receipt pad, slipping it onto his desk. As he examines it, the trust I've built with him over the years shatters. Mason, my rock, grabs my hand and nods, urging me to go on.

"As much as we've worked to keep it out of the press, I'm sure you've heard what's going on. Dustin, the man calling himself Azrael, has killed eight of Silas's former jury members. Now he's threatening to kill one more and the governor's son unless Silas is released. That's why I've come forward with this information. To save Jack's life. And maybe catch a killer."

Gellman's frown deepens. "You're asking me to prosecute you in order to release a man we've believed to be a serial killer for five years, based on the threat of another killer who you can't find?"

I nod, my voice trembling. "Yes. I have to try everything I can to stop him and save future victims and Jack."

"Off the record, you and I both know this isn't the first time a cop's done what they needed to do. If you want to retract what you just told me and walk out of here, I wouldn't blame you. But if you're determined to go through with this, you realize you could face criminal charges? Perjury's a maximum of seven years. Did you testify about the warrant under oath?"

"No," I whisper. "Office Dale found the receipt in Silas's trash and did the affidavit for the warrant. And the judge refused to look at it during Silas's trial."

"That's good for you, then. I'll have to charge you with tampering with evidence. That's a maximum of two years. The best you could hope for is your attorney arguing for a misdemeanor, and the judge agreeing based on your record."

I nod, the weight of my decision pressing down on me hearing Gellman spell it out like that. "I understand. I accept whatever punishment comes my way."

Mason puts his hands on Gellman's desk, leaning forward. "Scott, we need you to arrange an emergency hearing with Judge Spadina. Jena will confess in court and plead guilty. We hope to secure Silas's release in exchange for Azrael's cooperation."

Gellman's eyes bore into me, searching for any hint of deception. "You're willing to put your career, your freedom, and your reputation on the line for this?"

I meet his gaze, fire burning in my chest. "Yes, I am. If it means saving Jack and stopping Azrael, I'll do whatever it takes."

Gellman leans back in his chair, rubbing his temples. "Do

you have a criminal defense attorney you can consult before the trial?"

"I do. Fred Thompson." Another friend of Mason's, and a friend to officers of the PBP who find themselves in trouble.

"All right. I'll make the arrangements for the emergency hearing. Since you're self-reporting, I won't ask the judge if I need to hold you."

I swallow, grateful Gellman's sparing me the shame of a holding cell.

"Sit tight." Gellman pulls out his cell phone and dials. "Hello, Judge Spadina. It's Scott Gellman."

As he conveys the situation to the judge, Mason squeezes my hand. "I've got you. I'll do everything I can to help."

Tears prick my eyes, and he pulls me into a quick hug. "Silas is guilty," I say. "You know it. I know it. But what I did to put him away was wrong, and I won't cross the line like that again. Not that it makes a difference now."

Gellman clears his throat, and we both straighten in our seats. "Given the urgency of the situation, Judge Spadina has agreed to convene in two hours. I'm going to run down the protocol with you so you'll know what to expect, okay?"

I gesture for him to get on with it.

"For an emergency hearing, the session will be brief, and focus on the new evidence and testimony you provide. Then Judge Spadina will decide whether to grant Silas a new hearing and schedule a date for your own trial. Understand?"

I nod and swallow.

I reach for the receipt pad, but Gellman says, "Leave that with me, please. I'll make sure it gets to the judge prior to the hearing. That's everything. I'll call Silas's defense attorney and inform him of the new development."

I try to speak, but nothing comes out.

Mason jumps to my rescue. "Very good. Thanks for your help on this, Scott. We really appreciate it."

"I'd say you're welcome, but that doesn't feel right."

Mason and Gellman shake hands. As we leave Gellman's office, the door clicks shut behind us. Nowhere to go but forward, down the path I've set in motion. It isn't a long walk. I don't even need to leave the courthouse.

41

JENA

Wednesday, 11:00 a.m.

THE SHARP CLICK of my heels against the marble floor echoes throughout the courtroom as I enter, my pulse racing. The grand space with its high ceilings and walls embellished with the symbols of justice serves as a stark reminder of how I've betrayed the system I swore to uphold. The atmosphere is heavy with tension. Word of the emergency hearing has clearly leaked, drawing a small crowd of spectators, many of whom appear to be Allegheny County Courthouse employees, to the wooden benches. They murmur amongst themselves, casting curious glances my way.

Up at the front, Judge Spadina's stern expression dominates the room from her elevated bench. I glance over at Mason, who is seated behind the prosecution. His small, encouraging smile is a welcome sight amidst the sea of hostile faces. And then I spot Mary. She whispers, "No," when I walk by, then starts bawling. As I take my seat, the gavel's sharp crack reverberates through the courtroom, silencing the audience.

Gellman approaches the bench, his voice steady and

confident. "Your Honor, we've called for this emergency hearing in light of new information regarding the case against Silas Halvard. Prior to this hearing, we have submitted new evidence—a receipt pad with the carbon copy of the falsified receipt, as well as the original receipt from Silas's trial—for your review. We request that you allow Jena Campbell to take the stand and share her testimony."

Judge Spadina's gaze shifts from Gellman to me, her expression unreadable. "Ms. Campbell, have you consulted with your attorney about your decision to testify?"

I flinch at the name. At the missing "Detective" that should come before "Campbell."

My attorney, Fred Thompson, who is standing beside me, interjects, "Your Honor, I've advised Ms. Campbell against this action, but she's chosen not to follow my counsel."

Judge Spadina nods, her face still impassive. "Ms. Campbell, you've been charged with tampering with evidence. Do you understand the charges brought against you?"

"Yes, Your Honor," I say, my voice barely a whisper.

"Very well. Mr. Gellman, call your witness."

With a deep breath, I rise from my seat and make my way to the witness stand, acutely aware of the dozens of eyes tracking my every move. I raise my right hand and swear to tell the truth, taking my seat as Gellman begins his questioning.

"Ms. Campbell. You've come forward with new information about the case against Silas Halvard. Can you please explain to the court what that is?"

Gathering my courage, I lock eyes with Gellman and begin my confession. As I detail how I falsified evidence in Silas's case, a susurrus ripples through the courtroom, shocked whispers filling the air. Judge Spadina's icy gaze never leaves me.

"Ms. Campbell, do you understand the implications of your actions? You could face imprisonment for falsifying evidence," she says, her voice cold.

My own voice trembles as I reply, "Yes, Your Honor. I understand, and I'm prepared to face the consequences."

Gellman's tone is somber as he continues. "Ms. Campbell, you've come forward with this information now because you believe it will help stop a current threat. Is that correct?"

"Yes. A man calling himself Azrael has threatened to kill ten people unless Silas Halvard is released. He's already killed eight. There will be two more, and the tenth victim is the governor's son."

"Please state the alleged intended target's legal name," the Judge intones.

"I'm sorry. Jack Taylor. It's too late to save the eight jury members, and I'll have to live with that. But my confession is an attempt to stop future killings and save Jack's life."

As Gellman turns back to Judge Spadina, urgency fills his voice. "Your Honor, with this new evidence and Ms. Campbell's confession, we request that Silas Halvard be granted a new hearing. We understand that this is an extraordinary request, but the situation is dire, and we believe it's the only way to save Jack and other potential targets."

Judge Spadina raises an eyebrow. "Ms. Campbell claims to have lied to prevent what she believed to be an injustice to put Silas away. Now, she has an incentive to lie again as she believes it will save lives. Why should I believe her now?"

Gellman hesitates, which makes me cringe. I know he is searching for the right words, but it is making him look unsure.

"Your Honor, Ms. Campbell is willing to risk her own freedom and reputation to bring the truth to light."

His tone is strong, but the words are weak. I'm disappointed. He could've done better.

Judge Spadina's eyes narrow and I know we're screwed.

"Or perhaps," she says, "Ms. Campbell fabricated the 'evidence'—this carbon copy of the original receipt. How can I be certain it's genuine."

This is spiraling down a path I don't like at all. I clear my throat and interject. "Your Honor, if I may, I can provide a writing sample to prove my penmanship matches the writing on the original receipt. I'm willing to cooperate in any way necessary to demonstrate the authenticity of the evidence."

"Very well." Judge Spadina nods, and the court clerk provides me with pen and paper. I write the word *bloodstone* in the same disguised handwriting I used on the receipt and pass it to the judge. After a moment of examination, she looks back at me, her expression still guarded but the wisp of doubt fading.

The courtroom holds its collective breath as Judge Spadina considers the request, her fingers drumming on the bench. Finally, she speaks, her voice measured and firm. "I am disturbed by the confession shared here today. We do, and should, expect better of Pittsburgh's finest. Justice is more than an ideal. It's a practice." Judge Spadina pauses, and I shrink like a mouse in my seat, properly berated and cut down under her glare. "Given Ms. Campbell's confession and the imminent threat to the governor's son," she continues, "I am granting Silas Halvard a post-conviction relief hearing, which will be scheduled as soon as possible. As for Ms. Campbell, she will be released on personal bond until her sentencing hearing can be scheduled."

A mixture of relief and dread washes over me as the gavel falls once more, its whack punctuating the weight of the judge's decision. The spectators begin to mutter again.

"Ms. Campbell," Judge Spadina says. "Please approach the bench."

I freeze. This ordeal should be over now. The judge should be leaving. What does she want with me? She crooks a finger and I step down from the witness stand, wriggling forward as she reels me in like a fish on a line. I steal a glance at Mason. His face remains a picture of quiet support, and I find solace in knowing that however bleak the future gets, he'll stand by my side.

Judge Spadina drops her voice low. "I hope you understand what you're doing. Once Silas was put away, the murders stopped. Serial killers don't stop killing. And what happens if he is loose again? Of course, I'm not privy to the information, but I had lunch with George Mazur after he completed Silas's evaluation. George is a seasoned forensic psychologist, and he was three shades too pale."

The venom in her voice nearly has me shaking. Beneath her words, I'm sure she has heard more about Silas's psych eval than she has let on. I'm glad it is information I don't have. It would only make it harder to live with what I've just done.

Psychological Assessment

Confidential: For professional use only. Professionals and clients should contact the service provider directly should the client wish to read or obtain a copy of this report. Please protect the confidentiality of this document in accord with ethical and legal codes.

Client: Silas Halvard

Date of Birth: 07/22/78

Indictment: SCI Fayette, 21-2019

Date of Testing: 12/10/19

Date of Report: 12/13/19

Reason for Referral: Mr. Halvard was referred for court-mandated psychological evaluation following a first-degree murder conviction. Records review and clinical interview were conducted for the assessment.

Background History: Silas Halvard, a 44-year-old, right-handed, Caucasian male had a challenging upbringing as documented in the Court Mitigation Specialist Report completed December 2019.

Mr. Halvard reported no sensory impairments, good sleep, and that his appetite was "just fine" although he only eats once a day. An MRI brain scan conducted December 9, 2019 was within normal limits. He is in good health and takes no medication.

Mr. Halvard completed 21 years of formal education. Prior to his incarceration, he was working as a professor of Biblical Studies at Geneva University. He is widowed and lives alone. He has no children. Suicidal ideation and homicidal intent, and

A/V hallucinations were denied. Mr. Halvard does not smoke or drink alcohol. Illicit drug use was denied.

Behavioral Observations: Cooperative during testing, he showed good attention span and effort. His affect was warm, and rapport was easily established. A charismatic communicator, he downplayed past issues, possibly indicating manipulation.

Tests Administered: California Verbal Learning Test, Third Edition; Delis-Kaplan Executive Function System; Finger Tapping Test; Grooved Pegboard Test; Minnesota Multiphasic Personality Inventory-3; Rey Complex Figure Test; Rorschach Inkblot Test; Test of Memory and Learning, Second Edition; Test of Memory Malingering; Thematic Apperception Test; Wechsler Adult Intelligence Scale, Fourth Edition; Wechsler Individual Achievement Test, Fourth Edition; Wide Range Achievement Test, Fifth Edition; Wisconsin Card Sorting Test.

Test Results:

Cognitive Skills: On the WAIS-IV, Mr. Halvard obtained a Full-Scale IQ (FSIQ) of 128 (97th %'ile, Very High). His performance on a sight-reading test was at the 99th percentile (Extremely High). These scores, together with his level of education and occupational history, suggest that his level of general intellectual functioning is Very High to Extremely High. He also had average to above-average attention, memory, language, and executive skills.

Emotional Status: In order to gain insights into Mr. Halvard's personality and current psychological state, several self-report and subjective measures were administered.

MMPI-3:

The MMPI-3 provides standardized data regarding various aspects of an individual's personality. Mr. Halvard's MMPI-3 response style was consistent with an attempt to portray himself as typical, with slightly elevated T-scores for Dissimulation, Positive Malingering, and Social Desirability scales. However, the test results also reflect underlying psychological complexities linked to a traumatic upbringing and reality distortions.

Despite the attempt to portray himself in a favorable light, Mr. Halvard's profile is one of the most common 2-point codes in both inpatient and outpatient psychiatric settings, with low, but still significant, peak elevations on the Psychopathic Deviate (Pd 4) and Schizophrenia (Sc 8) scales. Standard interpretive sources have described similar patterns in others as odd and peculiar in thinking and behavior and as mistrustful in relations with others. They see others as hostile, rejecting, and unreliable. Defective empathy and difficulties in the expression of anger are chronic problems. Crimes committed by such individuals tend to involve bizarre and violent behavior. However, the murder for which Mr. Halvard was charged was far better planned and executed than is typical of individuals endorsing this pattern, likely due to his high intelligence.

Overall, Mr. Halvard's MMPI-3 profile emphasizes his alienation from others and from himself, and a hopeless attitude toward the world and his coinhabitants.

RORSCHACH INKBLOT TEST:

The RIT is a semi-structured, standardized, personality assessment. The RIT stimulus consists of ten inkblots; five are black-and-white (and shades of gray), two are bichromatic, and three are multicolored. They are presented in a standard order according to a structured administration procedure. Mr. Halvard's responses to the stimulus were indicative of positive impression management, portraying images as harmless and pleasant, possibly masking deeper complexity. For example, Card 4 is most often described as a looming, ominous shape, gigantic in scale, and possibly riding toward the examinee on a vehicle such as a motorcycle. To this card, Mr. Halvard responded, "Oh, there is a fluffy bunny just hopping with joy. Fills me up with calmness." Card 5, most often described as a bat in flight, he described as "a dainty butterfly with wings all aflutter," representing "freedom and transformation." Other cards he described as kittens, flower gardens, and "a charming dance of ribbons."

THERMATIC APPERCEPTION TEST:
The TAT is a widely-used projective test designed to reveal an individual's perception of interpersonal relationships. Selected cards from thirty-one black-and-white illustrations of people or scenes serve as stimuli for stories and descriptions about relationships or social situations.

Mr. Halvard's descriptions of the cards again showed a pattern of positive impression management. For example, he described a picture of a crowded city street with faceless people rushing past each other as showing "the interconnectedness of humanity." He also described a picture of a child peeking out from behind a curtain with a look of fear on his face as "a thrilling game of hide-and-seek." The only negative reaction shown on this test came in response to Picture 13MF that depicts a woman with her facial features obscured lying on a bed with exposed breasts. In the foreground, a man walks away with his head down and a forearm covering his eyes. Mr. Halvard objected to the "moral tone" of this illustration, with visible reddening of the face and flared nostrils, and refused to give a description.

Summary and Impressions:

Mr. Halvard possessed average to well-above average cognitive skills and abilities. Based on the results of the MMPI-3, Rorschach, and Thematic Apperception Test, Mr. Halvard's complex profile includes trauma, extremism, and distortions, including a strong need for atonement. While he projects resilience and control, underlying disturbances are apparent. Further evaluation is advised.

Recommendations:

Post-traumatic stress related symptoms, religious delusions, and antisocial tendencies are the most significant areas that require intervention or treatment. Cognitive-Behavioral Therapy and Interpersonal Psychotherapy are both intervention strategies that have been shown to remediate symptoms. However, pharmacological intervention may also be required in conjunction with treatment. A medical evaluation with a psychiatrist is strongly recommended.

Thank you for the opportunity to participate in this client's care. If you have any questions, please contact us.

G. Mazur

George Mazur, Ph.D.

Division of Psychology

42

JENA

Wednesday, 11:55 a.m.

AS I'M ABOUT to exit the courthouse, Mason catches up with me.

"The vultures are outside," he warns.

"Oh no. You don't happen to have a paper bag to put on my head, do you?"

"We've got this," he says, holding the door open for me.

I take a deep breath and force myself to move. When I step outside, a swarm of reporters and videographers descend on me. The bright lights from the cameras are more blinding than the afternoon sun as the barrage of questions begins.

"How does it feel to be stripped of your badge for corruption?"

"Do you think Silas Halvard is innocent?"

"Are you responsible for the governor's son being in danger?"

Overwhelmed and disoriented, the world spins around me. I drop my head down, avoiding eye contact with the media, but there is nowhere to hide.

Mason takes charge, wrapping his arm protectively around me and guiding me through the throng of journalists. His voice is polite, but firm as he addresses them. "Please. Give us some space. We have no comment at this time."

"Has Detective Campbell retained you as her legal counsel?"

"No comment," he says again in his well-practiced tone.

The reporters continue to press for answers, but Mason remains a shield, protecting me from the onslaught of questions. We finally push our way through the parking lot to my F-150. As I climb inside, I let out a shaky breath, getting a temporary reprieve from the media circus outside. Until they start swarming the vehicle, pressing their cameras to the window.

I start the truck and slowly part the sea of reporters, a careful balance to not hurt anyone but to keep driving. When I get on the road, my shoulders loosen a fraction.

"Thanks, Mason," I say softly, my voice hoarse from the strain.

Mason offers a sympathetic smile. "It's what I'm here for. We'll get through this."

"Where's your car? Is it in the parking lot?"

"Don't worry about it. I'll get it later," he says as his phone buzzes with an incoming message.

I glance over as he quickly scans the contents, his expression serious.

"It's the court clerk," he says. "Silas's post-conviction relief hearing has been scheduled for tomorrow morning. It is going to be a closed hearing, but given the high-profile nature of the case, I have no doubt the media will be out in full force."

"Shit. This is going to blow up, isn't it?"

"Nothing you can do about it for the moment. Let's get you home."

As I drive through the busy Pittsburgh streets, I can't help but feel sick about Silas's hearing. I can't see how Judge Spadina could make any decision but to overturn his conviction. Not with the evidence I provided. And once Silas is free? What will happen to Jack, to Dustin, to me?

The sun is blazing as we arrive at my apartment. Uncharacteristic sunshine for Pittsburgh this time of year. It is like the sky is mocking me with light and warmth in my darkest time. Highlighting a moment where I have nothing to do but sit on my hands and wait and hope. The street outside my apartment is quiet, disconcerting after the chaos of the courthouse. But I'm sure the media will make their way here soon enough to camp outside my front door and harass me. I spot the surveillance car and the officer inside. He doesn't meet my eyes.

I park in the underground lot, and Mason walks me to the building's entrance, his hand on the small of my back. He stops as I open the door to the stairwell.

"Are you coming in?"

He shakes his head. "I can't. Lots of work to do."

"Any of it on my account?"

He smirks. "Maybe some."

"Do you want me to drive you back? You didn't have to come home with me."

"I'll get an Uber. Lock your windows and doors, okay?" he says gently. "The media and Silas's zealots are sure to be buzzing about."

"You know I always lock them. I have surveillance. And I still have my personal gun. Word is, I'm a pretty good shot."

"Right." Mason sighs. "I know I don't need to remind you to be cautious. I worry. That's all. I'll come over and check on you after work."

"Don't you dare. You're going to be swamped prepping for tomorrow."

"You're more important."

I shove him in the direction of the lot's exit, but he is too solid for me to move, and he smirks at my effort. "I'm exhausted. I really want to be by myself tonight. You know how I get."

"Oh, believe me, I know. But this isn't like another rough day at the office."

"It's exactly like another rough day at the office. I'm going to have a hot shower and go to bed. And if you show up, I'm not answering the door."

"I'll climb in the window."

"I told you I lock them."

He throws his hands up. "What am I going to do with you?"

"Listen to me, that's what. Go," I say. "Get your work done. You'd better go to the Pirates' game tomorrow night, too. You've been obnoxious about it for weeks."

"I'm skipping it. I'll be here right after Silas's verdict."

"I won't be in any mood for company. And you deserve some stress relief. If you don't go to that game, I'm going to call Bob and take the extra ticket myself."

He sighs in surrender, then kisses the top of my head. "I'm going to call you every five minutes."

"You'd better not."

"Try to get some rest. Tomorrow's going to be a long day."

I manage a weak smile. "I'll try. Thanks. For everything."

Shuffling up the stairs to my apartment, the weight of the day's events catches up to me. As soon as I'm inside, I flop onto the couch, my thoughts spiraling. I can't handle anymore shit today. So, of course, my laptop dings on the coffee table. The dread sinks low in my stomach when I see the message's sender. A DM from @azrael.

Dear little bird,

You kept up your end of the bargain! Here's a round of applause for you. 👏 👏 👏 *Which means no one else dies and Jack stays alive! For now. I'll be watching the results of Silas's hearing tomorrow very closely.*

Tick tock, little bird. Tick tock.

~ Azrael

My hands tremble as I shove the laptop away. How the hell does Dustin know the hearing is tomorrow? Fucker has eyes everywhere. Maybe including inside Mason's phone. Dammit. I screenshot the message on my burner phone and forward it to Mason.

I type: *Looks like you may be hacked.*

Within seconds, he calls me back, his voice tight with concern. *"Jena, are you okay?"*

"I'm fine," I say. "But I'm so sorry. About your phone. That I've dragged you into this."

Mason lets out a deep sigh. *"It's fine. I needed a new phone, anyway. I hope you're resting."*

"Yeah. I'm about to take that shower and have a hot tea."

"Okay, good. I'll talk to you soon."

As I hang up, my original phone rings. "Walking on Sunshine" by Katrina and the Waves. Mary is calling me.

"Hey," I answer.

On the other end, Mary's bawling. *"I still can't believe…you just…why didn't…"*

"Shh," I soothe. "It was the right thing to do. Thanks for coming to the hearing."

"I'm so mad at you."

"For the lie? Or for trying to get Silas out."

"Both." Mary sniffs. *"You and I know what Silas is."*

"I can't let Jack or anyone else die."

"And you're hoping with the kid comes something that will lead us to Azrael."

Mary knows me too well. "Yeah, that, too."

She sighs. *"If they make Jersey my new partner, I'm quitting."*

I give a small, mirthless laugh as I pull up Silas's and Dustin's case files. The only thing that will keep me from completely losing it is keeping busy. Time is running short, and I need something that points me to Dustin. I need to be ready if—*when* Silas is released.

Confidential Case Notes of Dr. Rachel Davis, Ph.D., Clinical Psychologist

[Audio Recording]

Recording Date: December 16, 2019

Location: SCI Fayette

Participants:

Silas Halvard, Inmate

Dr. Rachel Davis, Court-Appointed Psychologist

[*Click of a recording device*]

Dr. Davis: Good afternoon, Mr. Halvard. I hope you're doing well today.

Silas: I appreciate that, Doctor. I suppose I am as good as can be, given the hand I have been dealt. But call me Silas, if you don't mind.

Dr. Davis: I'll do that. Thank you. As you know, this is court-appointed therapy. And while it's not voluntary for us to be here together, your participation is, of course, up to you.

Silas: Got it. Do your magic, Doctor.

Dr. Davis: Well, I'm not sure about magic, but I hope I can give you some tools and insights that may help you cope with some of the emotional stressors you're no doubt facing.

Silas: Well, jail is no picnic, that is for sure. But I have my faith to lean on. I am not the kind of man who easily gets rattled.

Dr. Davis: Faith can be a wonderful support and way to cope with difficult situations. Before we go any further, I need to go through the informed consent process with you, okay?

Silas: Sure thing.

Dr. Davis: What's said in these sessions between us is confidential except for if you tell me you're in imminent danger of hurting yourself or someone else. I'm required to report that by law to the proper authorities.

Silas: Got it.

Dr. Davis: Also, if there's anything you share with me that the Warden would need to know about for the safety of his inmates, I may be required to report that as well.

Silas: Roger that.

Dr. Davis: I make use of recordings to help me recall our conversations for future sessions. These recordings are confidential and will be deleted once our sessions terminate. Is that okay with you?

Silas: That is fine by me.

Dr. Davis: Great. Now that we have that out of the way, let's dive in. I'd like to start at the beginning if you don't mind. Sometimes delving into the past can help us understand the influences that have shaped your current situation. Can you share anything about your childhood?

Silas: Let me set the record straight, Doctor. I am not guilty. I didn't do what they say I did. What got me here? Nothing but phony evidence. I am sure of it. As for my childhood, nothing much to talk about. Good folks, good home, nothing bad to speak of. Just the kind of upbringing you would expect from an innocent man done wrong.

Dr. Davis: I understand your frustration, Silas. I'm sorry to hear you were falsely accused.

Silas: You are just going through the motions.

Dr. Davis: No. I believe what you're experiencing is real.

Silas: But subjective.

Dr. Davis: Your guilt or innocence isn't the focus of these sessions. You tell me you're innocent, and I've heard you. But the fact is that you're facing a lengthy incarceration. I hope I can help you achieve and maintain mental well-being during your incarceration.

Silas: Well, I do appreciate that, Doctor. You have a good heart. I can see you are just trying to do right by your fellow man.

Dr. Davis: Everyone carries their own burdens, Silas. Inside or outside these walls. I'd like to fully understand your experiences so I can better help you. Were there any significant events or incidents during your early years that impacted you?

Silas: I hate to disappoint you, Doctor, but it was plain and simple. Nothing out of the ordinary. I wish I could point to something, something that would give us something to work with, but it is just not there. Close-knit family, loving parents, good times with the siblings, ball games on Sundays, and all that. Did all right in school, too. Became a scholar. Moved from New Orleans to Pittsburgh to work. Really, my faith is my rock. But I am curious, what about you? What is your faith like? I think it might help me trust you more if I knew.

Dr. Davis: I don't like to get into my personal circumstances or beliefs, as it's not relevant to our therapy sessions. But if it helps you, I'll share that I do respect the realm of faith and admire religious practitioners.

Silas: That is a roundabout way of saying you are not a believer, isn't it? I never could wrap my head around folks who don't see what God is offering. All that hope, all that healing. There has got to be something that eats at you. Something that needs a higher power to fix. You said it yourself; we all have struggles. So, what weighs on your mind?

Dr. Davis: [*A momentary pause*] While I appreciate your concern, it's not my place to talk about personal struggles. Our session centers on your well-being. Let's refocus on your experiences and how they have shaped your beliefs and actions.

Silas: Beliefs, huh? Well, I have always believed in atonement, Doctor. That heavy burden of guilt. That constant chase for redemption. You ever felt that? The weight of guilt pressing down on you, the hunger for absolution?

Dr. Davis: *[A long pause]* I'm sorry. I want to be transparent that your question puts me in a difficult position. I need to maintain the boundaries necessary for our therapeutic relationship.

Silas: I get it, Doctor. But you see, we are all searching for something. Something to take the edge off. Right now, I believe a little prayer might do me some good. Would you be willing to join me?

Dr. Davis: [*Throat clearing*] In the spirit of fostering a therapeutic relationship and addressing your needs, I'm willing to participate in a moment of prayer with you.

Silas: I appreciate it. If you could bow your head... My God, I am sorry for my sins, with all my heart...

[*The recording captures a long prayer session*]

Silas: Amen.

Dr. Davis: Amen. Thank you for sharing this moment with me. It's rare to witness such vulnerability and depth of emotion with my clients so quickly.

Silas: Your willingness to show some vulnerability means a lot to me, Doctor. Reminds me we are all in this together, each with our own battles to fight, our own faith to cling to.

Dr. Davis: That's very true. Life is often a bumpy journey, filled with darkness and uncertainty. We all must seek comfort in whatever sustains us. However, our shared goal toward understanding and wellness should remain our priority.

[*A long stretch of silence fills the recording*]

Dr. Davis: Silas, in this session, we've started to explore your beliefs. As we move forward, I hope we can maintain this open dialogue, allowing your thoughts and experiences to shape our path.

Silas: I am with you on that, Doctor. I feel a kinship with you, like there is a mutual respect and trust forming. I think these sessions could make a real difference in this dark time in my life.

Dr. Davis: I appreciate you saying that. Together, we'll continue to seek your truth, letting your experiences guide us. Your resilience and determination in facing your present circumstances are inspiring. And I'll support you through this difficult journey.

[*The recording fades out*]

[End of Audio Recording]

43

JENA

Thursday, 4:39 p.m.

THIS MORNING'S POST-CONVICTION relief hearing went exactly as predicted. Silas was clean, except what was found based on my false evidence. Everything recovered in his house because of the warrant had to be thrown out, just like Mason said. Fruit of the poison tree. Judge Spadina overturned Silas's conviction and returned him to SCI Fayette to wait for his release. I never understood why an inmate had to go back to jail after receiving a ruling that they be freed. Administrative stuff, I've been told. With Jack's release dependent on Silas's freedom, the lengthy process has never seemed stupider. But my wait is almost over, Silas's liberation imminent.

I watch it unfold on *Pittsburgh's Action News 4.* The media is in a frenzy, journalists swarming SCI Fayette, live aerial footage of the prison from overhead. It is on every channel. Interrupting everyone's game shows and soap operas and whatever else the few people who still have cable watch in the late afternoon.

My phone buzzes with a text from Mary. *They're releasing him.*

I type: *When?*

Now.

Text me if you hear anything about Jack's return.

I will.

Promise me.

I promise.

I turn my attention to the breaking news. The reporter is a stern-looking man with high cheekbones and a face like a blade. Someone who can make the most mundane matter sound grave. "Here at SCI Fayette, I'm told Silas Halvard will be released shortly. And today, one day after the fifth anniversary of Silas's incarceration, many of his followers are here to support him."

Whoever is in charge of the camera footage shows closeups of Silas's fan club holding up signs like god is good and believe. The video splices back to the reporter, who is interviewing an old man in a flannel jacket.

"We all knew Silas didn't do that murder." The old man grins, showing a mouthful of yellow teeth with a missing upper canine. "He's a good man. Five years he served, and for what? So the police had someone to pin those killings on to look like they were doing their job. Police corruption is the real problem here."

The reporter nods sympathetically. "And what do you think should happen now?"

"Can't nobody give him those years back. But the whole lot of us will follow that man wherever he goes." The old man makes a sweeping gesture at the crowd. "The Church of Silas. And this is the start-up congregation right here."

There is whooping and hollering from the horde. Cheers and applause.

The reporter touches his earpiece. "I've just received word that Silas is on his way out the front door of SCI Fayette."

The volume of the crowd rises to a fever pitch as the camera zooms in on the prison's entrance. The mechanical door slides open, revealing Silas in black pants and a black-collared shirt, a guard at each side. Silas steps forward, crossing the threshold that divides Fayette from the ordinary world. The two guards stay where they are.

Silas emerges into the afternoon sunlight. Uncuffed. Unshackled. Unrestrained. The sight of him as a free man turns my stomach.

His followers open their arms to receive him, and Silas stretches his hands out toward them, his cult-leader charisma in action. His right hand stays mostly closed. I see a glint of what is inside. One of the personal effects stripped from him when he was incarcerated.

A bloodred jasper stone.

Confidential Case Notes of Dr. Rachel Davis, Ph.D., Clinical Psychologist

[Audio Recording]

Recording Date: December 23, 2019

Location: SCI Fayette

Participants:

Silas Halvard, Inmate

Dr. Rachel Davis, Court-Appointed Psychologist

[*Click of a recording device*]

Dr. Davis: Good afternoon, Silas. I hope you're doing well.

Silas: Thank you, Doctor. Your visits are like a bright spot in some mighty dark days.

Dr. Davis: Let's pick up where we left off last time, okay?

Silas: Sure thing. But I can't help but notice something, Doctor. You seem to have some troubles weighing on your mind. I can see it. If you let it out, it might make me more inclined to share my own thoughts.

Dr. Davis: [*A short pause*] As we talked about before, Silas, this time is about you, not me. Let's keep the focus on your well-being.

Silas: Fair enough, Doctor. But I am picking up something in you. A heavy burden. Who do you talk to when you feel down? I can't help but be distracted. Maybe if you reveal it, I will be more inclined to open myself up, too.

Dr. Davis: [*A long pause]* I appreciate your concern, but boundaries are there for a reason. Our focus should be on your experiences.

Silas: I understand, Doctor. But you have to know, as a man of faith, I am here to listen and offer a moment of peace if you need it. It would give me a bit of relief, too, knowing I can trust that you will do the same for me.

Dr. Davis: [*A very long pause*] Silas, I... [*A sigh*] Okay. In the spirit of helping you see my humanity. I'll admit my husband was in a bad car accident six months ago. He's still recovering, and we don't know if he'll ever heal, in his body and mind. It's been hard.

Silas: Thanks for opening up, Doctor. I can hear the hurt in your voice. Let your faith be your guiding light in this storm. Trust in Him, and He will show you the way.

Dr. Davis: I have to say, you do have a way with words. It's like you have a deeper understanding than the rest of us.

Silas: We are all just trying to make our way through this rough and tumble life, Doctor. My calling is to help guide lost souls back to the path of redemption. Your dedication to your patients, your steadfast commitment, speaks volumes. Together, we can make our way through the darkness and find a brighter tomorrow.

Dr. Davis: Your words have a warmth that is truly comforting. I'm sure the other inmates appreciate it.

Silas: You are strong, Doctor, and your journey through this sea of grief will lead you to a renewed sense of purpose. Trust in the divine that is within you, and you will come out of the shadows stronger than ever. Maybe through our shared exploration, you can not only help me but also find your own healing and salvation.

Dr. Davis: Tell me, why do you want to give others this spark of hope? You seem to have a deep understanding of pain.

Silas: Faith is the key to transcending pain. We can all rise above our circumstances and reach for a higher purpose that is waiting for us.

Dr. Davis: You've certainly got a fire in you.

Silas: Have you ever looked beyond psychology to find meaning, Doctor? Can't you feel it right there, within reach?

[*A long silence*]

Silas: I think our searches for meaning and healing are on the same track. With faith and devotion, we can both rise. Don't you think we are kindred spirits, both driven by a shared purpose?

Dr. Davis: [*Throat clearing*]

Silas: As we walk this path together, let us be beacons of light, helping guide others toward their own redemption.

Dr. Davis: You have some compelling ideas. It's almost like you're the therapist and I'm the client. [*Nervous laughter*]

Silas: Doctor Davis, are you ready to explore the depths of faith and purpose that are waiting for us?

[*The recording fades out*]

[*End of Audio Recording*]

44

JENA

Thursday, 7:04 p.m.

SUNSET. MORE THAN two hours since Silas's release. I'm parked in my F-150, across the street and down a few car lengths from Silas's house. I keep my eyes trained on the exits. Front door. Windows. Sides of the house in case he leaves through the back door. No lights have flickered on inside yet.

I'm trying to be patient. Dustin set the deadline as midnight, and releasing a hostage takes time. But I can't stand the helplessness. No badge. No authority. I'm hamstrung, but I never did know when to stay down. I prepped to stay here all night to keep an eye on Silas. My night-vision goggles are on the floor of the passenger seat, my Sig P320 concealed beneath my jacket. But Silas hasn't come home.

I fire a text off to Mary: *Any news on Jack?*

Mary responds: *Nothing yet. I promised to let you know, remember?*

Right. Thanks. I close the text and put down my phone.

My stomach sinks. I knew I couldn't trust Dustin to keep his promise. He has had his chance. Time for me to take matters into my own hands. On personal bond or not.

A tap on the driver-side window interrupts the message I'm about to send. A young police officer glares at me through the tint. I recognize him, but don't remember his first name. His name tag says T. Yeobright. It doesn't help jog my memory. I roll down the window.

"You can't be here," he says, eyebrows squished together.

"It's public property," I muster, keeping my gaze locked with his. Not glancing at Silas's house. Definitely not glancing down at the night-vision goggles.

"Move along," he says. "This isn't your fight anymore."

I nod, working to hide the burn of humiliation in my cheeks from this rookie. Sitting outside Silas's house has been fruitless anyway. "No problem. I'm going. Have a good night, Officer Yeobright."

I start the engine and drive away. Slowly. Taking my time. A bit of a middle finger to the rookie, maybe, but I'm not breaking any laws. I take a left, keep going for a few blocks, then pull over again. Time to send that message.

I open my alternate social media account on my burner phone and type a DM.

Dear Dustin,

I met your demands. Silas is a free man. Let the kid go.

~ Little Bird

Dustin responds almost immediately.

Dear little bird,

But he's the completion to my magnum opus. The best way to honor our heroes is by outshining their deeds. Don't you think?

Here's to becoming legendary,

~ Azrael

I fling my phone onto the passenger seat with a snarl. He is going to kill Jack. Even though Silas is free. He'll stay in hiding, and go on killing, giving my team nothing. And Silas will kill, too. Making my confession good for nothing except destroying my life. My rage dragon is roaring, bringing down an avalanche of rocks and stalactites from inside his cave. But I need to find my calm so I can think. I breathe in through my nose and out through pursed lips. Why demand Silas's freedom if that wasn't the goal? Or not the only goal?

Because he wanted Silas to see what he was going to do. No, he wanted Silas to help with the last victim. For it to be their shared final victim.

Dustin wanted Silas free so they could meet. The realization sends a shot of adrenaline through me, my leg juddering up and down like a jackhammer.

But where would they meet?

I retrieve my phone and text Mary again: *Does anyone have eyes on Silas?*

We don't, Mary responds. *Captain's orders. He's a free man. We have one patrol near his house to make sure no one bothers him, but that's it. Wouldn't look good for us to hound him right now with all his followers ready to riot and the media buzzing. He left Fayette with a crowd. He's probably out drinking Kool-Aid with his new churchgoers.*

Shit. Shit, shit, shit, shit, shit.

I keep trying to breathe from my diaphragm, but the air gets stuck in my throat. I'm pissed at myself for being so stupid. And for continuing to be so stupid. I have no clue where Silas is. Whether he and Dustin are meeting. Where they would meet. How they would have communicated that to each other…

Wait. How they communicated with each other.

The Bible verses. Silas's words resurface to haunt me.

What does it mean, little bird? What does it mean?

Sweat drips down my spine inside my t-shirt. I can't remember exactly what the verse said. Something about an altar. But I have copies of the originals. I scoop up my phone and reopen the photos Kyle shared. I zero in on the two we couldn't figure out.

Isaiah 40:40, Every valley shall be lifted up, and every mountain and hill be made low; the uneven ground shall become level, and the rough places a plain.

Isaiah 27:9, So in this way Jacob's sin will be forgiven, and this is how they will show they are finished sinning: They will make all the stones of the altars like crushed limestone, and the Asherah poles and the incense altars will no longer stand.

And then there are the pen strokes cut off at the bottom.

Valleys. Mountains. And Silas recited the words about the limestone. I have a hunch forming deep in my gut, and my hunches are almost always right. If Silas and Dustin are meeting for a joint killing, it must be tonight. The tenth plague day. The killing of the firstborn son.

I think back to the floors in the governor's house, those

Pittsburgh-limestone floors common to so many homes. Every Pittsburgh local knows where the stones come from. Including Silas. I open Google Maps and type in Ridge Limestone Quarry, Saltsburg, PA. As the address loads, the memory of the map to the quarry I found in Silas's basement haunts me.

When the program locates the quarry, I click to find the coordinates.

Latitude: 40.58 2693 8436 6419 5

Longitude: 79.38 7789 9310 6939

I scramble to find an old receipt and a pen in my glove box, then hurry to write the coordinates down. Then I hold the paper up to the pen strokes cut off at the bottom of the Bible verse. Despite the different handwriting, it is a close match. My pulse is beating bongo drums in my throat. Dustin and Silas are on their way to a quarry. The perfect spot for a stoning. Possibly the spot Silas had picked out for his twelfth victim. Maybe that was why he had the quarry map.

I have to let Captain Price know, get the team deployed, stat. I have no time to lose. Jack's life is hanging by a thread.

Then a message pops up on my phone screen. From the @*azrael* account. I swallow hard, my fingers shaking. I'm already too late.

DISCIPLINARY ACTIONS – March 2020

PENNSYLVANIA STATE BOARD OF PSYCHOLOGY

Allegheny County
Joe Forthe, Ph.D.

Joe Forthe's license, license no. PS006384L, of Pittsburgh, Allegheny County, was suspended for one year, stayed in favor of probation, because he is unable to practice the profession with reasonable skill and safety by reason of illness, drunkenness, excessive use of drugs, narcotics, chemicals, or any other type of material, or as a result of any mental or physical condition. (3/4/20)

Rachel Davis, Ph.D. (former member)

A hearing before a Panel of the Discipline Committee of the Pennsylvania State Board of Psychology took place in Pittsburgh on March 6, 2020 concerning allegations of professionalmisconduct against Rachel Davis, license no. PS005015L, of Pittsburgh, Allegheny County.

STATEMENT OF AGREED FACTS:
As stated in a statement of agreed facts,

1. Dr. Rachel Davis was a psychologist and licensed to practice psychology in Pennsylvania until 2020.
2. In 2019 Dr. Davis was employed as a Staff Psychologist at a State penitentiary in LaBelle, Pennsylvania, where she provided psychological services to inmates.

3. Between December 2019 and February 2020, Dr. Davis provided these services to a male inmate who was serving a life sentence for first-degree murder.
4. On February 14, 2020, the inmate's cell was found unlocked. Following a search of his cell, Dr. Davis's Access Card was recovered, along with a collapsible ladder and grappling hook, likely for use to scale the perimeter fences. Dr. Davis had reported that she forgot the Access Card at home on this day.
5. The inmate had the means for possible escape, however, the inmate stated that Dr. Davis's conduct and attempt to aid in an escape were unwanted actions and reported them to a prison guard.
6. When questioned about this, Dr. Davis broke down, insisting that she acted because the inmate was innocent and did not deserve to be incarcerated for life. Dr. Davis was arrested and taken into custody.
7. Two days later, Dr. Davis was charged with attempting to arrange a prison escape, to which she pleaded guilty. She was convicted and sentenced to four months in prison.
8. Shortly afterward, Dr. Davis resigned her membership with the PA Board of Psychology.
9. The Panel notes that Dr. Davis's lack of personal and professional judgment, her inappropriate professional relationship with her client and her subsequent actions were serious breaches of ethical and professional standards which put a vulnerable client in a moral dilemma. It is fortunate that, in this case,

the inmate showed higher ethical standards than Dr. Davis by reporting the incident to the appropriate authorities.

(3/6/20)

45

JENA

Thursday, 7:16 p.m.

JACK'S DEAD. THAT is the thought-spiral of doom my brain is tail-spinning down. When I open my DM, there is a video frozen on an image of Jack tied to a gurney, along with a message. I read the message first.

Dear PBP,

Oh wow. It's not addressed to me. Dustin sent the message to the entire police department. My heart seizes in my chest, but I force myself to keep reading, slouching down in the driver's seat.

> *What's a better spot to hide out in than one that's already been searched? Trick question. The answer is, none!*
>
> *Do you remember that delightful little apartment where you sent your fine SWAT officers to look for Jack? Great waterfront view, right? And you know what they say the key factor is in real estate. Location, location, location! That baby is the*

perfect home base to hang out in before a meetup. You can sneak out by tunnel, bridge, boat, or car! After that, it's easy to disappear among 22,000 people.

That's right. The Pirates game is going on! And they're winning. Against the Phillies! Great to keep things local, don't you think? What better place to unleash the final plagues but in front of such an incredible fanbase? And the best part? They won't be spectators for long. I've always believed nothing ups the hype of a finale like audience participation.

Okay. Enough talky talk. Gotta run. It's my first blind date. I'm so nervous! Do you think Leviticus will like me?

~ Azrael

I tap the video and watch Jack immobile on the screen. He is strapped to a gurney in the apartment we stormed with the SWAT team. The lighting is dim, casting an eerie glow over the flotsam and the peeling wallpaper that clings desperately to the walls. Jack's peacefulness is unnatural, his chest rising and falling in a steady rhythm. His eyes are closed, his head lolling from side-to-side. Probably sedated.

The scene shifts. Jack is now slumped in the passenger seat of a nondescript sedan, its engine humming as the car glides through the streets. A jammed parking lot flickers into view through the window behind him, bathed in the orange hue of the setting sun. The air outside carries the faint buzz of anticipation, the electric atmosphere that comes before a big event.

As the car turns a corner, the camera angle captures a glimpse of PNC Park in the distance. Its distinctive yellow exterior walls and black steel support beams rise like a fortress against the darkening sky. Shadows stretch across the pavement, and the rumble of the crowd grows louder, their voices melding into a single, pulsating beat.

The video cuts once more and Jack reappears, this time slouched in a wheelchair. His head hangs low, but his breathing remains steady. A pair of gloved hands—I presume Dustin's—grips the handles, propelling him forward with purposeful strides. They weave through a sea of fans, excited chatter bubbling up among arms spilling with popcorn and hot dogs. The crowd, clad in team colors, waving pennants and foam hands, is a blur of faces, their attention focused on socializing as they find their seats.

Jack and his captor move deeper into the stadium, swallowed by the throngs of people, their presence going unnoticed as the tension in the air mounts. A voice-over starts up. A woman with a British accent speaking in the didactic tone used for educational videos. It is a text-to-speech, and I'm sure Dustin programmed it to say whatever the hell he wants it to say.

"Bomb innovation requires artistry combined with explosive power," the voice-over begins. "A propulsive force large enough to destroy the intended targets."

"An impressive bomb will soon detonate for your viewing pleasure. A cloud of destruction that will obliterate whoever gets in its way—baseball players, security guards, law enforcement, 22,000 fans —while providing spectacular entertainment. Please prepare yourselves for the post-game fireworks."

It makes me sick. I need to focus on Jack, but all I can think of right now is that Mason is at that game. I want to punch myself for telling him to go to the game instead of spending the night with me. My stubbornness, my need to always put on a strong façade, could mean his life.

The voice-over changes to Dustin's distorted vocals. "*Where are we, Pittsburgh Bureau of Police? Can you track down our tickets? Pinpoint the location of the bomb I hid? Maybe I stuffed it under the stands. It's easy to sneak things in when escorting a poor unfortunate soul in a wheelchair. Pity causes people to overlook so much. Luckily, I'm lacking in the sympathy department. And that's what will make me great. What will help me carve my name into the history books in the biggest, boldest font. Happy hunting, Pittsburgh's finest!*"

And then, the video ends with a green screen shot of a mushroom cloud over the stadium.

46

JACK

Thursday, 7:27 p.m.

JACK'S MIND DRIFTS in a daze, the muffled roar of a thousand voices echoing in his mind. He can almost hold on to the scent of fresh-cut grass, can nearly taste the stale popcorn clinging to his tongue. But the outside world keeps slipping away. There is a crack like a baseball bat smacking a ball. And then he remembers. He is at PNC Park, lost among the crowd.

A cold, shivering presence clings to his skin, pulling him down into darkness. He feels motion, someone pushing his wheelchair up an incline, but then the slope changes direction and he is sliding down. He hits the ground. A jarring impact. The cold creeps in, pressing down, surrounding him bit by bit.

Jack can't open his eyes. Metal hits dirt. Labored breathing next to his ears. A gradual weight embraces him, squeezing tighter, trapping him. He starts to panic and flail. Dirt. That's what is encasing him. He is being buried. The dirt is up to his chest, the load compressing his lungs. Making breathing a battle. Each inhale more difficult than the last.

"Shh," Shadow whispers, a haunting lullaby that sends a

shiver skittering down his spine. "It's okay, Jack. This will all be over soon. You'll finally be able to rest."

Rest. The thought brings a tsunami of terror, followed by an ebb of relief. Maybe death would be a welcome comfort. Freedom from this torment. The sounds of the stadium surround him, whispers of exhilaration coming from far away.

A faint melody reaches his ears. A familiar tune he struggles to grasp, the notes guiding him back from darkness.

Bah dah bah bah-dah baaaahh daahh. "Take me out to the ball...game."

Shadow is humming, the melody accompanied by the rhythmic thudding of Jack's heartbeat. He has never heard a sound so terrifying.

As darkness threatens to consume him, Jack summons his failing strength. He clenches his right hand into a fist and releases it, the earth giving way beneath his fingertips. With deliberate, shaky movements, he moves his hand in small circles, careful not to give himself away as he displaces the damp soil. It is a silent act of defiance, a whisper of hope in the face of despair.

Shadow continues to hum, the notes haunting the void. Jack can't help but listen to the tune, his mind clinging to the song's familiarity. The song is a lifeline despite the way Shadow's voice twists a sweet memory of happier days.

Jack continues to work his hand, soil shifting, grit collecting beneath his fingernails. Each rotation grants him another sliver of space. It isn't much. It likely won't be enough. But it is all he has.

47

JENA

Thursday, 7:31 p.m.

I CLOSE THE video, the mushroom cloud over the stadium disappearing off the phone screen. My heart is pounding, my mind racing. No way Dustin brought Jack to PNC Park. It makes no sense. I'm confident in the information I've pieced together about the quarry. The baseball game is a decoy. A distraction. Right? It has to be… Mason…

I dial Mason's number on my burner phone. No answer. Shit, shit, shit. I try again, then send a text: *Call me. Urgent.*

I need to get to Collins. See if the video is a fake. I switch back to my original phone and dial his direct line. It rings, rings, rings. No answer. My muscles tense, my shoulders raising up to my ears as I dial again. Same thing. I dial again.

"Campbell," Collins clucks. *"I'm a little busy."*

"The video."

"Yes, ma'am. That's what's got me in overdrive."

"Is it faked? I mean, you checked, right? That the footage is real?"

"Of course I checked. It's real."

I pause, my mind turning over the new info.

"Anything else, ma'am? I'm scrambling and, no offense, I'm not supposed to be talking to you since you don't work for us anymore."

"No, that's all. Thanks, Collins. For taking my call, I mean."

"Once a brother, always a brother."

I suppose I should feel honored at the Marine sentiment. I'm about to hang up when something strikes me. "Wait."

"Ma'am?"

"Is the video from today? Did he record it today?"

Collins hesitates, and I hear the clicking of keys. *"No way to tell. He's scrubbed the time stamp."*

"Thank you. I mean it. Thanks a million. I owe you one."

"You realize you're making that promise to a Marine, right? I might collect on it someday."

"Noted."

"I really need to go, ma'am."

With that, Collins hangs up. Already, I've pulled the video back up on my phone, and I'm rewatching it, the footage of Jack in the wheelchair. He looks too healthy. Rosy-cheeked. I'd bet my F-150 that isn't a recent video. I pull up the video of Jack that Dustin live-streamed as Captain Rock. Jack is thinner. His cheekbones sharp. Skin pallid. I'm 100 percent on this. Well, at least 99. That is an old video.

My next call is to Captain Price. He doesn't pick up. I call a second, third, fourth, fifth, sixth time. Dammit. Either he is in emergency mode with this crisis, too overwhelmed to answer, or he has disowned me. I leave him a message, then call the next best thing. Mary. She doesn't pick up the first time either, but I get her on the third try.

"Jena!" she shouts over the wail of sirens. *"I can't talk now."*

"I saw the video."

"What? Did you say video?"

"Right. I think it's a decoy."

"Yes, exactly," she barks over the blaring bells. *"That's why we had to deploy."*

"Not deploy. Decoy. Decoy!" The knot in my stomach tightens.

"A bomb. Sweet mother, he wants to kill the whole stadium. The entire department's been mobilized. I gotta go."

And just like that, Mary is gone. Fuck. I shoot her a text, even though I'm not sure she'll see it. *Pretty sure PNC is a decoy. I think Jack is at Ridge Limestone Quarry. Remember the map we found in Silas's basement? Please call me!*

Flooded with adrenaline, I squeeze my phone, palms sweating. I go down the line calling every number I have. Jersey. Weisz. Dale. No answer. I send them all the same text. I call the clerk, but he refuses to relay any messages on my behalf.

My body shakes, my skin flaring with heat. I clench and unclench my fists, considering my options. The way I see it, there are only two. Do nothing, or follow my hunch. My gut says I'm right about this. I close my eyes, taking deep breaths. It is okay. Everything is going to be okay. Because I'm going to make it that way.

I glance down at my night-vision goggles and pat my Sig P320, the gun's weight a comfort as I throw the truck into drive and floor it.

48

JENA
Thursday, 8:06 p.m.

I'M FLYING EAST on I-376 in the Ford F-150, speeding well over the limit. Weaving between lanes, I hope I don't get pulled over. Wouldn't that be ironic? I'd laugh at the thought if Dustin hadn't torn every shred of humor from me in the last ten days.

The quarry is over an hour away, but not with the way I'm driving.

I keep calling Mason on the burner, but he is not picking up. I want to punch my steering wheel. Anger would be far better than the panic that has overtaken me. But I need to focus on my reckless driving.

The further I get from the heart of Pittsburgh, the more the traffic thins. When I-376 turns to 22—or Old William Penn Highway—there is almost no one on the road. I turn left onto Sardis, taking it easy on the accelerator as the streets become more country and less well lit.

Finally, Mason calls back. The background noise is chaotic, a melee of distraught voices and police sirens.

"What's going on?" I can't help the way my voice pitches up and cracks.

"It's madness!" he shouts over the crowd. *"They got the players out first, of course. I'm trying to get out, but—"*

Mason cuts out, only screams and sirens coming through.

"—evacuation is a joke."

I exhale hard, relieved to hear him again.

"People are stampeding, and the swarm of police—"

More cries and shouts. I think I hear a megaphone. I stare at the phone, willing Mason back on.

"—isn't enough to keep control."

I've been glaring at the phone so hard I've drifted, my wheels crunching over the gravel shoulder.

"Wait, are you driving?!" he yells. *"Where are you? You're not coming here, right?"*

I wince, guilt gnawing at me. "No. Ridge Limestone Quarry. I think I figured it out and Jack is there. Silas had a quarry map in his basement when we arrested him. Could be Dustin and Silas are planning a joint kill. I don't know."

Mason's voice is laced with worry. *"Jena, don't play hero. Did you call it in? Are the police on their way?"*

"No. I tried, but the entire force is at the stadium. If I'm right, there's no time."

There is a sound like thousands of footsteps thundering on concrete before Mason comes back on. *"Are any of your colleagues letting you in on what's going on here?"*

Ex-colleagues, I think to myself. "No. Guess they have their hands full."

"Yeah. Yeah, they do. I'll keep you up to date."

"Get the hell out of there, Mason. I'm serious."

"I'm trying," he says, his voice strained. *"It's not easy with all these people trampling each other like a pack of elephants."*

"I wish I was with you."

"I'm glad you're not. I mean—"

The roar of the crowd surges.

"Mason, please, do whatever it takes to get out."

"I will."

My mind races. What if I'm wrong? What if Jack is at the stadium, not the quarry? What if there is really a bomb in the stadium? I can't bear the thought of losing Mason.

"I'm going to make a run for it. I'll leave the phone on speaker, okay?"

"Okay."

When he switches the phone over to speaker, the sounds of the frightened crowd turn deafening, shouts of chaos and confusion.

Over the other voices, Mason yells, *"Damn it!"* and my stomach flips.

"What's wrong?!" I shout. He doesn't respond, and my heart punches up and out of my throat as I yell, "Mason?! Mason!! Mason?!!!"

49

JENA

Thursday, 8:29 p.m.

NO REPLY FROM Mason. I can't think straight, and nearly pull over on the shoulder to turn around. But then I hear the phone rubbing against his face before he answers, still on speaker.

"Shit." Mason makes grunting sounds.

"Mason?!"

"I'm here. It's my ankle. Got knocked down. I—" There is more grunting, then, *"I'm in a corner. Safe, for now."*

There is a boom and I slam the brakes. The bomb has gone off. I know it. But then there is…a guitar riff? Another boom underneath the music, and another. Rhythmic. Heavy metal.

"What the hell is going on?" I screech.

Mason is shouting into the phone. *"There's a video. On the jumbotron. Wait, I'll call you back on FaceTime so you can see."*

"No! Mason! Just go! Go!!"

But he has already hung up. As I start driving again, I can't hold back punching things anymore, opting for the dashboard over the steering wheel. Don't want to hit the horn and announce my presence on the dirt road. I'm about five minutes away from the quarry, so I kill the headlights.

When the call connects again, I shake out my hand, my knuckles throbbing. I see a view of the jumbotron on Mason's phone camera. I struggle to keep my eyes on the road as I watch the screen. It is Dustin in darkened silhouette, using his favorite green screen trick to show different types of bomb detonations in the background. His distorted voice echoes over the heavy metal blaring in the background. I think I recognize the song. It is one Papich plays a lot. "Angel of Death" by Slayer. I don't like the implication of that title. Not at all.

"Hello, ladies and gentlemen of Pittsburgh's law enforcement community. Shall we play a game? Hmm? I love a good scavenger hunt. Where is the bomb, dear officers? I've left you some clues, if you can find them in time."

I don't catch what else Dustin is saying because I'm screaming at Mason. "Listen to me! You have to get out, now! Please. Just get the fuck out of there."

"I know. I will. After. Ah, crap. My ankle's not doing so great."

I'm maybe two minutes from the quarry now. I pull off the dirt road into a tall copse of trees to hide my truck. I turn off the engine, hunching over the steering wheel, my breath heaving like I've run a marathon. I'm paralyzed. I don't know what to do. Stay with Mason and watch the video or go to the quarry?

There is only one right answer. Only one where I can make a difference.

"Mason. Please. Get out. I'm at the quarry. Jack needs me. And if Dustin is here, maybe I can stop whatever is going on there. I have to… I can't… Just please, get out. Please. I don't know what I'd do without you."

Mason's voice is calm. Too calm for my liking. *"Okay. I… I think I can. I see the stairs. I'll go. Now. I promise. You've got this. And don't you leave me after what you just said, you hear me? I can't live without you, either."*

I open my mouth to tell him I love him, but the line is dead.

50

JENA

Thursday, 8:48 p.m.

I HOP OUT of the truck, greeted by the quiet of the night. Crickets. The hoot of a night owl. The rustle of a breeze through high grass. The remoteness of the area sends chills up the back of my neck. It is just me and my hunch out here. No partner. No backup. No police available to show up, and no way that they could make it in time now, even if they were free. At least one person listened to me. Mason. But I need to put him from my thoughts, lock him up in a different compartment of my mind if I'm going to do this job well.

I take a few steps forward, getting my bearings. The terrain would be challenging enough to navigate in the daylight, but the night has cranked this obstacle course up to eleven. Weak moonlight fails to break through a blanket of cloud cover, giving almost no visibility. Not wanting to risk anyone spotting a flashlight, I pull on my night-vision goggles and see my surroundings in various shades of green. I draw my gun, taking no chances of getting caught unaware or unprepared.

I hoof it to the quarry, conscious of every second ticking

away. Soon, I come to a no trespassing sign nailed to a tree. The warning hangs next to a heavy chain stretched across the gravel road to prevent unauthorized vehicles. I slow my approach to a crawl, taking stock of the place.

I move in a low crouch and stay a few feet away from the road, although it hardly counts as a road. It is more like a muddy rut carved out by the wheels of heavy equipment, with the occasional sprinkling of gravel. Enough for one-way traffic.

I cross the threshold into the quarry, and my line of sight is blocked in every direction by gigantic machinery. There is a contraption to my right with an inclined conveyor belt that looks like it is meant to separate rocks into a giant bin. Beyond that, there is an excavator and a massive quarry truck. To my left, a front loader and a bulldozer. The pits are difficult to see, even with the goggles, but there are at least three. I don't see any movement. No silhouettes creeping through the night.

The closest pit is by the excavator, perhaps ten feet in front, and five feet from the quarry truck. Maybe less. I sneak over, cursing the gravel each time it crunches beneath my feet and risks giving me away. Using the massive machine for cover, I slide along the side until I'm hidden behind the sharp teeth of the bucket. The heavy-duty scoop rests with the top of its head on the ground. I hold my breath and listen. For a minute, the only sound is the blood rushing past my ears. But then there is faint moaning, the shuffle of feet over gravel.

My guts clench and then release in an explosion of butterflies. An internal *"I told you so."* My hunch was right. They're here. I take off my shoes to make my approach silent; they won't hear me coming in my socks as I step quietly toward the pit. I keep my weight on the balls of my feet, the rocks sharp and cutting as I move, but pain is a small price to pay for the element of surprise. When I'm near the edge, I flatten myself, chest to the ground, counting on the darkness to hide me. I inch toward the lip until I get a view of what is inside the hole through the hazy green of my night-vision goggles.

Fifteen feet below, Jack is exposed from the middle of his chest up, the rest of him buried beneath the dirt, including his arms. He appears to be sedated, his head lolling back as he moans. A ring of tangerine-size rocks surrounds him. The perfect size and shape for close-range hurling. Not much smaller than the softballs I pitched in college. Scanning him, then the steep sides of the pits, I realize how difficult it will be to get him out of there. Impossible, if both Dustin and Silas are in action. They'll need to be neutralized. But right now, I only see Dustin in the pit, pacing back and forth like a caged animal.

He is waiting for Silas. He wants his mentor's participation, a final touch to his masterpiece. But Silas isn't here. Looks like my hunch was half-wrong; Silas hasn't shown up. How long will Dustin wait before he ends Jack's life?

51

JENA

Thursday, 9:11 p.m.

DUSTIN STOPS PACING and moves over to a folding tray table that holds a laptop and ring light, both of them off. There is other equipment below the table. A remote maybe? I can't be sure from this distance. Looks like he is planning to live stream the main event.

It is like Dustin can read my mind because he leans over and turns on the laptop. The screen casts a bright glow in my goggles, and I need to squint to see. The laptop screen shows PNC Park and the swarm of police cars surrounding it. Dustin's watching the scene with the sound muted. He murmurs something to Jack I can't make out, but his tone is filled with glee.

Dustin clicks something on the laptop, I assume to start recording, but I can't be sure. His ring light is still off. Then he picks up a rock. I take careful aim with my Sig P320. The Sig has a different feel than my Glock service pistol, which I'm more comfortable and practiced with, and this isn't a shot I can miss. Dustin winds up, drawing his arm behind his head. I inhale, ready to pull the trigger.

Before I can shoot, a blur, green-tinted in my goggles, hits my hand. Pain shoots up my arm as my bones crunch. I cry out and drop the gun. I roll onto my left side, looking to see what the hell hit me. A baseball-size rock lies next to me on the ground. White-hot heat flames through my hand. Two fingers are definitely broken. Maybe three. I'm in a lot of fucking trouble. I don't see my gun anywhere. It would be a challenge to fire it well left-handed, even if I could find it. And I can't breathe, afraid of where the rock came from.

I peer into the night in the most likely direction, looking at the scoop of the excavator, which stands out bright green against the background. I don't see anything, but I'm conscious of Dustin in the pit below, and that if he had a way down, he has a way up. I'm about to make a run for the excavator when I see motion. A figure descends the front stairs of the quarry truck next to the excavator. Silas, also wearing fucking night-vision goggles. His arm flings, like he is pointing at me. I see the rock's green streak before it hits my goggles dead center. My vision turns to static. I'm on my feet, running blind, scrambling for what I hope is the cover of the excavator. I keep my broken hand sweeping in front of me as I tear off my shattered goggles with the other. When I rip them free, I see the glint of the metal machine in the feeble moonlight right before I take a hard strike to the back of the head. *Damn, Silas has a good arm*, is all I can think as my vision dances with stars and my knees give out.

52

JENA

Thursday, 9:32 p.m.

I WAKE FIFTEEN feet below ground level in the bottom of the pit. The moonlight slices through the cloud cover, offering me the gift of sight. It is cold, my breath expelling in ragged puffs of frost, my heart pumping overtime inside my shivering body. The back of my head and my broken fingers scream with pain. My vision is a carousel of starbursts, my body spinning with vertigo. But I'm alive. That is more than I expected. I inhale through my nose, thankful I'm conscious and alert, despite the circumstances.

My back is pressed against the wall of the pit, my wrists secured behind me, bound with zip ties. As much as I despise the cold, I'm also grateful for it. Makes escaping plastic bindings a hell of a lot easier. I blink away the disco lights inside my eyelids and focus on the people in front of me.

Dustin and Silas stand five feet away with their backs to me, their silhouettes illuminated by the glow of a monitor. Nearby, just outside the screen's light, Jack moans, weak and pitiful. On the screen, there is an aerial shot of the chaos inside the stadium.

Must be one of Dustin's drones shooting the footage. Pittsburgh police search the area. Probably looking for Dustin's bomb.

"Exciting, isn't it?" Dustin asks, his voice dripping with anticipation.

"As if we are witnessing a biblical revelation," Silas replies. There is underlying sarcasm in his voice, but Dustin appears to miss the subtlety.

I need to get out of these zip ties and stop whatever is about to happen. And I need to do it quietly.

Before I can make a move, a wicked chuckle slices through the air. Dustin holds his hand out to Silas, revealing a remote control. "Show time!"

The picture on the screen changes to a closer shot of the jumbotron behind one section of stands. Dustin presses a button on the remote, and I hold my breath. Waiting for the detonation.

But the explosion doesn't come. Instead the jumbotron expels a massive, shimmering cloud. For a moment, it looks beautiful, spreading over the striped grass of the playing field, before its trajectory sends whatever it is made up of slicing through the crowd. Spots of red appear as wounds open on skin, people dropping to their knees, uselessly swatting at the glimmer.

Dustin leans in closer to the monitor, pointing to the shimmering cloud. "You know what that is? It is made up of fine silica shards. They're cutting through the fans like a hot knife through butter. Goooooooo, Pirates!"

A beam of light shoots from the jumbotron, projecting a holographic angel with a massive wingspan onto the death cloud.

If the crowd wasn't hysterical before, it is in an absolute frenzied pandemonium now. People crashing into each other, dropping, rolling, swiping at the air.

Dustin pumps his fist. "Now that's what I call entertainment!"

Silas clicks his tongue. "You revel in the chaos of now, but Ecclesiastes says, 'There is nothing new under the sun.' True artistry seems lost on the young."

As I watch Dustin's drone zoom in on different people, I feel sick to my stomach. The drone's picking up the heavy metal music still playing in the background, the only good part about it that it is drowning out most of the screams. I can't help scanning the faces for Mason, praying he got out of the stadium in time.

My heart clenches, but I can't look away. People screaming and writhing in pain as glass shards tear through flesh. Blood stains the ground, and the wounded struggle to escape the deadly cloud. The agonized cries of the injured blend with the escalating heavy metal soundtrack, creating a horrifying shriek of suffering and chaos.

Family members try to shield their loved ones, only to fall victim to the glass storm themselves. A mother cradles her injured child, her own face covered in cuts as she weeps blood. A young couple clings to each other, their bodies riddled with deep gashes, their clothes torn and soaked in crimson. The stampede of petrified people tramples over those who have fallen, limp limbs flinging upward under the pressure of a stomping.

As the holographic angel of death looms over the stadium, its glittering wings spread wider and the panicked crowd surges and pushes, trying to escape the carnage. Some are crushed against walls and barriers in their attempt to flee, while others are tossed over railings, bodies crashing onto the unforgiving concrete below.

The relentless glass rain continues to spread havoc. The

injured stagger and crawl, leaving trails of blood in their wake. The avatar may be an angel, but it is a scene straight out of hell.

The picture zooms in on a few Pittsburgh Police, gas masks on, trying to help usher people out in an orderly fashion, but it is a losing battle. The cloud is coming for the fans.

I'd recognize the shortest officer anywhere. Mary. I can only watch in horror as she pulls her mask off and gives it to a small boy, maybe five years old, strapping it onto his head, before red lines streak her face. I think of her husband, her two-year old daughter, and want to scream at her for being such a soft-hearted idiot. She'd better not die. I couldn't bear it. My insides are screaming in tormented rage. But I need to stay silent, even as the tears prick my eyes.

Dustin watches with an unsettling rocking motion, clearly enjoying every moment of the destruction he has caused.

Silas looks unimpressed, picking at a fingernail. "Quite the show you are putting on," Silas says, his voice now dripping with sarcasm. "Are you hoping for a standing ovation?"

Dustin isn't aware of Silas's barb, his eyes glued to the monitor. "Here's to becoming legendary," he whispers to himself.

I clench my jaw, trying to block out Mary's torn up face. *Keep it together, Jena*, I silently plead with myself. I need to save Jack and make it back to Mason. To bring Dustin to justice for what he has done.

Pressing my back hard into the wall of the pit, I tuck my knees into my chest, passing my zip-tied wrists beneath my stocking feet to bring my bound hands in front of me. Then, I bring my hands to my mouth and bite hard on the strip of excess plastic, yanking the cuffs even tighter, thanking whatever god is listening for the cold weather that shrinks my wrists. I raise my hands, praying the heavy metal in the stadium masks the sound as I slam the piece of plastic joining my wrists onto a sharp rock. The zip ties pop open. Skin scrapes off. The impact sends a flash of pain shooting through my broken fingers. I bite the inside of my cheek to keep from crying out.

"What is that?" Silas says, and I'm sure I'm caught. I'm too close to them. They must have heard.

Waiting curled up, I tense my muscles, ready to spring and make a run for it.

But then I see he is pointing at the screen. To me.

What the hell?

The drone shot tightens, showing my face, gouged and bleeding.

53

JENA

Thursday, 9:49 p.m.

"WHAT KIND OF foolery are you pulling?"

Silas's statement echoes my thoughts.

"How's that for true artistry? This is the future. Virtual horror."

"You are saying this isn't happening in real life?"

"Not yet. I wanted you to experience what I can bring to the table before I bring on the biggest ninth plague of darkness you've ever seen. The news will block out all the good parts. Sanitize it for viewer consumption. But the theatrical version I'll air afterward… People around the world will see the beauty of what really happened with my masterpiece. It'll go viral. Everyone will know what I'm capable of."

"Well, now." Silas says. "Isn't that something."

It sure is. It means there is still a chance to shut the glass death cloud down.

"Thanks," Dustin says. "Think of what I can do in the future. How I can manipulate and terrorize. But hey, you're the godfather. It never would've happened without your inspiration. I read about it in the news, and it lit a fire under me."

"So, you did your homework on me, huh?" Silas says. "Then you should know my reasons. But I don't know yours. Tell me, why did you take out those jurors? Why kill all the folks in the stadium?"

"They're the means to an end," Dustin says, head cocked to the side, appraising his hero, Silas. "The steps on the path to immortality. Does it matter?"

"Humor me. One straight answer. What did Jack do to deserve what you did to him?"

"Nothing," Dustin says. "But this is what you wanted, right? One last kill to be legendary? Think about it. We'll go down in history, completing the last kill of our mission together. It's never been done before, bringing two solo quests together for the final endgame. Isn't it beautiful?"

Dustin pushes a button on his remote, and the monitor changes, showing *Pittsburgh's Action News 4.*

The stadium is still chaos. The stampede of fans mashes up against the police, trying to control them.

I need to get that remote away from Dustin. Stop the death cloud. Save the people in the stadium. I scan the pit for my gun, but don't see it anywhere.

"Let's do this last one together," Dustin says. "You your way, and me mine." He flips on the ring light and presses what appears to be a recording button on the laptop.

Silas's profile is illuminated, and he has a rock in each hand. That realization makes my guts churn. He is staying out of the camera's line of sight.

"Ready?" Dustin says, his thumb hovering over a red button. "Three..."

Jack groans, but no one is paying attention to him except me. I can't wait any longer.

"Now just hold on a minute," Silas says.

"Two."

No gun, but no choice.

I charge Dustin. Drive my shoulder into his kidney. He stumbles forward, the remote flying from his hand and skittering across the gravel. The people in the stadium are safe, Mason's safe. For now.

I retreat, putting as much distance between us as I can. Hands up, I'm ready for a fight. Trapped in the pit with two killers, I know this battle will be my last.

"What the fuck?!" Dustin screams as he spins around. "You're dead."

Dustin moves toward me but stops when Silas chucks a rock at the laptop, taking out both the computer and the ring light.

Dustin turns. "Why the hell'd you do that?"

Silas's hand shoots out, grabbing Dustin by the throat. Dustin is slight in stature, his years of video game expertise floundering under the direct strike of Silas's raw strength. He tries to bat Silas's arms away, but he is no match for Silas's muscle.

"Life isn't some damn video game," Silas taunts. "Ever heard of Leviticus? 24:20? 'Breach for breach, eye for eye, tooth for tooth: as he hath caused blemish in a man so shall it be done to him again.'"

Silas raises Dustin in his grasp. Dustin's feet leave the ground, kicking and flailing in Silas's outstretched arm.

"You tortured folks who didn't deserve it," Silas intones. "Murdered innocents. That is punishable by stoning."

54

JENA

Thursday, 9:54 p.m.

DUSTIN IS CHOKING and making strangled cries. At the same time, Silas both thrusts Dustin into the ground and raises the stone in his hand, slamming the rock down on Dustin's head. Blood pours out, black in the moonlight. A waterfall of midnight issues from Dustin's scalp as he drops to his knees. He is whimpering, cowering, covering his head with his hands.

I look at his battered body, unable to wrap my head around what is happening, that Dustin, responsible for turning the last ten days of my life into torture worse than I've ever known is now a victim, his high-tech knowledge and planning no match for Silas's real-world strength.

Maybe I should burst with joy at Dustin's demise. Drink in the satisfaction this murderer's life is about to end. That he is being brought to account for his crimes and will never hurt anyone again.

But I'm overcome with dread. I'm trapped in the pit with Silas. My wits the only thing between me and certain death.

Still I can't worry about my own neck. I dive, snatching up the remote.

Silas brings the rock down a second time, smashing it into Dustin's skull with a sickening thud. Dustin topples over, face planting a foot or two away from Jack. Silas raises the rock again.

I don't stick around to watch. The clock is ticking, and my time is growing short. I need to get out of this position and get a weapon if I have any hope of saving Jack. I stuff the remote into my jacket pocket, shoot to my feet and scramble to the side of the pit. Using whatever footholds and handholds I can find, I climb up, dirt and loose gravel tumbling down. My mouth fills with silt and grit with each inhale.

My broken fingers scream with pain, and I need to use my left hand to take most of my weight. The injury slows my progress. My spinning head doesn't help either. And as the rocks slice into my feet, I curse myself for taking off my shoes in the name of stealth.

I inch up the dirt wall, two feet, then four. Seven feet up, I hoist myself onto a ledge peppered with loose stones and a few small boulders. I've just found my feet when I'm struck hard in the back between my shoulders.

"Son of a…"

Silas. He has struck me with a limestone fastball. Again.

I duck behind a small boulder for cover, then turn around. Cautiously, I peer over the outcropping. Down below me, Silas drops a stone next to Dustin's lifeless corpse. The weak moonlight is enough to reveal what lies discarded in the mud. I catch sight of the iron red glint. The jasper stone. That makes Dustin the twelfth victim and means Silas's mission to dispense the foundation stones is complete. But as Silas walks over until he is right below me, smiling up with my gun in his hand, it is obvious he isn't done killing. Lucky for me, he doesn't have a clear shot.

I wedge myself between the wall and the boulder, my legs coiled like a spring, feet on the rock. I hide the remote behind a small rock pile for safe keeping, listening for sounds of him climbing, but only picking up my own heartbeat.

As a distraction, I call out, "Just let Jack go, and…" I test the rock's weight. It is heavy, but with a good heave, I think I can move it. "And I won't come after you. He's an innocent."

"He might be. But you are no saint, little bird. Lying through those pretty teeth."

"What I did was a crime, yes, but my actions weren't wrong. Putting you away was justice."

"The judge didn't seem to think so."

My chest expands and I breathe deeply. "Yeah? Well, the DA thought I should recant and walk away. What do you say to that? Tell me, when are laws wrong, Silas? When can they be bent or broken? Doesn't the Bible say 'Thou shall not kill?'"

"Sometimes killing is just."

"You've done what you set out to do. You've atoned, right? Killing Jack's not justified. He's done nothing wrong."

Silas clicks his tongue, his vexation echoing in the night. "Don't I know it. If I kill him, I will owe a debt. But don't think you call the shots here. His fate? That is on you."

"No," I cut him off. "It depends on you. You can walk away right now. Twelve victims. Your mission is over." I tense my quads and hamstrings, waiting for his answer.

"There is no end to purging the wicked," he cries like a wolf with its leg in a trap. A wounded animal. That is what he is beneath that glossy shell. "Jack is no devil, true. And if I kill him, I will have a tab to clear. Need to start fresh. And there are plenty more souls out there to guide my salvation."

That is all I needed to hear. I strain against the pit wall, back wrenching, feet bleeding, head swimming. In one explosive burst, I kick out, thrusting the rock over the ledge. It plummets into the pit, knocking Silas down.

Silas screams. A loud bang like a balloon popping reverberates through the quarry as he fires my gun.

55

JENA

Thursday, 10:03 p.m.

THE BULLET ZIPS past me, burrowing deep into the clay next to my head. The gun's report shatters the dark stillness of the night. And then there is nothing.

I drop to my belly, ears ringing from the blast, my breathing labored from dislodging the boulder. I'm panting as I peer over the cliff, sweat dripping from my brow. Silas lies on the ground, one leg trapped beneath the boulder, my gun still in his hand. He raises the barrel so quickly I barely register the movement before he fires again. I stumble back, arms windmilling as I crash into the pit wall.

"Show yourself, little bird," his voice rings out below. "Or the boy gets my next shot."

Jack's moaning turns to sobs, weak and fading. Lost to the high-pitched squealing in my ears.

My mind races, searching for a plan, a way to save Jack. And myself. Silas is injured and pinned. That makes him vulnerable. But he still has the advantage with the gun. I can't just charge him. I need to outsmart him. Which is why the only plan I have is to do something stupid enough to catch him by surprise.

"Fine," I say, my voice cracking. Maybe the crack is too much, and I should've gone with a weary tone instead. Silas is too damn good at sniffing out other people's bullshit. "I'm coming down so we can end this. Just don't hurt Jack."

Silas chuckles, a cold, sinister sound. "At last, you are catching on."

Maybe he believes me. Or maybe he is playing me. Guess I'll find out.

Taking a deep breath, I scoop up a baseball-size rock, like my glory days pitching college softball. With my broken fingers, it is difficult to grip the stone, but I squeeze as tight as I can, ignoring the pain. Then, I creep to the edge, trying to gauge Silas's position and the distance between us. Silas has the gun aimed at Jack. No time to lose.

I back up as far as I can, then launch myself off the ledge, whipping the rock at his head as he trains the gun on me. The rock misses its mark, smashing into his hand as he pulls the trigger, jerking his arm to the right. There is a sharp bite in my left shoulder. I'm hit. I land hard, the impact knocking me off my feet. Warm liquid seeps down my arm, soaking my shirt. When I look up, Silas is shaking out his hand. The way his middle finger is bent, I'm sure it is broken, but he is still clutching the gun. I scramble to retrieve the rock, but it is too late. Silas has the gun pointed at me. I inhale, waiting for the shot.

Something hits Silas in his injured hand, startling him into lowering the gun. A small, red object. The jasper stone. Jack freed his right arm from the dirt and threw it at him. Giving me enough time to retrieve the rock.

Silas gives Jack a death stare, and Jack's face becomes a mask of horror. He doesn't think I can save him.

56

JENA
Thursday, 10:08 p.m.

I MUSTER ALL the strength I have left and send the rock flying. The projectile connects, hitting Silas in the wrist. The gun flies from his grasp. I dive for the weapon, my swollen fingers hot as they wrap around cold metal. Silas tries to scramble away, but his leg is still trapped under the boulder. I transfer the gun to my left hand, pointing the muzzle at him, my hand shaking.

"Stop!" I shout. "Don't move!"

Silas gives me a wicked grin, whirling onto his side and hauling himself upright. His bone snaps as he frees the trapped leg. Silas howls, face pale from the shock, leg twisted at a grotesque angle. Still he rises on the other leg, letting the broken one dangle. Then he lunges.

Without hesitation, I fire. The bullet hits him in the upper left chest. Not the head. Because I misjudged. I thought he was coming for me, when he was aiming for Jack.

He slides on one knee, like a baseball player skidding into home plate, his broken leg trailing behind. He wraps a big, meaty arm around Jack's emaciated throat, putting him in a sleeper hold, hiding himself behind the boy.

"Stay still, little bird."

I raise the gun.

"Oh, little bird." He squeezes tighter and Jack lets out wet gurgle. "If you are so inclined, see if you can hit me before I snuff the spirit out of him."

Jack coughs, his neck stretching as he struggles against Silas's grip.

"Put it down."

I drop the gun. "Let me help him. There's no reason for him to die."

"There is reason. For me to live. If it is the Lord's will you both perish, so be it."

"It's your will, and you know it."

He wrenches Jack's head up, testing, and Jack hacks and chokes.

"I'm sorry," I say. "That was rude. Don't hurt him because of me."

Silas eyes me up and down. "Your concern should be with your own saving. That shoulder is crying out. Charging at me, getting shot—not your wisest move."

I glance down and see my white shirt has gone red beneath my jacket. I press my hand to the wound, but it only results in blinding pain that nearly knocks me out. "I'll be sure to get it looked at."

"You have some wisdom, little bird. I didn't expect you to decipher the path here. To the quarry."

"I remembered the map in your basement. Is this where you were planning to stone your twelfth victim?"

"Arriving badgeless and alone," Silas continues, ignoring my question. "Brave move."

I suck in a deep breath and try to look unflappable, despite the vertigo and nausea whirling inside of me. "I'm not alone. 911 still comes when you call them. They'll be here any minute."

Silas's eyes flash. "Deceit. You didn't call them."

"Just go," I say. "We're no threat to you."

"And you promise not to strike me down as soon as I turn my face from you?"

"You have my word."

"The word of a liar. What is that worth?" A touch of madness dances beneath Silas's eyes. His grip tightens and Jack squeals.

"No. Stop. Please. Don't punish him because of me."

Silas's grip relaxes, and his eyes flash to the top of the pit. I pray that means he is thinking about leaving, because I'm not sure I have the strength to fight. My vision is flecked with static, my knees rubbery.

"You are a pale shadow," Silas says. "Such a wound. Might it be retribution for the five years you took from me?"

Silas splits into two, then merges back into one. I can't stay conscious much longer. I want to put the next shot right between his eyes. I'm ready for Silas's haunting presence in my life, stretching from when I discovered his first victim until now, to be over.

Jack's stopped moving. I can't tell if he has passed out or if Silas is crushing his airway. Either way, I need Silas's attention off Jack and onto me.

"You should've been slapped in the chair, and you know it. What the hell is all this about? Twelve victims for what? Some sort of religious show-off?"

Silas cocks his head, scrutinizing. "Therein lies the distinction between Dustin and me. Dustin sought his own glory. I walked in the Lord's shadow."

"Oh, bullshit. You did it because you needed to feel like a righteous hero. Rationalize it to yourself any way you want. You and Dustin are the same."

Silas narrows his eyes, drawing himself up. "Matthew says, the path of righteousness is narrow, and few find it. I have dedicated my life to illuminating it, to cleansing it."

"You can quote scripture all day, but you know what? Even Jesus died at the hands of those he tried to save. Seems to me you're on the wrong side of salvation."

Silas blinks, and maybe for a moment there is uncertainty behind those stormy eyes.

A wave of dizziness washes over me. The pain in my shoulder intensifies, the blood loss taking its toll. I stumble and fall to the ground, my vision narrowing.

Jack gives a hoarse scream of "Help me!"

I struggle to get back up, scanning the ground for the gun. But it is too late.

Silas releases Jack with an animalistic growl and pounces.

I dive, scooping up a rock with my left hand as Silas crashes into me. Pain explodes in my chest, Silas's weight crushing as my back smacks into the ground. He presses a behemoth forearm against my neck. I work to suck air. Weak from blood loss, my strength is ebbing. I can't give in. I stretch my arm out to the side and smash the rock into his temple.

Silas grunts, his head bobbing like a drunk. He is disoriented. I try to roll out from under him, but he is too damn heavy. I manage to wriggle back a few inches, taking the pressure off my windpipe. I fling my arm out again, this time stabbing the rock into his temple. Silas screams. I scream, too, my fear turning into a cry of rage as I do it again. He screams. I scream. I hit him again. He screams. I scream. Hit him a fifth time. Our chests press together, sticky with blood, his and mine. I strike him over and over, the wound in my shoulder tearing as I fight him. But he has stopped fighting back.

I listen to his breathing, the way it changes speed, filled with gasps and pauses. Silas's brain shutting down as it fills with blood. Gore from the gash on his temple drips onto my face, hot and sweet. I lie still as Silas breathes his last, his weight making my own breathing difficult.

I manage to wrestle my right hand free, searching my coat pocket, my hand slick with blood. I fumble, but finally retrieve my phone, dialing 911. When the dispatcher answers, I give our location and details. Come quickly. Three down. One dead. Two dying.

57

JENA

Two months later

DARK RAIN FALLS outside the courthouse, tapping on the windows. Almost like the storm is trying to get my attention, letting me know it is waiting to wrap icy fingers around me when I'm done here. Inside, the courtroom is a clamor of hushed voices and the creaking of wooden benches. Dozens of eyes bore into me from the front, side, and back.

My right hand is in a cast, and my left shoulder throbs with a dull ache. The forty-seven stitches dissolved weeks ago, but the mass of scar tissue and limited mobility remains. My life weighed into my decisions that night, and I don't regret my actions. My only regret is the lengths I had to go to, falsifying evidence to get the warrant to search Silas's home. Even though it turned out I was right about him, it doesn't make what I did right. Checks and balances are there for a reason. And if it had turned out I was wrong… No matter the outcome of today's verdict, forging that receipt will continue to weigh on my conscience.

Judge Spadina sits behind her bench, stern and imposing. Her expression is unreadable, but whatever she thinks professionally, the weight of her personal judgment bears down on me. She doesn't care for me one bit, hasn't since the first time I appeared before her to testify that I falsified evidence.

The courtroom is filled with people waiting to hear the final word—lawyers, journalists, curious spectators, Silas's followers; "The Church of Silas" more zealous than ever now that Silas is their martyr. The hearing has been going on for forty-five minutes now. The proceeding should've taken no more than twenty minutes, but several of the Silas devotees have been restrained or kicked out, this legal process turned into a zoo of feral, rabid animals. The same way they've brought chaos to my life.

After the quarry, I couldn't go home when I was released from the hospital. Silas's disciples had thrown rocks through my apartment window, several wrapped up with threats written on paper and secured with rubber bands. So I was moved to a safe house. Just like Dustin's victims. The irony isn't lost on me. The worst part is that they targeted Mason, too. The best part is that he insisted on moving into the same safe house. Two months of forced living together has gotten me over my commitment phobia. Everything else in my life may be shit, but Mason and I are good. Really, really good.

Now, my gaze shifts between the seal of the Commonwealth of Pennsylvania and the American flag. I may be agnostic, but I'm not above praying to symbols of justice that I might be absolved of wrongdoing. My lawyer, Fred Thompson, is quiet by my side, his arguing on my behalf over. My fate is up to Judge Spadina.

The wait is excruciating, the silence in the courtroom bearing down on me, as heavy as the weight of Silas's body lying on top of me as he died. I watch the clock on the wall. With each tick, my emotions swing between relief and hope. Relief this will soon be over. Hope my sentence will be light.

"Ms. Campbell." Judge Spadina is talking to the courtroom, the press, as much as she is addressing me. "The court recognizes the extraordinary circumstances of your case. Without your actions, the events in the stadium and the quarry could've taken a much darker turn. There is no doubt that you saved thousands of lives that night."

Her words hang in the air like ghosts, a chill making me shiver as the rain continues to drum on the window.

"However," Judge Spadina continues, "a member of the police force, falsifying evidence, that is inexcusable." The judge levels her gaze at me and I swallow hard, my throat bobbing. "In your ardor to bring Silas Halvard to justice, you disregarded principles you swore to uphold, becoming that what you sought to fight. You crossed the line that separates law enforcers from law breakers. Am I clear?"

I nod, unable to breathe.

"In light of your previous exemplary service, and the fact that your actions did, in fact, prevent a potential massacre, the court is willing to show leniency. But this doesn't absolve you of your crime."

My knees knock together as the judge studies the documents in front of her.

"Ms. Campbell, I sentence you to two years of probation and a fine of five thousand dollars. Further, you will serve five hundred hours of community service. This court hopes this sentence will serve as a reminder not to cross the line again. The court clerk will provide the necessary paperwork to your attorney. You're free to go. This court is adjourned."

The gavel strikes the sound block with finality, the smack

echoing through the high ceilings. The courtroom erupts into a flurry of activity, reporters typing and texting, cameras flashing, spectators murmuring. I'm grateful she saw my act as a misdemeanor. I know I'm getting off easy, and I could have done jail time for this. But she still managed to make the sentence steep. I can't help thinking Judge Spadina crafted the punishment as much for the press's benefit as mine. Five thousand dollars! On a civil servant's salary. I suddenly feel a need to commiserate with Papich. The warden would sympathize with the financial burden. I turn around to face the gallery, seeking and finding Mason's gaze. There is pain in his eyes, at what this means for me, for my career. But there is reassurance, too. I'll make it through this because we'll be together. And sitting next to him, Mary smiles at me with bubble gum pink lips. I almost have it in me to smile back.

As I rise, my legs shaking, I thank Fred Thompson and leave the courtroom. Mason joins me on the walk, taking my hand. He leads me out of the building and down the courthouse steps, once again shielding me from the press and, this time, protecting me from Silas's followers. The rain pours down, soaking my hair and plastering my shirt to me like a second skin as he escorts me into his Range Rover.

I cast one last backward glance at the horde of spectators and spot a figure looming off to the side of the courthouse staircase. The person is dressed all in black. Black shoes, jeans, hoodie. Black sunglasses. A skeleton gaiter pulled up over their face. My heart hammers in my chest as Mason pulls away, the skeleton's image still haunting me. He is dead. He can't be there. Maybe the stress, the storm, has me seeing things wrong. As the Range Rover lurches forward, the storm shows no sign of letting up.

58

JENA

Two months and one day later

THE SAFE HOUSE is an antiquated farmhouse tucked away in the rural outskirts of Pittsburgh. It has a quaint, rustic charm that might have lured in city folks looking for a weekend escape once upon a time. But now, it is just the wallpaper to our confinement, the hardwood floors creaking underfoot to remind us of our seclusion.

A chill drafts through the cracks in the walls, creeping over me like an unwelcome guest. I wrap my arms around myself, glancing over at Mason. He is sprawled out on the worn-out couch, eyes locked onto the ceiling, the same sense of cabin fever that I feel reflected in his gaze. I get it. There is only so much you can do to pass the time when you're trapped in a place like this. We've scrolled to the end of the Internet, played every board game in the house twice over, read through the small collection of musty old novels, and I've lost count of the number of times we've walked the narrow, twisting path that circles the property.

I never thought somewhere so open could be more confining

than my small apartment. But neither Mason nor I are used to having nothing to do. I'm currently unemployed, and Mason has taken some time off. Waiting until the risk of Silas's disciples following him here from work die down.

I wriggle in the armchair, trying to get comfortable. But the chair is like a big pillow, cozy no matter how I sit. I'm just restless. The sun dips low, painting the room in long, brooding shadows.

Mason stirs from his reclined position on the couch, sitting up. "I'll start dinner."

I nod, not moving as he rises and shuffles off to the kitchen. I find myself counting the seconds, listening to the silence punctuated only by the occasional creak from the house settling.

The gravel crunches outside, a car engine humming softly before cutting off. I pull open the drawer of the side table, pulling out my Sig with my left hand and concealing it under the armchair's cushion. The old screen door creaks open, then slams shut with a bang that echoes through the house. I look over at Mason, who has popped out of the kitchen, his gaze now fixed on the entrance to the living room. Footsteps echo on the hardwood, and then Captain Price steps into the room.

My heart races at the unexpected visit, and I release my hold on the Sig. Mason says, "Hey, Price," with a wave before returning to the kitchen.

"Captain," I say, trying to keep my voice steady. "What a nice surprise."

He stays a few feet away, looking me up and down, his face unreadable. "Boredom's not a good look on you." For once, he doesn't sound like he is trying to shout over a crowd.

"Yeah, relaxation and I don't know what to make of each other."

Price leans against the wall. "As mad as I am, *was*, at you, we both know you don't belong here, sitting on your duff, doing probation."

"The law says otherwise."

"The law isn't always the same thing as justice."

"'Sometimes you have to do what is right even when it is wrong.'"

Price's eyebrows squish together. "Come again?"

"Something Silas said to me once."

"Well, there's irony for you." Price's lips twitch, almost a smile. "I've brought you something."

Touching my shoulder stitches, I half-heartedly joke, "A new arm?"

Price's smile turns to a chuckle, the sound bouncing around the vast space. "Sorry. Fresh out."

I hold up my right hand with the cast. "How about a hand?"

Price responds with mock applause.

A chime cuts through the air, pulling our attention away from the moment. Price pulls his phone from his pocket. A quick glance at the incoming message before he turns the screen to me, revealing an incoming video call from a private number. With a flick of his finger, he accepts the call, and Governor Ted Taylor's face appears on the screen.

The governor is in his office, dressed in a navy blazer and matching tie. He is on a laptop. He sits up straight, his hands clasped together on the edge of a dark wooden desk. Heavy forest green curtains make up his backdrop.

"Campbell. How are you?"

"I've been better," I admit.

He nods sympathetically. *"Well, I hope this will help. Not only did you save a stadium full of people, you saved my son, and I'm grateful."*

A wistful smile tugs at my lips. "I'd say I was just doing my job, but, well…"

The governor's eyes soften. *"I've been giving it a lot of thought and a lot of prayer this week. I'm granting you a pardon."*

I don't know what I was expecting him to say, but it wasn't that. "Thank you," I whisper. I don't say anything else, afraid I'll break down in front of the governor and Price.

"Thank you for your service to the city, and for bringing my boy home safe," he says. He leans forward and ends the call, the screen fading to black.

I turn my face away from Price, blinking back tears, my mind still grappling with the news. Price puts a hand on my good shoulder. When I meet his gaze, he is grinning.

"Looks like today's your lucky day."

"Seems like it," I say with a sniffle.

"You deserve a second chance, Campbell. Just don't blow it."

I expect him to release my shoulder and leave, but instead, his grip tightens. I look up and he locks eyes with me, his stare intense.

"There's something you need to know." Price drops his voice to a murmur. "Silas had a thumb drive on him the night he died. O'Reilly discovered it, and Collins decrypted it."

My heart pounds, anxiety clawing its way back in. "What was on it?" I ask, struggling to form the words.

Price purses his lips, deciding how to break it to me. "It's biblical-style text, written by Silas about himself."

"Seems right for his ego. But why is that so troubling to you?"

"After Silas's death, the Church of Silas went into hyperdrive. Silas sent out copies of the text. To dozens of them. They're calling it a new book of the Bible. The Church is planning to continue with Silas's vision of ridding the world of evil, and we're already seeing an escalation of...stoning violence. Even though Silas is dead, his ideas are alive and thriving. We've kept it under wraps so far, but I'm afraid the PBP is going to have their hands full."

"We can't let them..." I start, but can't bring myself to finish.

"Right. Which is why I wish I could give you your old job back, but even with the pardon, your confession of evidence tampering makes that impossible. You'd never be able to sign an affidavit or testify again. The defense attorneys would have a field day with you. No offense to Mason. Or you."

I swallow. "None taken. I didn't expect—"

"Before you say anything, I want you to consider going private. You'd have my support. Covertly. And I'm not the only one. Understand?"

Price holds his hand out, and I only hesitate a moment before giving it an awkward, left-handed shake. As I accept Price's olive branch, my mind flashes back to the skeleton standing outside in the rain next to the courthouse, wondering how, or if, he fits into this mess.

THE BOOK OF SILAS

Silas 1

The Call to Atonement

1. In the beginning, the word of the Lord came to Silas, saying, "Arise, my chosen one, for the time has come to deliver my message unto the world. Though you have stumbled upon the path of righteousness, I shall grant you forgiveness if you devote your life to undoing the wrong and bringing about greater good in the world. For those who have erred can find redemption, and those who have fallen can rise to great heights."
2. Silas bowed before the Lord, humbled by the divine mercy, his heart filled with humility and purpose, for he knew the path set before him was one of sacrifice.
3. Thus spoke Silas, "Lord, as you have chosen me as a vessel of righteousness, I will spread your word of truth."

Silas 2

Living a Moral Life

1. And the Lord said, "Behold, the world is filled with darkness and corruption. But I say unto you, resist the temptations of sin and walk in the path of righteousness."
2. Silas proclaimed, "Let no one be deceived, for the wages of sin are death. Turn away from the evils of this world and embrace the light of righteousness."
3. For he knew that to live a moral life was to honor the Lord and pave the way for salvation. And that through

his actions, he would inspire others to seek forgiveness for their transgressions and to atone for their sins.

Silas 3

The Stones of Justice

1. The Lord bestowed the foundation stones of the heavenly city upon Silas, a reminder that the Earth could achieve purity and divinity with the eradication of sin. And Silas said, "As it is written in the Book of Revelation, the twelve foundation stones symbolize the triumph of righteousness over evil."
2. And Silas spoke of the ancient practice of stoning, saying, "Let the stones be a reminder of the divine justice that awaits the wicked. For in the face of evil, it is our duty to rid the world of sin."
3. He named the sins that warrant stoning: unjust murder, rape, serial adultery, sex trafficking, possessing child pornography, bestiality, and other abominations that corrupt the purity of the innocent.

Silas 4

Metaphors of Faith

1. Silas, a wise and knowledgeable instructor, imparted his teachings to his students through thought-provoking parables and allegories. He said, "Blessed are those who build their lives upon the rock of righteousness, for they shall withstand the storms of temptation."
2. To the incarcerated, he likened the path to salvation to a narrow gate, saying, "Enter through the narrow

gate, for the wide gate leads to destruction. Strive to walk the righteous path, though it may be difficult."

3. To his supporters, Silas declared, "I am the shepherd of the lost, guiding them toward the light. Follow my voice, and you shall find solace and eternal salvation."

Silas 5

The Martyr's Revelation

1. Silas knew that his time on earth would be marked by sacrifice. He recorded his words for his disciples, saying, "Behold, I tell you this: I am prepared to lay down my life for the sake of righteousness. In my martyrdom, my message will be etched into the hearts of those who seek the truth."
2. He wrote of the coming kingdom of heaven, saying, "Go forth, my disciples, and continue the mission to rid the world of evil. Preach the gospel of atonement and lead others to the path of righteousness."
3. For Silas believed that through the disciples, the divine message would spread like a wildfire, illuminating the darkness, and preparing the way for the kingdom of heaven.

Silas 6

The Call to Action

1. And Silas concluded his writings, "My disciples, go forth into the world, for the time is near. Proclaim the truth, stand against evil, and embrace the call to atonement. Together, let us pave the way for the kingdom of heaven to be revealed."

2. "My disciples, your purpose is great, and your mission is sacred. Spread these words far and wide as a testament to your faith and commitment to righteousness."
3. "As you venture forth, you will encounter challenges and opposition, but your resolve must remain unshakable. You will face persecution and ridicule, yet you will persevere, knowing that your cause is just and your mission divine."
4. "Call upon all to cast away their sinful ways and seek atonement through righteous living. For those whose ears are deaf to the call, take action to eradicate their evil from the world. Heavy are the stones of the faithful. Remain steadfast in your mission, and usher in the kingdom of heaven."
5. Let those with ears listen, and those with eyes see the path that leads to righteousness. Let the words of The Book of Silas guide and inspire, for it is a beacon of light amidst the darkness, a testament to the unwavering faith and unwavering commitment of those who dare to seek a better world.
6. May the teachings of Silas resonate, and may the disciples uphold his vision, until the day when the kingdom of heaven is at hand, and righteousness prevails over all.

59

JENA

Two months and two weeks later

JACK REACHES OUT to me, wanting to meet for lunch. As a thank you, he says. We agree on a pizza place that I suspect he'll appreciate more than I will, given my attempts at healthy eating and his teenage appetites. The moment I step inside the restaurant, the aroma of greasy cheese and tomato sauce fills my nostrils. Jack is already inside sitting in a dark wooden booth with red vinyl seats. Nice and private. He waves me over.

"Hey, Detective," Jack greets me. He is wearing a black hoodie and sunglasses pushed up into his thick hair. For a second, my mind flashes back to the skeleton outside the courthouse. I shake the thought away and smile.

"It's just Jena, now," I say.

"Right." He gives a goofy grin, trying to cover up his discomfort.

Jack looks so much healthier than the last time I saw him. His gaunt face has filled back out and regained its color. I don't see any trace of lasting injury on him. Not on the outside, anyway.

A server comes by, and we order. Jack opts for pepperoni

only. I go with the veggie deluxe, trying to trick myself into believing I'm ordering something with nutritional value.

When the server leaves, I ask, "So, how have things been going?"

Jack lets out a small sigh, then takes a sip of water. "Could be better," he confesses. "I'm having awful nightmares. Sometimes, I even hear Shadow's voice during the day. My therapist says it's common, you know, 'auditory hallucinations' after experiencing what I did. Looks like I have PTSD."

"I'm sorry," I say, my heart aching for him.

I don't tell him what Collins has discovered. That someone released the VR games he was forced to play—and they're making a killing. That wouldn't help his PTSD at all. Would probably kick it up a couple notches.

He continues, his voice trembling. "When I was trapped in that VR hell, I thought no one would find me, that no one would save me."

I swallow hard, not wanting to say out loud that I'd had the same fear. "If you hadn't thrown that jasper stone at Silas when you did, he would've killed me. You helped save yourself."

He looks at me, his eyes welling up with tears. "I never looked at it that way. Thanks, um…Jena. Seriously, thank you. For showing up. For caring enough to find me."

Our server brings our pizzas, and Jack dives in, the cheese stretching between his mouth and the slice. My right hand is still out of commission, so I pick up a slice with my left hand. The limited mobility of my shoulder along with using my non-dominant hand make it tough for me to grip. I clumsily bring the slice to my mouth.

Jack's eyes widen, but he is too polite to comment.

"You should see me use a fork," I joke.

"Guess I'm not the only one with scars," Jack says between bites. "I'm trying to work through it all. Mom and Jude have been coming to the family sessions, too."

I notice he doesn't say his dad is participating, and there is unspoken tension there. Not that I blame him. If my dad had the power to pardon in exchange for my release and didn't use it, I don't think I could forgive him, either. Especially when that same dad pardoned the cop that found me. I'm surprised Jack doesn't resent me for it, but there is no trace of contempt in his face or his tone.

"It's hard to let go of what happened, you know? But on the bright side, my VR stream is popular now." He grins, trying to find a silver lining. "And I have a group of friends I met in my support group. We hang out together all the time."

"That's great, Jack. Really."

I attempt to take another bite of my pizza, but my left hand slips, causing a glob of tomato sauce to splatter on the table. Jack chuckles and hands me a napkin.

"Thanks," I mumble, wiping it up.

I try to keep my mind on what he is telling me now, about the games he is live streaming, and how he is earning an income, but I'm distracted by the thought that Jack might find out someone is profiting off his pain. Even though Collins is working on the situation, and keeping me informed, so we can shut it down. But what has really been bothering me all week is how whoever is putting this out there got access to Dustin's games. I don't understand enough about that world to know where Dustin might have stored his games and what type of person could've hacked into them. That is best left for Collins to puzzle out, but he doesn't have any answers. Yet.

When we finish our pizza, the server brings the bill.

"Thanks for lunch," I say. "It's great to hear you're on the mend, and that things at work and with friends are looking up."

I reach for the bill, but Jack snatches it away. "It's on me."

I smile. "How about we split it?"

"I insist. This was my idea. My way to say thank-you. It's the least I can do."

I put my hands up in defeat, not wanting to insult him. Once he settles up, giving his card to the server, who quickly returns with it, we exit the booth and head for the parking lot.

"Well, I guess this is good-bye, Detective…uh, Jena. I'm hoping we don't have any unexpected run-ins again. No offense."

I can't help but chuckle. "None taken. Wishing you an awesome life, Jack."

"I'll give it my best shot."

We part ways, me heading to the back of the lot to my F-150 while Jack hops into his burgundy Honda Civic. The car's color triggers a memory of Silas's prison uniform, and I shake off the recollection with a shudder.

I wave good-bye as Jack drives past, then climb into my F-150 to head back to my new office. There has been another violent incident involving stoning, and Price has been feeding me information to help me track down the members of The Church of Silas. It is a lot of pressure. Working for myself, while still trying to meet PBP expectations. I grin as I realize I wouldn't have it any other way.

At the stoplight, I glance around, taking in the city's bustling life. The workday lunch crowd escaping their cubicles for a bite. As I wait for the light to change, I can't shake the sensation that I'm being watched. My eyes flick to the lone pedestrian not crossing the road with the rest of the horde, his gaze glued to his phone. As his stare rises to meet mine, I don't glance down at his shirt. I've already read it. The same damn slogan I've been seeing everywhere. Spray-painted on buildings, tagged on trains, written in bathroom stalls.

"Heavy are the stones" - Silas 6:4

About the authors

J.D. Barker

J.D. Barker is the New York Times and international best-selling author of numerous novels, including DRACUL and THE FOURTH MONKEY. His latest, BEHIND A CLOSED DOOR, releases May 13. He is currently collaborating with James Patterson. His books have been translated into two dozen languages, sold in more than 150 countries, and optioned for both film and television. Barker resides in coastal New Hampshire with his wife, Dayna, and their daughter, Ember.

Christine Daigle

A clinical neuropsychologist by day, Christine Daigle's work includes brain-computer interface, translating brain signals into commands that can control technology. As a writer, her novel was selected for the Pitch Wars industry mentorship program. An anthology including her short fiction was a finalist for an Aurora Award. Her co-authored, pen-named work on Kindle Vella was consecutively one of the top 250 serials for several years. In addition to her writing, she also co-hosts the Writers, Ink podcast. She lives in Ontario with her husband, son, and mercurial cat. You can find her at christinedaiglebooks.com